All Things New

EK Jonathan
Cover design by EK Jonathan
©2016. All rights reserved.
ISBN-13: 978-1536858891

Dedicated to Mom and Dad.
Because I wouldn't be here–or there–without them.

Foreword

The idea behind this novel first occurred to me in 2010. During the summer of that year, I tried my hand at a few passages, but the result was bland and riddled with issues. Disappointed, my motivation for the project evaporated. I knew that if I wasn't enthusiastic about writing it, no one would be enthusiastic about reading it.

And so the fledgling idea remained just that–a few pages of text in a remote file on my laptop's hard drive. I'd stumble across it occasionally, reading through what I'd written with mixed feelings. I knew there was a solid concept in there somewhere, and I wished *someone* would develop it, but I wasn't sure that someone should be *me*.

One of my foremost concerns was how a book like this would be received. I assumed that some would be offended by my portrayal of post-Armageddon society. Perhaps they would feel that my book was a transgression in over-speculation. At the very least, there would be a flood of those who disagreed strongly with my depictions. Maybe it was best to just keep my ideas to myself.

And then 2013 came along. Two things happened that made me reexamine my project. The first was that year's District Convention, which featured two dramas set in the future–one at the start of the Great Tribulation, the other after the Resurrection. The second was the yearly calendar, which featured six vivid paintings depicting the New World. In the corner of each page, a small question box encouraged us to think about what we wanted to do in Paradise.

I couldn't help but think back to the writing project I'd abandoned. A myriad of questions begged answers in my head that I wanted desperately to explore on paper: *How would the U.N. attack false religion? How would the Witnesses later be targeted? How would Jehovah protect his people? What would Armageddon be like? What (and who) would be left? How would we reorganize? Communicate? Travel? Rebuild? What would return to perfection be like? How would a perfect child think?* And, perhaps the most intriguing question of them all: *What would the Resurrection be like?*

Thus, in August of 2013, I returned to my novel. I wrote at a swift pace, with a loose quota of 2,000 words a day and an ultimate goal of 100,000 words, the length of a average paperback. As you might imagine, writing a novel takes determination, and writing is just half the effort. It involves hours upon hours of research, editing, and–in the case of a story with spiritual themes–lots of meditation.

Of course, the stories here are fictional. The events and characters are nothing more than my imaginative renderings of what *could* be. Still, I've done my upmost to align the details of the stories with our current understanding of Bible prophecy. Where that understanding is unclear or incomplete, I have bridged the gaps with reasonable hypothesis. Where some aspect of a story resembles a Biblical account, I've tried to conclude the *likeliest outcome* based on precedent. After all, Divine destruction is nothing new; neither are Divinely-backed construction projects.

Does this mean that I believe future events will play out as the stories describe? Not necessarily. They might, but I expect it'll be much more surprising (and more miraculous) than anything I could invent or write. So please, as you read through the novel in your hands, remember: I'm not making predictions. I'm merely exploring one stream of possibilities.

But one thing I am certain of–as are you, I'm sure–is that whatever happens in the end, each one of us will have a story to tell. Let that story be one of courage, integrity, and faith.

-EK Jonathan

Prologue

I have never written a book before. Even as I tap these words out on my heavy, clumsy typewriter, I feel a special nervousness about the stories compiled here. After all, the voices behind these tales will outlive mere pages in a book and will no doubt recount them with greater finesse and detail than I ever could. Still, putting these events down in writing, to record a sliver of the last century's stories, is important to me. I want the reader to feel what it was like to experience these events as they unfolded, from the start of the Great Tribulation to the massive restructuring and reorganizing of the present.

The stories herein are factual to the best of my knowledge. However, with so much having been lost in the last few decades, certain records are impossible to recover. Thus, it is required that the reader rely somewhat on the memory of the storytellers. Since these memories will become clearer and more perfect over time, I plan to revise this volume and add to it in further editions.

The accounts have been compiled in the sequence I first heard them, starting with the experiences in my hometown and moving westwards towards the Pacific Ocean and beyond.

My wish is that you, the reader, are able to feel the exhilaration of passing through the old system of things and on into the New World. May we never take for granted the great way our Creator and Friend, Jehovah, delivered us from the hand of our enemy!

Dedicated to Emma and Jacob, who I lost for so long.

-Mitch Hanson

The Envelope

My heart surged as I walked down the dusty road to my cedar cabin between the waves and the vineyards. Beneath my arm I held the envelope I had waited on for nearly six decades. A smile tugged at the corners of my face as I thought of my son, who would be full of questions, and his mother. My hands, I noticed, were slightly damp.

Entering the cabin, I flipped on the solar lantern, flooding the room with a warm light. I sat down in my red leather recliner and took a deep breath. Then, after a brief prayer, I tugged at the tear cord of the envelope and reached inside.

But before I continue, and before the significance of the envelope's contents can be fully understood, allow me to explain the events that built up to that climactic moment in the New World. Events that had unfolded decades prior and thousands of miles to the west. Events that would forever reshape our society, our lives, and our relationships with our Creator.

New Beginnings

When the dust had settled and everyone had been accounted for, our Organization began providing us with the details we needed to take our first steps into the New World.

Atlanta, the city I had lived in during the decade leading up to Armageddon, was mostly ruins. What hadn't burned to the ground was hardly fit to live in; and besides, no one was eager to stay in a crumbling city that reeked of death and decay. The suburbs that rubbed shoulders with the city hub, on the other hand, were mostly in livable condition, and many of our friends 'upgraded' to these areas, usually moving in with groups (and in some cases whole congregations) of other Witnesses.

The passing of the Old World, however, brought a sense of adventure for those who weren't ready to settle, including many who'd previously been in full time service. Theirs was the idea that *The world was so big and so full of possibility*, and *Why the rush to settle?* After all, the Organization had put out a call for volunteers who were willing to travel.

For a guy like me, who had always wanted to be a part of the action (but was too busy), this was the perfect opportunity. I had no sales quota to fret over, no family responsibilities, no mortgage on a house I could barely pay for. I was ready to go. The Resurrection was decades off, we'd been told, and I wanted some sort of legacy to pass on to my family when I saw them again.

So I grabbed my old hiking backpack from what remained of our attic, stuffed it with a few essentials, and headed to the local recruiting area, a sprawling Wal-Mart parking lot not far from my neighborhood. There were still a dozen or so parked cars in various spaces. Cars from before the Great Day. Cars that would never be driven again.

At the far end of the parking lot, next to the *Home & Gardening* sign, a small throng of volunteers had gathered. Many had already helped themselves to folding cots and camping chairs from inside the store and were sitting in the shade of the carport, waiting. A folding table had been set up in the entrance to the store, with several brothers working busily behind it.

At exactly 10 o'clock, one of the brothers, whom I recognized from a nearby congregation, stood up with a bullhorn.

"Brothers and sisters, could we please have you attention. In the next few minutes we'll be going over a few items and if you could all gather around we can answer your questions and get you all signed up." The bullhorn clicked off and the friends shuffled towards the table.

A few minutes passed. There were over a hundred of us there waiting in a knot of anticipation.

"Ok, first of all, congratulations. You have all made it through the Great Tribulation, meaning that you are the Great Crowd. We all had to face a lot to be here today, and the brothers want to express how happy we are to see all of your faces."

A thunderous round of cheering and applause shot through the crowd. It was a kind of release, making all that noise, a way to express the many emotions that had been roiling inside us. Excitement. Relief. Joy. Trepidation?

"Of course, Jehovah has given us work to do, and through his Organization, he's directing that work one step at a time. Now, it's still very early, so we don't have all the details; however, we do know that the Organization has formed several new Regional Committees to spearhead the cleanup work. You probably all heard about this through the letter that was read in your congregation meeting two weeks ago, but just as a refresher, we now have a Regional *Salvaging* Committee, a Regional *Demolition* Committee, and a Regional *Transit* Committee.

"The RSC is in charge of collecting as many usable goods as possible from homes, stores, shopping malls, warehouses, and so forth. These goods will be catalogued and stored for everyone's use until we can get production underway for our own goods. The RDC will be in charge of the heavy cleanup, meaning wrecking balls, bulldozers, and explosives..." A few chuckles of approval rippled through the crowd around me. "The RTC will be in charge of communications and shipping logistics, meaning lots of travel between cities carrying goods and mail and so on."

"Now, we don't know how long each of these crews will be out there, and we're only asking for as much as you're willing to give. If you want to volunteer for a year, five years, ten, it's completely up to you. Of course, if you decide not to sign up, you'll be involved in more or less the same work anyway, but it'll be a little less specialized, more local cleanup. The RC's are going to be on the move constantly. If you stick with one of the crews, there's a good chance you'll get to travel to other cities and possibly, down the line, even other countries." There was a nudge on the brother's shoulder and he pulled back for a moment while someone whispered in his ear.

"Oh, sorry, not countries. Other *regions*," the brother said with a smirk. "Any questions?"

Several dozen hands poked up above the sea of heads.

"Can families sign up?" Asked a brother who held a small child in his arms.

"The direction from the branch is that 'mature young ones who are capable of strenuous physical labor' are welcome to join with their families. If a child is eighteen or older, he can join independent of his parents. If it's a young child, though, it's probably best to wait until the child is a little older. Like I said, there will be plenty of local work to do..."

The brother with the child nodded and withdrew quietly from the crowd. I heard his son say, "Daddy, are we going home now?" as they walked away.

"Any age restrictions for the elderly?" Asked a white haired sister in jeans and work boots. Her hands were on her hips and she had a serious look.

"Nothing here about that. We're all getting younger, after all." The sister nodded, satisfied.

"What about tools? My house is gone, I have nothing," said another voice.

"Not a problem. Tools will be provided by the committees you are assigned to. All you need is a couple changes of clothes. Anyone else?"

"Any word yet on the Resurrection?" It was an elderly brother. He was wringing a baseball cap in his knobby hands.

"I'm sorry, brother, but we have no information on that yet."

The questions were endless, but if anyone was feeling impatient, they didn't show it. Rather, the crowd seemed to be paying rapt attention, not wanting to miss a detail. Finally, the brother with the bullhorn said, "All right, if you'll now please line up and fill out some papers, we can get you assigned."

"Paradise paperwork," whispered a voice jokingly somewhere behind me. The brothers behind the table took seats as the crowd funneled into a long line. Eventually, forms fastened to clipboards were passed out to quicken the process, but it still took the better part of the day to get everyone squared away.

When I finally received my own form, I realized the sensibility of it all. All the old systems of keeping track of people–passports, drivers' licenses, social security numbers–were a thing of the past. Incidentally, so were cellphones and the internet; if someone needed to get a hold of you, you had better tell them where you'd be and how long. The details we entered on the forms allowed the branch to better organize us, an especially tricky task given the fact that massive teams of volunteers were constantly going to be on the move.

Other questions on the form asked about work experience: *Construction? Plumbing? Cooking? Sailing? Operating heavy machinery?* I filled in a straight column of checks in the No boxes and sighed. For the last ten years I had been a salesman for an international insurance agency. Statistically, I would later learn, even experience in telescope repair would've been more useful. But I was willing to do anything, and the brothers were appreciative.

"How would you feel about a rotational assignment?" They asked when I handed my form in at the table. I didn't understand the jargon so they explained: "Basically you'd be on one assignment for a year or two and then have an opportunity to try something else, if you wanted. It'd give you a chance to build skills in a number of areas, skills that you'll likely use again later. I noticed here that you said you'd be willing to travel around, so this might be a good option for you."

It did sound like a good option, and I said so. Grinning, and feeling a like a little kid on the first day of kindergarten, I handed the form in and looped my thumbs under my backpack straps.

I spent the night right there in the parking lot, unfurling my sleeping bag on a small, triangular patch of grass. I had parked right next to this exact spot so many times. *Get the milk, get the eggs, get the soda on sale and GET OUT OF HERE.*

What were we so busy for?

***

"Just beautiful, aren't they?" Said a voice to my right that night. I looked over to see a couple roasting a package of hot dogs on a red hibachi. It looked new. A folded paper tag was still hanging from its wooden handle, flopping in the slight evening breeze.

"The hot dogs?" I asked.

"No, I meant the stars. Saw you looking up at them," the brother said, chuckling.

"Oh, yes. They seem especially vivid tonight. Have you noticed?"

"Mm-hm. It's been like that since the Big Day. Probably because all the lights are out now. No light pollution." That made sense. There was a depth to the night sky I'd never seen before, even when I used to go camping in the mountains near Yosemite as a kid. It was as if I could see through the smoky eternity of the cosmos.

"Maybe it's not just that," said the brother's wife, looking up. "Maybe the universe is welcoming us back to the family."

Her husband chuckled thoughtfully, munching on the end of his charred dog. Then, looking at me, "You want one?"

"No thanks, I had some canned beans."

"Ah, ok. Just thought I'd offer. Might be your last chance to, you know, get a taste of meat," he winked. It wasn't. In the months ahead, I would have my fill of canned meats, thawed sausages, and, of course, spam. No one really missed it when it finally ran out.

I laid there late into the night, gazing up at the speckled universe as it swung slowly around me in a cool, cloudless sky. I thought about my family and I thought about the work ahead. Then I prayed.

Thank you, Jehovah. Thank you for letting me be here...

The next morning, after grabbing a packaged pastry and canned coffee from the deserted Wal-Mart, I waited for the trucks to show up. I was told to look for the ID number of my caravan, R77, but in the end it didn't matter; the sister in the passenger seat had my name on her list and called for me. Waving goodbye to a few of the friends I'd spent the night with, I hopped into the back of the truck and headed off for the port city of Savannah, Georgia, a five-hour drive to the east.

Don & Carol Keene

"Carol, honey, have you seen this flower? It's just... beautiful!"

The man delicately plucked the flower from between the roots of the ancient oak. He was wearing a pink hardhat and neon-green reflective vest. He cradled it like a newborn in his pudgy hands, bouncing back towards the lunch line. A golden retriever, as if to mimic his movement, bounded after him, its tail and tongue wagging jocularly.

"Isn't it just...*amazing?*" He exclaimed.

The woman let out a sharp gasp, turning a few nearby heads.

"Oh, Don! Where did you find it?" The woman looked to the man beside her in line, tapping him on the shoulder, "Excuse me, could you tell us what kind of flower this is? I can't quite remember the name..."

"Uh, hey Margaret, what're these pink flowers called?" Asked that man to the woman in front of him.

"Ah, those are perennials. We should be seeing more and more as they come into season. Very fragrant," the woman replied, reaching for a plate and silverware.

"Ah! That's right!" Said the woman named Carol. She brushed her fingers against the delicate petals and brought the flower close to her face. "Just look at these colors. So... bright and... " Carol looked up and closed her eyes.

"Vivid?" Her husband offered.

"Yes! Vivid. That's the word."

Don gently lifted the perennial to the side of his wife's head, sliding it behind her left ear. After a group prayer, the couple sat down at one of the cafeteria tables with their lunch trays.

This was my unofficial introduction to Don and Carol Keene. They had been in Manhattan when the Tribulation began, a nightmare that had turned their city into a battleground. They had come down south shortly after Armageddon and had ended up here in Savannah.

We had been tasked with removing debris from one of the docks on the waterfront there. The Organization had given priority to these sorts of projects in an effort to establish intercity (and later, intercontinental) ferry routes. Although I had no notions of writing this book at the time, my casual conversation with Don and Carol made me realize that everyone had a story worth telling, and I decided that I wanted to hear and remember as many as I could.

Our conversation began after lunch and a discussion of *The Watchtower*. The dog, now sprawled out between Don and Carol's feet, lazed contentedly in the afternoon sun.

"So, New York during the Tribulation. That couldn't have been easy," I said.

"It was hard everywhere. But, New York. That place was something else." Carol frowned.

"We were in our seventies when the Tribulation began, and we'd lived there our whole lives," said Don. "We'd experienced dozens of protests, and even a few riots when we were young, but nothing like the Tribulation."

"People were like animals," said Carol. "And I don't mean that figuratively, like it might sound. They were like rabid, feral dogs." She was shaking her head.

"Do you remember a point," I asked, "when you realized it wasn't just another protest or riot, that what was being experienced was worldwide, part of something greater, part of prophecy?"

"I do," Don said. "I mean, a lot of events sort of bled together. We heard reports of false religion toppling in different parts of the world, and of course there had been anti-religious sentiment in our city for years. But when the Witnesses locally began to be attacked, beaten, and even, in some cases, killed, there was no mistaking it."

"Did you two ever face any of that personally?"

Don and Carol looked into each others' eyes and then back to me.

"We did," said Carol.

"Before the tribulation started, despite having our share of trials and disappointments, life was OK. We had our jobs, we had our congregation, and we had each other. I was an elder, Carol was a regular auxiliary pioneer, and we were happy patiently waiting for the end. But the Tribulation changed everything for us.

We didn't have a car, and in fact neither of us learned to drive, so we'd always take the subway to and from the meeting each week. We didn't mind it, it was kind of relaxing in a way, and we had more time to talk to each other, to talk about the meeting that night..."

"Or to put together a last-minute part," Carol said with a smile.

"Or that, sometimes, thank you dear."

16

Carol nodded.

"But one night," Don continued, "and this was before any official bans on our Organization, we were stopped by a group of young men on our way home from the meeting. They wanted to know if we were Witnesses. I explained that we were."

"I'll never forget the look in those boys' eyes," said Carol. "A look of cold, unfeeling darkness."

"My first thought was to protect my wife," Don explains. "I didn't know what they had in mind, I just wanted to be sure Carol was safe. 'Here, please, take all my money, anything you want,' I said. I took it from my pocket and offered it to one of the young men. Without saying anything, he knocked it from my hand and spit in my face."

"That got me going!" Said Carol, "Here Don was trying to be so kind to these hooligans, and we were old folks, you know, and I just couldn't see how anyone could be so awful."

"It didn't matter to me all that much," Don continued. "I was just scared at this point, and wishing I had taken up the offer of one of our friends to drive us home that night in their car. I spent years regretting that decision."

"Finally, one of the boys leapt at us," Carol said. "It happened in an instant. I can't remember what he looked like, I just remember looking at a black, New York sky, laid out on the sidewalk, and that horrible burning in my eyes."

"Burning?" I asked.

"Yes. We're not sure what it was, though it smelled a little like the bug spray we used in our kitchen when we had cockroach problems. Toxic, but with a fake flowery smell."

"And they sprayed it in your eyes? Why?"

"Both of our eyes. Who knows? Maybe they were on drugs? Maybe they hated Witnesses? They never told us the reason. After they attacked they just ran off, cursing and laughing."

"What happened then?"

"It took a few minutes to think straight. The pain was very intense. I may have been unconscious for a time as well after falling down, I'm not quite sure. When I finally had my wits I tried using my cellphone but it was hopeless. I couldn't operate it without being able to see it clearly. Finally, a neighbor heard us and called an ambulance and the police. But by the time we had gotten all the way to the hospital and a nurse had examined us, it was too late."

"Too late?"

"Our vision was ruined permanently. We were blind," Don

explained grimly.

A line of kitchen volunteers emerged from behind one of the trailers next to the dining tables, balancing trays of cupcakes in their hands. One of the volunteers, a young blonde sister, set a tray in front of us, explaining that they were made from local elderberries. I waved my hand, *No thanks*. "I see what you mean about changing everything for you," I said.

"Yes, our whole life flipped upside down. We had to learn to use walking sticks. And then Braille. Can you imagine, at our age? And then, of course, we suddenly had this strange new animal in the apartment to take care of. We weren't exactly dog people, either, but the doctor insisted on us having one to help us navigate the city."

"You continued living in New York City? Why not move somewhere a little..."

"Safer? We thought about it. But where? We knew the city and nothing else. We didn't have children to move in with, no family in the Truth, there was nowhere to go," Carol said, biting into her cupcake.

"But the friends really became our family. It was then that we fully understood the words at Proverbs 17:17. 'brother' and 'sister' weren't just words used for acquaintances at the Kingdom Hall; it was *really* the way we felt about the friends. We became so much closer to them, even if at times we felt like a burden," said Don.

"I know we were difficult to be around, especially right after the incident. We were frustrated with having to re-learn how to do everything, angry at having our old lives taken from us, and sometimes ready to quit. But the friends were always there for us, often staying in the apartment with us when we couldn't manage things on our own. Without them, we wouldn't have made it. We thanked Jehovah every day for that family." Carol shook her head slowly.

"And still do. And for Misty, our seeing-eye-dog, of course." Don bent down to stroke the golden retriever. "Couldn't have done it without her."

The dog rolled over, adjusting itself in the sunlight, and I saw its eye open slightly, looking back and forth between Don and Carol. And then, with a satisfied huff, Misty went back to sleep.

Hank Haynes

I spent the first few months in Savannah at the seaside ports, making preparations for the traffic we were soon to receive. On the first few boats over, brothers and sisters sailed in from Miami, Havana and the Bahamas. Most of them came on 30- to 50-foot sailboats. One group of Haitian brothers arrived in an expensive yacht. They later explained to us that they'd been praying for a way to Maryland, where some of them had family and friends. The next day their request was answered when they found the five-million dollar yacht sitting in the bay of their poor seaside town. Apparently, it had mysteriously unmoored from ritzy Pétionville and drifted right into their backyard.

A lighthouse at the end of the pier helped to guide the boats. A watchman was stationed there around the clock, and by way of long-distance walkie-talkie, he would contact the inland welcome center when any ships were spotted. If the brothers sailing them managed to get their HF radios working, they'd often scan for our signal and give us advanced notice. Either way, as soon as the passengers unloaded onto the harbor, we welcomed them and escorted them to downtown storefronts that had been partitioned into small apartments.

My job, for a time, was to make sure these guests settled comfortably in their temporary homes. Most of them only stayed for a few nights before leaving for a port up north. At this point, we'd already been through one New World winter, and it had still been relatively cold and stormy on the coast. We all expected the weather would even out as we passed into Paradise, but no one knew exactly how long that might take. Well, no one except for Hank Haynes.

Hank had, among other things, studied meteorology in the Old World, working for a time for the United States military. He explained that, even under ideal circumstances, weather patterns and global seasonal shifts would likely take decades. In the meantime, many of the friends from the upper northern hemisphere migrated south to be closer to the equator, where warmer living conditions meant less time preparing for and struggling with harsh winters, which in turn meant more time for the ever-important clean up efforts.

But there was more to Hank than just weather analysis. In fact, of all the stories I heard in the New World, I still think of Hank's as the most bizarre and incredible.

When I first saw him, he was kneeling at the prow of a 35-foot sailboat named *Diana*. One hand was resting on his knee and the other was gripping the pulpit. He had a white-blonde crew cut and his brow was furled. I remember thinking his clothes were a little odd, too. He wore what looked like a fireman's uniform: baggy orange pants held up by suspenders, heavy black boots, and a tight navy blue undershirt with an insignia I couldn't make out through my binoculars. When he stepped onto the dock next to me, I finally got a good look at it, with wide, unbelieving eyes.

"NASA?" I asked, staring at his shirt. He nodded.

"That's right," he said, shaking my hand firmly and stating his name.

"My name is Bro–uh, Mitch. Mitch Hanson. You can just call me Mitch."

"Pleasure to meet you."

I stared at the man silently for a few moments while the other men and women in the boat piled onto the dock and were quickly swept away by volunteer escorts. I realized Hank was waiting for me, and, apologizing, I led him to one of the empty apartments. I could tell he was exhausted, and likely confused. I showed him the room, the shower, and mentioned our dining arrangements before leaving him alone to rest. When I didn't see him again for another two days, I was a little worried, and finally went back to his room to check on him.

He came to the door after the third knock. He'd been asleep the whole time, and explained that he'd been through a lot recently. I nodded, as if I somehow understood. Of course, the reality was that I had absolutely no idea what he was talking about. I offered that we go get some food together, and he heartily accepted.

When we'd finished brunch in the cafeteria, we sat together silently at the table. Hank noticed the daily text wedged in between the napkins and the condiments and began flipping through it.

"So Hank... You're not... a Witness, are you?" I asked.

He shot me a side glance as his fingers continued turning the small book's pages.

"That obvious?" He said.

"How much do you know?"

"Only what I heard on the boat. Sounds like a whole lot went on down here in the last year."

"*Down* here?"

"I was on a five-year mission at the International Space Station when your... *Armageddon* struck."

"You were in space?"

Hank nodded, but wore a doubtful expression.

"And did you know what was happening?"

"I got the gist of it. The noises came through pretty clear in the station. I accessed one of the remote satellites and could see a lot of destruction going on on the surface. I thought it was a war, at first. That made our situation on the ISS dangerous; at the time there Russians and Chinese onboard with me. Radio contact with the ground was cut off so I couldn't be sure what country started the war. So I just sealed myself in to the USOS–the American section of the station–as a preventative measure. I wasn't sure what was going on, but I'd been trained to always protect the interests of my country, and that's what I did.

"But then I got the full report from the ground. It was judgment day, and God was wiping the slate clean. A few minutes later, our station was visited by a strange man wearing a white robe and carrying a sword. There were eight of us on the ISS when he arrived. When he'd gone, I was the only one left."

"What was that like?"

"Well... I felt that it was time to reconsider my atheism."

Hank finished off the last of his buttered toast and scrambled eggs and began helping himself to seconds. He was ravenous.

"Why you? Have you wondered that?" I asked.

"Of course. It's all I could think about. I kept trying to hail mission control... Whole lotta nothing came back. The others were dead, completely vanished from the ship except for a cloud of ash. The dust was so thick in some compartments that it almost shut down the air filtration system as it cycled through the intakes. But the fact is: I'd never heard the name *Jehovah* until that day."

"What? How is that possible?"

"My father and mother were both in the army. I grew up on military bases, went to military schools, and later trained with the Air Force. I rarely watched television, rarely even opened a newspaper. I was completely honed in on my career, and it paid off when I was selected by NASA for space training."

"So you're up there, by yourself, without any direction from the ground. How did you survive?"

"Survival wasn't the hard part. There was enough food, water, and O2 on the ISS to sustain a single life for years. The problem was what to do *next*. I stayed put for about eight months, trying to make contact with the ground every day. I checked all known frequencies, even foreign agencies like Moscow's Roscosmos and CNSA and CASC in Beijing, but it was the same across the band. There was simply nothing left. I couldn't even pick up radio signals on long-range scans, which was especially worrisome.

"I finally realized that I had to get down. I needed to be sure what had happened and see if there was anyone else left. And I needed to know why I was spared. Anyway, it's not healthy to be alone in space for so long. You start...losing it." Hank tapped the side of his head with his middle finger.

"So you decided to return to Earth."

"Speaking long-term, it was the only option."

"How'd you do it?"

"Well, for the first time ever, I tried praying. It was a little weird, for me, not believing in God my whole life. So I tried to remember the few times I saw people do it in movies. I bowed my head, clenched my hands, and started talking to Him. I did my best. I thanked Him for letting me live. I asked Him to help me get home. And I promised that if I made it safely, I'd do my best to get to know Him and His purpose."

"And then what?"

"Then came the tricky part. You see, typically, astronauts returning from the ISS would either travel in the American-made Apollo command module or the Russian-made Soyuz space capsule. Unfortunately, a team had left for Earth just a week before the attack in the Soyuz, and the US command module had been damaged when a solar flare fried its electrical systems. So I was forced to take the PPTS, a reusable Russian transport ship that had just been assembled on-station. In theory, it was supposed to replace all the other module ships we'd been using since the 1960's, but in reality, it wasn't fully tested, and I'd only been on it twice.

"It was a lot smaller than the other modules I was used to, and frankly it looked too flimsy to survive re-entry into the atmosphere, but I had no other options. If I didn't make it, I'd end up exactly like the others–a cloud of dust somewhere above the planet.

"So I suited up, strapped in, and did my best to re-familiarize myself with the controls. Fortunately, the systems were practically identical to the ones I was used to. I was scared out of my wits to be doing it alone, though. The modules, of course, are built so they can be operated by a single pilot, but that's only worst case scenario, and I hadn't run a solo simulation in over two years. So far as I know, I'm the only one that *actually* had to land it alone.

"I plotted my course and let the computer time the launch. The space station moves at an incredible speed around the Earth–15 orbits per day–so the timing has to be *exact*.

"Once the coordinates had been set–right off the Florida coast–I sat and I waited. I had no idea what was coming next, but I guessed I was probably going to die. And even If I made it back, I knew Earth wouldn't be the home I'd left, and it wasn't likely anyone would be there to welcome me.

"As the rockets fired off behind the ship, I watched the station spin away slowly into the distance in my rear screen. It was what pilots called *PNR*–the point of no return. If I didn't make it back to Earth, I would die in space, or on reentry."

"But you did make it."

"Yes, somehow. I kept worrying that there'd be a malfunction in the module. Anything, even the slightest rocket misfire, would be enough to throw me miles off course. I was sweating bullets, and not just from the heat of the atmosphere. But somehow, while I was passing through, I blacked out. Probably the force of reentry.

"When I woke up, the module was bobbing somewhere off the East coast of Florida. The electronics systems weren't working properly so I couldn't confirm my position by satellite, and since I had been out of contact with ground control for months, I knew there would be no scheduled coast guard pick up. I was all alone, drifting in the Atlantic Ocean. I had gone from being stranded in space to stranded in the waters of my own planet. It was little comfort.

"I sat there for a whole day in the module, wondering what to do. There was just *nothing* left. I thought I might be the only human on Earth, like some awful sci-fi movie. But the nights were beautiful, worth living for. The ocean was calm enough that I could climb up on the hatch and just sit there looking back at the stars. It made me think about why I'd wanted to be an astronaut in the first place, why, at some point in time, *every* kid wants to be an astronaut.

"But you know, you get out there in space and it's just not as fulfilling as you'd hoped. If you can manage to even get past the atmosphere of Earth, you quickly realize just how incredibly hard It Is for humans to survive anywhere else. We take a lot of things for granted on this planet: the water cycle, gravity, being able to produce our own food and oxygen. Well, you stop taking that stuff for granted real quick when you're out there.

"The tiniest particle crashes into your suit and, in all likelihood, you're dead. You somehow run out of oxygen or food or water and that's it. A fan backs up somewhere and the computer fails to catch it and you suffocate, or die from inhaling a poisonous gas.

"Any one of a million things could go wrong up there and it's all over. You ever hear of the Space Shuttle Challenger explosion? It was caused by a gasket on one of the boosters called an O-ring. There was nothing wrong with the gasket, per se–it had just gotten a little too cold prior to launch, and it failed. 73 seconds after liftoff, it killed the entire crew of seven because the temperature the night before had been a *few degrees too low. That* is the reality of space travel."

"Being up there, thinking about all those factors, never made the Earth seem special to you? You never thought it was the work of a Creator?" I asked.

"No one denies that the Earth is special. That's a main reason that programs like NASA always drew a large share of critics. They knew–as we did–that the chances of finding a planet even remotely similar to our own was infinitesimal.

"And as for as thinking about the existence of a Creator, sure, the thought crossed my mind. You'd have had a hard time finding an astronaut that didn't imagine at least once that there was a God. But the act of *considering* a possibility and *believing* are completely different. And the other thing is, there's no money in it. You don't have to go in space to believe in God. NASA wanted astronauts, researchers, scientists, and theorists that were looking for answers *out there* so they could keep their projects funded. The idea of a God was fundamentally contrary to their goals, if that makes sense. So no, I never thought deeply about a Creator's existence."

"So what happened after you landed the module in the sea?"

"Well, on the second day, I was sitting in there trying to get the sat phone working, when I started hearing strange noises, a sort of clicking and chirping sound. I first I thought it was the radio, but the radio wasn't working. Nothing was. then I realized that the sound was coming from outside the hull, somewhere below me in the water. I put my face against the wall and listened carefully as the sound got louder and more intense.

"And when I looked out the window, there was another face staring at me.

"It wasn't a human face, though. It was an elongated, rubbery dolphin face. And it was watching me. Soon there were more, maybe twenty or so, and they seemed to be in a frenzy once they realized I was inside. I had heard dolphins were friendly with people, but they seemed very frantic, and possibly hungry, so I stayed in the module just to be sure.

"After awhile, they left, but the next day, around the same time, they were back. It was the same thing: frantic swimming, excited chirping noises, and then they were gone. When they came back on the

24

fourth day, they were wilder than ever, and kept jumping into the air and splashing around the module. Then I heard a sound that about stopped my heart:

"*CLANG! CLANG! CLANG!* Something hard was knocking against the outside of the module. And then, the sweetest sound ever: that of a human voice.

"'Anyone in there?' Just three simple words, but that's all it took. I started sobbing like a little baby.

"There were a dozen men and women on the sailboat. They were as perplexed as I was exhilarated. They simply couldn't believe I'd come from space, or perhaps it was the fact that I'd been saved that amazed them. Either way, they were happy to have me, and began filling me in on the details I'd been wondering about for so long.

"They told me about your Organization, your preaching work in the past, and the work that's being done now. To be honest, while it was all very interesting, more than anything I'm just happy I'm not the only one left. I know I've got a lot to learn about this place, and you people. But I plan to keep the promise I made to God, and that means keeping an open mind."

Hank sighed and looked around the kitchen. In the late morning sun, the tent was starting to heat up. He unbuttoned his cuffs and began rolling up his sleeves. Then, suddenly, he stopped.

"Huh. That's odd," he said with a frown.

"What's that?" I asked.

"I used to have a scar here on my left forearm. Cut myself on some barbed wire when I was just a kid..."

I smiled. "Yeah, you won't ever see that scar again."

Hank squinted into my eyes intently. "And that's because?..."

"I'll tell you what–wait here a second and I'll grab a couple of books from my room," I said, swinging my legs out from under the table.

And that's how I started my first study in the New World.

Tyrel Rodriguez

After a year or so in Savannah I was given the option to head north to Baltimore. It wasn't easy leaving Hank, whom we now called Brother Haynes. He had been a quick learner, and had taken to the truth eagerly. We had become close friends in our few months together, and he'd already made a huge contribution to the restoration work when I finally boarded a repurposed Coast Guard speedboat and began my way up the coast.

Baltimore had been more developed than Savannah in the Old World, so a larger cleanup operation was needed. When brothers and sisters from the surrounding suburbs had finished their work there, they moved into the city to help tear down the skyscrapers and apartment complexes that dominated the skyline next to the harbor.

One of those brothers was Tyrel Rodriguez. He was rolling giant spools of electrical cables away from a building that was about to be detonated. What had intrigued me about Tyrel was the tattoos on his arms and neck. They had obviously been etched in his skin over a period of many years and had only half-faded into oblivion. They piqued my curiosity about Tyrel's story, so I decided to talk with him that evening. We found a quiet bench in a park several hundred meters from the tents and bonfires.

I asked about his tattoos.

"Oh, these... You aren't the first to mention them. I guess it's pretty rare now to see someone with them," he said. Tyrel twisted his arms around, glancing at the various designs. He looked almost surprised to see them, as if he'd forgotten they were there.

"The truth is, I guess I'm trying to forget some of the memories behind these markings. I feel like I'm getting there a little bit each day, and I suppose the ink fades bit by bit...under a new layer of skin, or something. Things were so different before all this." Tyrel motioned with to our surroundings with the swing of his arm. The trees were alive with birds settling in for the night. The smell of Spring was heavy in the air. Foraging deer peeked at us curiously from nearby bushes.

I asked him if he was willing to tell his story, and after a momentary pause, he nodded.

"I guess I should tell it from the beginning, when I was a little boy living in Oakland, California. My family lived in a dangerous part of town, but there wasn't much we could do about it. It was just us two boys, and my mom and grandmother. My dad had left when I was still a baby, so I never knew him, though honestly I sort of hated him all the same for making life that much harder for us. But as I grew up, my mom would tell me again and again that I was like my dad, and so I hated her for awhile too, because I didn't want to be compared with him.

"School was, in some ways, even more dangerous than the streets that surrounded my neighborhood, and I was always a smaller kid, so I was pushed around a lot by the other boys. They were boys a lot like me–many of them didn't have dads, or moms, or either. Some were already experimenting with drugs and sex, and this was in elementary school. There were no good examples. Even the teachers were bad. Some of them would sell or buy drugs from the students. No one did anything about it, no one seemed to care. Where we lived, we were like dirt swept under a rug. And, after awhile, you start thinking of yourself that way. *Nobody wants me*, you'd think. *I'm trash*. There was no reason to push yourself to be a good person, to do good things. It made no difference.

"There were only two positive influences in my life at that age. The first was my grandmother, Nattie Brooks. Nana was the counterweight to all the bad things in my world. She was warm and kind and loving and patient and honest. Nana was one of Jehovah's Witnesses. She urged my mother to study the Bible with her, but mom never did. Looking back, I think it scared her. I think she knew that if she studied she would have to make changes. The people she worked with (and drank with), the men she dated (and was abused by), would all have to go. And my mom wasn't strong enough to do it. So Nana worked on us boys.

"Every Tuesday after school Nana would have a Bible study with Nate, my older brother. Nate was about eight when they started studying. Nate was an amazing kid, the second good influence in my life. Despite everything, Nate studied hard in school and never got into trouble. Sometimes mom would come home late from work, smelling like alcohol and screaming or crying, and Nate would be the one to put her to bed, making sure she was lying on her side with a pillow under her head so she wouldn't vomit in her sleep and choke to death. Nate was the closest thing our family ever had to a father.

"But for a reason I could never understand, mom never liked

28

Nate. When we were little, I remember mom once pushing him down to the ground, maliciously. They were in the kitchen and she had gotten angry. As he lost his balance, he fell and hit his head on the corner of the table. He had to get rushed to the hospital. They put six stitches in him for that. Mom lied and told the doctors Nate had fallen while chasing me around the house. I remember that blank, horrible stare in Nate's eyes when he heard her. We never told anyone about that, not even Nana.

"As I got older, Nate tried to share with me what Nana taught him from the Bible. She was getting older then and was gradually succumbing to Alzheimer's. She would wander around the house aimlessly; once she almost burned the building down after forgetting a fire she was using to cook with.

"Nate was a good teacher to me, but when mom found out what he was doing she was furious. I remember her screaming: 'You think God is going to save you, Nate? Yeah? Well did he save Nana? Look at her! She doesn't even know who God is anymore!'

"But mom was wrong. Although Nana forgot and confused a lot of things, she always remembered Jehovah. After she died, we found a crumpled piece of paper inside of her nightgown pocket. The handwriting was very shaky, but we could still read it. They were her favorite scriptures: *Revelation 21:4, John 17:3, Psalms 37:10,11*.

"Nate took that paper and hid it away in our room somewhere. I would sometimes catch him looking at it at night with a flashlight, crying and praying to Jehovah under his sheets. Nate did his best to continue teaching me what he'd learned. Before mom would come home from work, Nate and I would climb up on the roof of our building and read a few chapters from *My Book of Bible Stories*. I'll never forget those afternoon studies. Nate taught me why I had to be honest with other people and do good things even when others weren't around, because God was always watching. Nate liked to read me the Joseph stories. They were his favorites, and they became my favorites, too.

"It wasn't until years later that I finally understood that Nate *was* Joseph: a prisoner in our house, despised by his own flesh and blood, doing his best to listen to and obey his God.

"Things got worse for our family after Nana's death. Mom drank more, came home later. Nate grew up faster. Soon he was in high school, which meant I saw him less and less. He was also attending meetings at a nearby Kingdom Hall. But mom wouldn't let me go.

"'If he wants to lose his mind, what do I care?' my mom once said. 'But not you, you're too good for that stuff, baby Ty.'

"So I didn't. And with no one to look after me at school, I was getting in with the wrong crowd. For awhile, Nate and I drifted apart. Then we started arguing. A lot. I thought he was just jealous; I was mom's favorite son. I was beginning to pick up mom's traits and habits. Even at 14 years old, I was cursing, losing my temper, drinking, and smoking. Sometimes all at once. In her twisted way, this seemed to please mom, maybe just because it hurt Nate so much.

"And then, one night, when I was fifteen, a knock at our front door changed everything. I remember those red and blue splashes of light coming in from the curtains and a crackling radio from the street below. The officer said that Nate had been mugged on his way home from a meeting. The mugger had a gun and had pulled the trigger. Nate had bled out on the sidewalk.

"He had only been carrying four dollars in his wallet at the time."

Tyrel twisted his left arm around so that his inner bicep was visible. The letters N-A-T-E were written in a furled, flowing script.

"How did your Mom react to Nate's death?" I asked.

"Well that was the worst part of it. You know, when that knock came, I peeked out of my room and I heard the police officer tell my mom what had happened, and that she would have to come to the morgue to identify the body of her son. And I just stood there, shaking, feeling somehow guilty for it all, but my mom, all she said was, 'I'll go tomorrow after work. It's been a long day.'

"And that was it. Like someone had come to pick up the recycling and she was too busy to deal with it. My relationship with my mother ended that night."

"How did life change after your brother's death?"

"I guess it didn't, really. I kept doing what I was doing, my mom kept doing her thing. She died at thirty-four from liver problems, so I moved in with the girl I was dating. I was sixteen at the time.

"When we first started dating, in high school, I promised myself that I would take care of her. I had never gotten over the anger towards my father, and I was determined not to repeat his mistakes. I told her all this, that I was going to be there forever, that she could count on me. But I could barely take care of myself at the time, much less someone else. I did alright for awhile, but then it just got too hard. I didn't see the point. So I left her, and left Oakland. Years later, I found out she was pregnant when I left. She had had an abortion.

"I didn't have any money when I left Oakland, so I knew I had to get a job, and either because of loneliness or fear, I felt I needed to make friends. It seemed that I had an answer to both of these questions when I met Sam, who lived in San Jose, not far from where I grew up.

"Sam seemed nice. He knew a lot of people, and he was very generous. He even let me stay in an extra apartment he owned for free. And he got me a job as a driver. It was a simple job, and I loved how free I felt having my own car. All I had to do was to deliver contracts between companies and businesspeople. Each trip paid well, about one hundred dollars.

"But something didn't feel right. The businesspeople didn't look like businesspeople, and I was getting the feeling they weren't just passing documents. Finally, one night while filling up the tank, I opened the trunk and jimmied open the lock on the "document" case. It was loaded with bags of fine white powder. Having grown up in a rough neighborhood, I knew the stuff immediately. It was cocaine.

"I was terrified when I realized what I had been doing, especially since I had been driving without a license and sometimes with a couple of bottles of alcohol in my system. I drove home that night, furious, ready to confront Sam. I wanted out. I would tell him I was grateful for his help and the work but that I didn't want to be trafficking drugs. I was nineteen at this point and was starting to realize that I wanted more out of life. I was thinking a lot about Nate at the time. I was also wondering how I could find the Witnesses.

"When I knocked on Sam's bedroom door, I had the words all laid out in my head. I had known guys like this back in Oakland. They could turn on you like wild dogs so you had to be careful. But before I could say anything, Sam opened the door with a smile and invited me in for a drink. Then he started talking.

"He told me I was a good driver, I had been reliable, and that he wanted to give me a raise. It was going to mean more responsibility, but he felt he could trust me, and so on. Before I could refuse him, he handed me a stack of bills and a fake license. *The car's yours now*, he said. He gave me the keys.

"And that was how I started a career trafficking drugs in California. I never used the drugs I sold; I had seen how much damage they could do to a person's life and body. More than a few of my mom's old boyfriends had been users, and I hated them all. I hated the people I sold drugs to, too, but I suppose that's how I justified what I was doing. I didn't care if they threw their life away—I was making tons of money. *Tons*.

"After three years working for Sam, I had enough money to buy my own duplex in the Valley, an uppity place near San Jose where Sam suggested I move to expand our business. Eventually we lived in the place together. The Valley had a lot of rich kids and their families, and they could spend a lot more money on drugs than the average junkie on the street. So we sold and we sold and we sold.

"As the months turned into years, I became more and more hardened in my view of the world. I hated what I was seeing on the news, the injustices, the corruption, the wars. But I was a hypocrite for all that, since I was only contributing to the very problems I criticized. So I began to hate myself, too. To make up for the lack of self-respect I had, I paid thousands of dollars to cover my body in tattoos–tattoos that would remind me of all the things that I wished or thought I was.

"Around this time, maybe 2015 or '16, Sam and I decided to expand our business to include the sale of illegal firearms. California, and really the whole world, was becoming more and more dangerous. Riots were becoming commonplace and everyone seemed unhappy and scared and looking to buy a weapon.

"One of our customers was a guy named Joe, or at least, that's the name we knew him by. Joe was not your average arms buyer. He was in his fifties at the time, slightly greying but still mostly blonde, well tanned, with a big smile. He seemed like a genuinely nice guy. Not that we hadn't sold guns to nice guys before–we had–but those guys were typically just in the market for a personal piece they could stick in their closet or in a dashboard in case of an "emergency". But Joe was buying *thousands* of firearms. For about three years he was our biggest client.

"Joe had an insatiable appetite for guns, and eventually it spread to other devices. He wanted machines that could kill, maim, mutilate, destroy. Whatever we could get, he wanted. Sam and I were terrified of the guy. And with every sealed deal, he'd simply smile and say *Thanks guys, I guess we're done here* and walk out, just like that.

"I was curious about what he was doing with the stuff, but Sam told me to stay out of it, that it was bad business to pry into a client's life. So I let it drop, and that was that."

"Did you ever find out what he was using the weapons for?"

"I did. One night Sam and I were up late watching the news, all this stuff about the economies of different countries crashing, and how the unemployment rate was going up, and on and on, and then suddenly we see this familiar face, with that big, toothy smile. It's Joe. And he's handing a five thousand dollar check to some homeless shelter in the city.

"And then the news anchor explains about how 'Pastor Mark Ritter has been known in the community for his charitable contributions to various organizations in need and how this latest act of goodwill is much appreciated by the' blah, blah, blah...

"Well, as it turned out, this "Joe" guy was actually a well-known pastor and had been reselling the weapons to a drug cartel in South America where he would often go on "missions" for the church. In return, they were supporting an incredible lifestyle for him there, with yachts, women, alcohol, and even, you guessed it, drugs.

"When I found out, I was angry beyond words. This guy, Mark Ritter, represented to me everything that was evil in the world. So, without telling Sam, I went one night to the church he worked at, and burnt it to the ground. Fortunately, no one was injured, though at the time I'm not sure I would've cared either way."

"Was that the beginning of the California Church Burnings?"

"I'm not sure if it was the first, but it's possible. There seemed to be a bunch of them all at once, before the government stepped in."

"But how did you get back to the Truth? At this point, your life seems to have been going in the opposite direction..."

"It was, but on the inside I was coming to terms with a decision I had known to be right ever since I was a little boy looking at *My Book of Bible Stories* with Nate. The problem was that after my act of arson I was arrested and spent the next few years in prison. All those Joseph stories came back to me and gave me a lot of strength, even though there were some...well, major differences between us at that point.

"The ironic thing was, before prison, finding the Witnesses had been easy. I saw the Kingdom Hall almost every day, in fact; it was only five minutes walking distance from our apartment. But now, behind bars, I had no way of finding them. Or so I thought.

"Still, I decided to pray about it. It wasn't easy, after all those years, opening up to Jehovah. The words weren't ready. But my heart was, or at least was starting to be, and I felt much better when I had said *amen*. Two weeks later, while I was laying in my bunk trying to recall pictures and passages from the *Bible Stories* book, an announcement came blaring over the loudspeaker:

"'Inmates with privileges are invited to attend a thirty-minute Bible sermon given by Mr. Mark Caffery from the Mountain View Congregation of Jehovah's Witnesses.'

"At first I didn't know how to react. I just lay there, frozen like a dead man in a coffin, gazing at the cinderblock ceiling. And then, hot tears were welling in my eyes and rolling down the sides of my face. Jehovah was there! And he was listening to me! I was ecstatic.

"But it's hard to change yourself in prison. As excited and eager as I was to begin studying and learning, it was dangerous to appear needy or weak to the other inmates. But those brothers, Caffery and others, had experience dealing with men like me, and their patience produced results. I was baptized, there in prison, about a year later, soon before the Liberation Act was passed. I was released from prison soon after that, but of course by then the world was in chaos."

"What happened to Sam?"

"Never saw him again. It didn't surprise me. He would have been putting himself in danger trying to make any kind of contact with me in prison. And the bond between criminals...well, it only stretches so far.

"When I went free, I decided not to return to my old apartment. I stayed with the Caffery family for awhile until I finally got a job working as an electrician for a brother in a nearby congregation. One day we had a job on the same street as my old apartment. As we unpacked our tools from the van, I saw an old woman emerge from the house I had owned before I went to prison. I wondered about Sam, where he was, if he was even still alive."

"You said earlier that, before going to prison, you'd made a lot of money. What happened to it?"

Tyrel shrugged. "I stashed it behind an air conditioning vent in my apartment room. I'm sure Sam found it before he left."

"You never went back to check?"

"You know, back when I had been locked up, I once asked Brother Caffery about that money, if there was any way I could keep it. Maybe donate half to the Organization and keep the rest? But Mark just smiled, tilting his head as he did when I got the answer wrong to a question in the *Teach* book.

"'Well,' he said, 'How do you think Jehovah views that money?'

"In any case, I really hope Sam used all that cash to get himself out of the 'guns n' thugs' life. Because, just a few years later, it wasn't worth a thing."

Tyrel stared off in the direction of the construction site, where the warm glow of a bonfire reflected from high-rise exteriors. "It's hard to believe so much of this happened within the last decade. It feels like it's been a lifetime on this side of the line. It's true–the things from the Old World, or at least the pain of it all–is fading quickly from mind."

And he was right.

Ferra Rockdale

When I first met Ferra she was ad-libbing poetry to the rhythm of a bongo clenched between her knees. We had just finished a meal of canned beans, corn, and homemade cranberry bread and were sitting around a bonfire listening to her perform.

I had to smile at her skill; she had a way of choosing the perfect phrases to match the sound of the drum. A scrape of her hand across the surface of the drum was paired with fitting words, each syllable coarse and bristled. When she quickened the tempo and began tapping the sides of the drum, her voice was like a spark trying to ignite a flame. I'd never heard anything like it, and added my hearty applause to the others' when she'd finished.

"So, what do you call that?" I asked her later that night.

"Most just call it *crazy*," said Ferra, and her wild eyes convinced me. Her inky black hair was parted down the middle and braided into ponytails that covered her ears. She wore an orange t-shirt and khakis rolled up to the knees.

"Well I thought it was great," I told her, meaning it. "Where did you learn...all that?"

"Mostly my Dad. He had Native American roots. They liked drums and chanting and campfires. I guess that blood runs pretty strong," Ferra shrugged.

"And you've got talent, too."

"Yeah, well, I try."

I asked her about her assignment.

"I'm with the East Baltimore Salvage unit. Our job is to go search out and salvage anything that can be used. Our main focus, of course, is nonperishable foods, like canned corn, beans, spam, jars of jam and pickles, seasonings, etc. But we look for lots of other stuff, too: toilet paper, paper towels, paper plates, plastic ware, cups, aluminum foil, light bulbs, and lots and lots of batteries."

"I noticed a lot of generators here run off of propane. Where does that come from?"

"Well since propane isn't commonly found in this area of the city, it usually has to get trucked in by crews working near city limits.

It's used sparingly, though. The generators are strictly used for tools and to power the kitchen. So we use bonfires for light at night, and generally people just go to sleep earlier these days."

I glanced at my watch and realized it was only eight o'clock. Most of the workers had already unrolled sleeping bags and cushions and begun settling in for the night. From our vantage point on the hill, we could see a handful of similar campsites glowing in the city below.

"How long have you been doing this?"

"Over three years now. I was one of the first to sign up when our congregation got the announcement that help was needed. It seemed like a great way to get involved, and I like this kind of stuff."

Ferra reached into her pocket and pulled out a switchblade, flicking the black, serrated edge out and jamming it into a fresh wood chopping in her other hand. She deftly ran the blade beneath the bark, peeling it from the wood.

"Here," she said, handing it to me.

"What am I supposed to do with this?"

"Throw it into those bushes over there."

I didn't understand but threw it anyway. I looked back at Ferra, but her eyes were locked on the bush in front of us.

"Just wait," she said, grinning. A moment later, the bush moved.

"Wild dogs?" I asked.

"Better."

From the hedge emerged a black snout, and then a head, and ears. And shoulders. And a large, dark body. In its mouth, the bear held the stick.

"Grizzly?" I asked, feigning composure. I had never been this close to a bear.

"Yep. And just a baby. You should see the mama."

"You've seen the...mama?"

The bear lumbered around the campsite, sniffing the workers in the sleeping bags and getting rubs and scratches from the others who were still awake.

"We call him Rory," Ferra explained. The bear, evidently on hearing its name, came over and plopped next to her on the grass. Ferra extricated the stick from its jaws with her thumb and index, let it hang limply in the air, and then tossed it in the fire.

"I told you Rory," she said as she rubbed his ears, "if you want to play fetch, don't get your nasty spit all over the stick." Rory grunted, lowered his head, and let out a heavy sign that rustled the grass.

"So what was the Tribulation like for you, Ferra?"

The girl took a sip of her hot maple cocoa and scratched her nose. "Brutal. I learned the truth when I was in college. I was studying to become a musician at a university not far from here. One of my classmates, named Alice, was a Witness, and from time to time we'd talk about God. Alice would ask me if I thought he'd exist, and I never knew how to reply. I'd read some of the magazines she'd given me, and from the parts I understood, it made sense that everything was created, but... it was hard for me to make any definite decision. It wasn't that I believed evolution; I didn't. I guess I just felt that a belief in God would turn me into a conservative religionist, and I was afraid that would stunt my creativity.

"I was, of course, really into music. I loved almost all of it, from classical stuff to the music of my parents' years to contemporary bands. I was at concerts two or three times every week, and was part of my own band, too. Music was my god, you could say, and I was more or less satisfied with that.

"But Alice was patient with me, and I liked talking to her. I respected the way she treated other people, her academic integrity, and clean lifestyle. I didn't know anyone else like that at school, and I could see that the way she lived really protected her. So many other girls in college would get drunk at these wild dorm parties and many became addicted to alcohol and other drugs. Some girls, after going to these parties, would later find out they were pregnant, or worse. They couldn't even remember who the guy was. But Alice never had to worry about that stuff."

"What finally got you studying?" I asked.

"In 2018, the anti-religious stuff was really heating up, especially on college campuses like ours. A lot of students organized anti-church rallies and demonstrations. It started off in response to the popularity of the WhollyEvil website, and was mainly anti-Catholic in the beginning, but later came to include most of the major churches: Protestants, Baptists, Pentecostals, Mormons, etc.

"It was during that year that I asked Alice what she thought about everything that was going on, and if she was worried about being a Witness.

"'Not at all,' she said, and that really surprised me. Then Alice explained that the Bible had prophesied a global attack on religion, and that things would only get worse over time. That really impressed me, and I agreed to study."

"Did your classmates ever find out about your studying?"

"I tried my best to keep my study a secret. I covered all my books in old sheet music and pretended they were textbooks. And I insisted that Alice and I only study off-campus. But eventually someone found out, and that was that. I was a pretty popular student, especially since our band was well-known in the area, and my studying the Bible was like scandal.

"I did my best to explain to those willing to listen that the Witnesses were different. They held to their principles, they were good people, and I wasn't joining a church after all, just learning a little. But you can't reason with people when they're in a mob mentality. No one seemed to understand me. Especially my band mates, since it had a huge effect on the number of people attending our concerts.

"One night, while we were playing a gig in a bar, a drunken college boy shouted, 'Hey Jehovah, sing us a Bible song!' I felt sick; I knew he meant me. My band mates had stopped playing and were glaring at me, the whole audience seemed to be sneering. I lost it.

"I screamed a curse at the boy into the mic. I instantly regretted it, of course, and felt even worse. I turned my head and saw the rest of the band storm off the stage. I turned back to the crowd at my feet just in time to see a green beer bottle hurtling at my face.

"When I woke up, I was lying in a bed in a lonely hospital room. My head throbbed like a kick drum. I could only see out of my left eye. I touched the right side of my face and winced in pain. The whole side of my head was swollen and bruised.

"I just sat there, wondering why all this was happening, and cried. I didn't cry often; I was a tough girl—and still am—but that night it all came out. My confidence, my popularity, my circle of friends, it all seemed to be disappearing from my life. With nothing left, I prayed to Jehovah.

"It was the first time I had really communicated with Him in prayer. Alice had told me a million times that prayer was important, and I had tried once or twice, but never with my heart. I barely found the words. I think my prayer was something like, 'Jehovah... Why? Help!...'

"After I was done, I felt so... calm. The pain—at least on the inside—had lessened. A lot. And a scripture popped into my head, one I had just read with Alice the week before. Jesus's words at John 15:20: *If they persecuted me, they will persecute you also.*

"And then Alice's words came to me, an echo in some chamber of my head: *Sometimes the persecution comes without warning, without cause, from unexpected places. But you WILL be persecuted. That's a guarantee...*

"She was right. At that moment, I really wanted to talk to her, to tell her that I wanted to get serious with this studying business. I was ready to move on with my life. I thought about calling her but it was already two o'clock in the morning.

"At that very moment, my phone started buzzing in my purse beside the bed. I leaned over and looked at the screen—it was Alice! She'd heard from someone about my accident and had tried calling earlier but I'd still been unconscious. It was so good to hear her voice.

"From that point on, we were like sisters. I studied as much as I could. My thirst for music was replaced by a thirst for truth. I quit the band, changed the way I dressed and talked, stopped going to parties, and began attending meetings with Alice. The ridicule from classmates continued, but I had the strength to face it. I was baptized the next year, in 2019."

The life had all but vanished from our fire. The final embers pulsed in an ashy pit. Rory's ears twitched in his sleep. Glancing around the campground I realized that I, too, was exhausted. It had been a long day with another right over the horizon.

I bid Ferra farewell and trudged back to my tent, where I dreamt of drums, bears, and poetry.

Baltimore to California

When we'd finished our assignment in Baltimore, the crews were rearranged and sent into the inland cities that needed workers: St. Louis, Cincinnati, Oklahoma City, and so on. It was around this time that I received a letter from an old friend living in Los Angeles.

Mitch,
We heard you were doing volunteer work on the East Coast with one of the crews out there, hope everything is going great. There are some incredible things happening out here on the West Coast. Have you heard of the New Monterey Aquarium? Really incredible stuff.
If you're ever in the area, please stop by. We have more than enough space for visitors! We'd love to see you.
Reply if you can, or just surprise us with a visit.

Sincerely,
Mark Raven

California! It had been a long time. I thought about my time there growing up, driving up the coastal highway to see relatives. It had been beautiful before the Tribulation and I wondered how it looked now. I decided to ask our overseer about a transfer.

"Well that's a coincidence," he said. "We just got a request in for volunteers willing to do demo work in Los Angeles. Interested?"

I was. "Why so late on demolitions there? I would've thought a major city like LA would've been a primary restoration site," I said.

"Long Beach was, and I'm sure that was the plan for Los Angeles too, but it's been inaccessible for months due to the fires. It's just now safe to go in. You still interested?"

"Yeah, sure," I said. He shuffled through a case of papers and withdrew my file. He made a few notes and checked his watch: 7:25 PM.

"Four twenty-five in sunny California. They should still be at their desks," the overseer said to himself. His name was Jared Hale.

He spun around in his chair and unlatched a metal bin. Sliding the cover off he withdrew a smaller case. He set it on the table and unfastened the clasps. The plastic hinges groaned open, revealing a rectangular black metal box. The overseer flipped a switch on its side, turned a few dials, and reached into a canvas bag, pulling out a coiled cable attached to a hand-operated transmitter. He plugged the cable into the box.

It was a radio!

Over the course of my travels to the West Coast I would see many more like it. While I was in Arizona I met a brother who was training overseers in their use. Salvaging crews in Fort Hood, Texas, had discovered a huge army depot full of these radios. (Stumbling on it had been a fluke; military bases were usually completely ignored since there was nothing usable, meaning either it had been destroyed or had no foreseeable application in the New World.)

The radios were a fortuitous find: they could send and receive signals within most of the continent and were easy to use. The brothers were soon organized into a training unit and sent in different directions across North America. It was hoped that they would run into other brothers from South America doing the same thing, helping to slowly establish an intercontinental network of speedy communication.

Until then, though, the brothers were instructed to set up mobile radio hubs, give the hubs unique call letters, and train the local overseers on their operation. Of course, boys being boys, the hubs rarely used their given designations in favor of nicknames. Though we were formally "Baltimore Oh-Nine", the brothers quickly adopted the moniker "Balti Badgers" in honor of one of the overseers, whose head of white-streaked hair hadn't quite returned to its youthful jet black.

"Baltimore Oh-Nine to So-Cal Oh-Eight. Do you copy?" Brother Hale released the button and waited.

"So-Cal Oh-Eight here. Reading you loud and clear, Baltimore. What do you have for us?" Came a voice on the other end. Its clarity surprised me.

Brother Hale explained my transfer request. A few numbers were read back and forth, and the paperwork was adjusted. In just five minutes, everything had been settled. It was amazing how quickly things could get done in a theocratic system free of red tape and bureaucracy.

"You're all set, Mitch," my overseer said as the clamped the radio box back together. "They're expecting you in a month, so that should give you the time you need to get over there."

It dawned on me that LA was over 2,000 miles to the west. "What do you think is the best way to get there?" I asked.

"Check with the garage unit. They've got a huge collection of vehicles. I'd set you up with a transport, but they don't move in a straight line; they stop here and there along the way, sometimes for days at a time. You'll probably be quicker on your own. I'll radio through to let some of the friends along the way know you're coming."

"Thanks."

"Don't mention it. You've been a nice addition to our crew and I'll be sad to see you go." Jared Hale shook my hand firmly and told me how to get to the Baltimore garage.

"Oh, and when you finish your book, please, send me a copy. I'd love to hear the stories from some of the friends in other areas, and I'm sure my wife would too."

The Garage

The Garage was only a twenty-minute walk from where I'd been staying. In the Old World, it had been the largest shipping warehouse near the Baltimore wharf. It was, due to its size and convenient location, one of the few buildings that wasn't slated for demolition. It still bore the orange-and-purple logo from the company that had owned it in times past.

The massive floor space (equivalent to the area of two football fields) was divided between the Salvaging and Mechanic departments. On the Salvaging side, volunteers with walkie-talkies and clipboards were zipping around crates stacked to the ceiling on metal scaffolds. Forklifts were weaving between the shelves, neatly slipping boxes of canned goods, clothing, and other essentials in and out of small nooks.

The Mechanic's half looked much like you might expect–a sprawl of cables, tools, pneumatic jacks, and a hundred other devices I couldn't name. Dissected vehicles of every imaginable type were lying in neatly organized piles on the floor: Cars, trucks, ATVs, motorcycles, scooters, golf carts. I even spotted the unmistakable windshield and propeller of a helicopter leaning against the far wall.

Moving closer, I realized that each piece had been carefully cataloged and tagged with a yellow flag.

"Hiya there! You Mitch Hanson?" Came a voice from behind a stack of tires. A hand waved at me and I walked over.

"Is it ok for me to walk through here?" I asked, poking my head up to get a better view.

"Sure, sure, just watch your step. There are lots of pieces here and there."

This was no exaggeration, I realized, coming across a mosaic of gears and bolts and plates of metal that I imagined once comprised a working engine.

"There you go, hi there," said the man as I finally rounded the tires. He had pulled the stained gloves from his hands and shoved them into his coverall pockets. He wore a backwards Orioles baseball cap that had been dripped on, smeared over, and worn to tatters. He stuck out his hand and introduced himself as Hammy Royce.

"Hi," I said.

"Jared rang us last night after you asked 'bout a transfer. LA, huh?" I nodded. Hammy squinted his eyes and looked at the ceiling, thinking. "Well, that pro'ly means you'll be takin' I-40, right?"

"Uh, yes, that sounds right."

"I can see why Jared sent you here, then. The transports go way off course when they run the I-40 route, and usually they stop for days along the way. He told you?"

"He did."

"Ok then. Well, you have your pick of the fleet." I looked around dubiously. Hammy must've noticed, because he said, "*This* is not the fleet, of course."

"Oh," I said. "You had me a little worried. What exactly is all this for, then?"

"Research, mostly," Hammy said. He removed his cap and ran his fingers through damp hair.

"Research?"

"Yeah, most of the mechanics here worked on sedans in the Old World, Hondas and Toyotas and Fords and whatnot. But the branch wants us to familiarize ourselves with anything with an engine we can get our hands on now."

"Why?"

"They want to keep everything as well-maintained as possible. No more car factories runnin', remember? Once all this stuff runs down–and it will, eventually–we'll have no way of makin' more."

"But what about the other vehicles? Is there really a demand for helicopters and ATVs?"

"You'd be surprised. We actually just sent out twenty ATVs yesterday to New York. Some of the rubble out there is so bad it's impossible to drive the transports through. The friends need to ride in one-by-one, on something smaller with wheels that can handle the uneven terrain. We've had one helicopter pilot come through here as well. He helped train our mechanics, in fact. And that's the other big thing: learnin' how all this stuff works!"

"I'll bet. How are you guys figuring all this stuff out?"

"That's the interesting thing, really. I can't really explain it, but I guess the example that comes the closest is Bezalel and Oholiab."

I was more than a little embarrassed as I struggled to remember the Bible characters.

"You remember, they were the craftsmen Jehovah blessed with the special abilities needed to build the tabernacle."

"Oh, right."

"It was sort of like that, for myself and many of the other mechanics–and some non-mechanics–that volunteered for this assignment. We may have had some small amount of skill in the Old World, but Jehovah has enhanced it and blessed us with new mechanical insight. It's... it's something else, really."

"So that's why you've got everything labeled and in pieces, then?"

"That's mostly for training purposes, really. The mechanics here have all been given an incredible memory for detail–something I don't doubt is straight from the Holy Spirit. They can look at a machine in pieces for a few minutes, figure out how it works, and rely on that memory to fix most problems they run into based on a similar mechanical design. Neato, huh?"

"It's incredible. Are there other garages like this out there? I've only come across this one so far..."

"Yeah, most are on or near the coast for ease of transport. Those ATVs I mentioned were sent out on a transport boat. By sea is the easiest way to move things around these days."

"So you fix up the vehicles here and send them out to other places. But what if they break down?"

"We expect them to, over time. So mechanical depots are being set up, as we speak, along the main highways. Sort of like the Old World: if your car breaks down you give us a call, we tow it in and take a look. Only difference of course, is we don't charge you an arm and a leg for it." Hammy punctuated the twinkle in his eye with a wink.

"And what about gasoline? Where is it coming from?"

"One of our first tasks was actually to go out to all the gas stations we could find and siphon out the gas and store it. Now, gas stored can actually go bad, and even with special additives it won't last more than two or three years, but again, miraculously, it's been ok up 'til now. We actually had a chemist come down and test it for us last month, and it's just like new. No degradation whatsoever. This is one of the big proofs that Jehovah is supporting our decision to use gas-powered automobiles, at least for now."

"Was that ever an issue, deciding whether or not it was ok to use all this once we entered the New World?"

"I believe so, yes. I was originally with Salvaging, before the Mechanics department was established. I just assumed, like most of us, that automobiles would be prohibited in the New World. Actually, to be honest, I had no idea any of this stuff was going to make it into the New World. I dunno, I guess maybe it would all disintegrate or get sucked into the ground or something.

"Well, it didn't. And after a few months working with Salvaging–I was in Boston at the time–my overseer asked if I could help out with Mechanics here in Baltimore. It was what I had done in the Old World, and it's what I love doing. I was surprised to hear there was a need for it now, though.

"But what about the pollution?" I asked him.

"The Branch has decided that with the current population, use of automobiles will have an acceptable impact on the environment."

He likened it to chopping a small patch of trees down to build a home. Yes, it had a negative effect on the environment, but it was temporary and acceptable in small quantities. Eventually the trees would grow back. The atmosphere and the air we breathe is similarly resilient, he said.

"The other thing we have to remember is that we're not doing this out of a selfish or careless attitude. Every automobile out there running is in some way related to the cleanup work. We're doing God's will. And we can see his blessing on our efforts by His maintaining the fuel. Of course, once it runs out, well, that's a different story."

We walked as we talked, circling various piles of parts. Whiteboards had been set up next to many of the work areas, covered in complex scribbles that could only be deciphered by the modern Bezalels and Oholiabs. I shook my head in disbelief.

Hammy finally led me to the back of the warehouse, which hadn't been visible behind the stacks of boxes in Mechanical. When the overhead lamps *thunked* on, I let out a little gasp. The entire area was filled with cars, trucks, motorcycles, and ATVs, lined up in slanted rows.

"Wow. So *this* is the fleet."

"Biggest on the East Coast of this continent."

"Looks like you've got a little of everything in here."

"Well, not quite. We've got a tight set of guidelines that a vehicle must pass to get added. You'll notice no sports cars here, for starters."

"Low mileage?"

"That and a dozen other things. No storage, usually only seat two passengers, and there's really no need for that kind of speed."

"What else didn't make the cut?"

"A lot of the SUVs. Mostly for the mileage reason. There are a lot of more economical cars that can do the same thing. And if people really have that much stuff to move across land, it's easier to just use one of the larger trucks." Hammy motioned to the far row of vehicles, a line of old U-Hauls.

"So how much stuff are you taking with you to California?" Hammy asked.

"Not much," I said. "I've got a backpack with a few sets of clothes, work boots, that's about it."

"Huh. Have you ever ridden a motorcycle?"

I couldn't hide my boyish smile as I shook my head. "Well, only once, around a block at a friend's house, but that was years ago."

Hammy nodded and walked me over to a line of sleek cruisers. "Let's give this one a try," he said, pointing to a red and silver Yamaha.

"It's a little big, but it runs smooth and gets almost 80 miles to the gallon. What do you think?"

"I think I'm gonna have fun on my way to L.A."

"Can't say I'm not just a little jealous. I've always wanted to bike cross-country."

The key was in the ignition when Hammy pulled the monstrous 1300cc motorcycle from its slot among the others. He wheeled it out the back door, handed me a helmet and jacket, and spent a few minutes refreshing me. I rode it around the building a few times, familiarizing myself with its weight and handling.

"All good?" Hammy asked as I coasted to a stop beside him on the fifth lap.

"I think so. It handles well, and it's not too loud."

"Yeah, we've tweaked the exhaust pipes a little to make them quieter. Make sure you take it slow on your way down to Cali. You won't hit a lot of traffic, but some of the roads aren't so good. And rest every few hours or when you feel even a little bit sleepy, OK?"

I nodded solemnly. Hammy slapped me on the back and I pulled on the throttle, slipping onto the lonely Baltimore roads and off into the west. Even at the leisurely pace I'd promised, it took me less than two weeks to reach California.

Otto Weber

I parked my Yamaha at the point where the redwoods formed the forest boundary, teetering high above the road like giants frozen in time. I had been here before, as a child, and it looked the same now. No smaller, no less awesome. I ran my hand over the coarse bark, felt its life against my skin. *I will outlive you, old friend.* The asphalt, however, was showing its age, with a web of cracks radiating across its surface like wrinkles.

I was only five years old when my parents first brought me here. My first camping trip. Mom got food poisoning from eating a bad egg and the mosquitos had been large enough to drain the blood from our beagle (or possibly carry it off whole to the nest), but the trip had been enjoyable all the same. Dad had taught me how to fly-fish, had even shown me how to make my own flies with bits of ribbon and wire. At night we roasted marshmallows and grilled trout on the campfire. The memories felt warm in my mind.

Maybe that's why I had enjoyed camping with all these different crews of brothers and sisters for the first few years after the Great Day. While many of the friends had gone right to building their dream house (or finding an existing one to claim), I was content to wander around with the ones who were still working. It made me feel like that adventurous little five year old, trudging through the woods with his fishing rod and pocket knife. Part of us always wants to return to nature, I think.

But I wasn't just back here for the nostalgia. Rumors about these woods had been whispered across the continent. It was impossible to separate fact from fiction, and I wanted to know just what was going on.

I hiked eastward over hilly terrain before finally seeing it: a lopsided cabin jutting from the slope. Everything seemed wrong about the small building. The angles were off, the steps were uneven, even the roof seemed to be swallowing itself. I considered that its appearance might have been the result of the Great California Quake, but couldn't be sure.

As I neared the cabin, my sense of balance seemed to wane. The ground didn't feel stable, or perhaps I hadn't had enough water during the hike? But each step became more precarious, so that I finally had to crawl my way to the odd wooden door.

I knocked.

No answer.

I knocked again.

From outside the cabin I could hear a low humming noise. It made me think of the washing machine we used to run in our basement when Jacob was still a toddler. I missed washing machines. Finally, the door creaked open.

"You are Brother Hanson?" Asked the burly man behind the door. He wore leather goggles with tinted lenses and a brown, swooping, perfectly-waxed mustache.

"Yes. That's me," I said, rising unsteadily to my feet.

"Come in and sit. It will take a moment to get your bearings here."

I stumbled into the cabin and sat on a hard wooden bench. The cabin, which had appeared to be a series of rooms from the outside, was actually one large space–a laboratory jammed with shelves of books, vials, various lengths and thicknesses of wires and cables, and plastic bins overflowing with mechanical parts.

In the center of the room stood a bronze coil as tall as a man. A section of planks had been pried from the floor, allowing the coil to plunge into the darkness below the cabin. Or maybe it had erupted spontaneously from the earth. My head was still spinning and it was impossible to tell.

But stranger still was the angle at which everything rested or stood in the cabin. Nothing was truly vertical or horizontal. Even my mustachioed host leaned at an impossible degree.

"What is this place?" I asked.

"I'm inclined to let you guess first." The man's back was turned to me now, but I could see he was jotting something down in a clipboard he'd held in his hand when he'd opened the door.

"Well, assuming you're Otto Weber..." I paused, waiting for his affirmation. None came.

"I would say this is some sort of... science experiment?"

"Yes, that much should be clear, but for what purpose, do you suppose?" Otto asked. He removed his goggles and began adjusting metal dials and levers on some sort of control panel near a window. I contemplated what this strange man could possibly be testing out here in the woods.

"Something to do with magnets? Electricity perhaps?" I

attempted.

"You are fifty percent correct. Although, I would estimate that some scientists from the Old World would have praised you with a perfect one hundred. Back in the Old World, this place was a bit of a tourist trap. This house was the focal point. Guests would buy tickets to tour this strange cabin on the hill, where all sorts of mysterious phenomenon were purportedly happening. Some even thought it had supernatural powers."

Otto took a wooden sphere from his white coat pocket and threw it to me. "Place the ball on that bench you are sitting on," he instructed. I watched in disbelief as the ball rolled slowly up the incline.

"How does it work?" I asked.

"Alas, it is all an optical illusion. This house, built on a slope, gives the impression of defying natural physics. In fact, it is all completely normal, and natural. There are many like it around the world."

"So what about your experiment?"

"That is where you guessed right. This is a geothermal energy coil. Not far from this cabin, as you may know, lies one of the most famous–or infamous, perhaps–continental transform faults in the world, the San Andreas fault. This fault separates two tectonic plate boundaries, allowing scientists like myself to test for geothermal energy with relative ease."

"So, assuming it was your decision, why choose this cabin as the space for your laboratory?"

"It was already here, and frankly, I like the place. And it amuses my guests, few as they may be." The pointy ends of Otto's mustache twitched as a grin wrapped across his lips.

"How are the experiments going?"

"Fine indeed. This coil has sped things up considerably. A new invention from a New World brain." Otto rapped a pencil against his forehead, still grinning.

"Geothermal power plants of the Old World were formidable undertakings. Expensive, large, difficult to maintain. Hot water had to be pumped from wells thousands of meters below the ground's surface, then pumped somewhere else to release the steam, and then cooled and returned to the ground. This coil does much the same thing, but without the steam and excess heat. It's a clean, easy, efficient way to produce electricity."

"No more batteries and generators..." I said.

"Yes, this is the goal. Renewable energy."

I thought for a moment about what this might mean for the

future, having running electricity in our houses as it was in the Old World. But frankly, I'd gotten so used to life without all my electronic devices that it didn't hold a strong appeal.

"What will we do with all this electricity?" I wondered aloud.

Otto and I stared at the coil and pondered the question together.

"Small things first. Light bulbs and power tools for the building crews, hot water for our home showers. We will see what comes next. Forever is a long time. My father used to tell me that Jehovah's greatest gift to us was our ability to study, learn, and create. I speculate, now, that electricity is fundamental to our future creations. Our technology in the Old World was significant, but it pursued the wrong goals and gave no thought to its consequences. Now, with perfection and eternity, we have the means to try again, and get it right this time."

Brother Weber's words infused me with a kind of curious wonder. We were, after all, built in the image of the Master Creator. Creation was in our blood, so to speak. What would the future hold? Some were still convinced we'd be heading into space once the Original Purpose had been fulfilled, but I was never convinced. Perhaps, though, our creations would, one day, take us somewhere else.

"Were you a scientist in the Old World?" I finally asked. His response was a slow nod.

"I designed air conditioning systems for Mercedes-Benz automobiles."

"In Germany?"

"*Ja*," Otto replied, momentarily breaking from the New Tongue.

"What kinds of trials did our German brothers face during the tribulation?" I asked. Otto scratched his head and sat down in a three-legged stool near the control panel.

"Much like the trials a previous generation had faced with the Nazis, actually. They had different names for the persecution lest anyone draw the parallel to the former nightmare, but it was fundamentally the same. The German government called a lot of these reformations and bans a kind of *freiheit*, or freedom, to depict the Witnesses' ministry as a sort of oppression or brainwashing campaign."

"How did our brothers there face those trials?"

"I'm proud to say that the vast majority stood firm. We had, as I mentioned, the support of an older generation who had experienced similar things spurring us along. This strengthened us. But the trials were difficult to face nonetheless. Especially the relocation. I wonder if they ever reported that in American news media?"

I did my best to recall the news we had heard from Germany during the Tribulation. I remembered the ban on the preaching work, which had happened around the same time in various countries throughout Western Europe, and the confiscation of kingdom halls and branch offices. There had been rumors of work camps camouflaged as "freedom factories", too. But I couldn't recall anything about a relocation.

I shook my head.

"Not surprising," Otto said with raised eyebrows. "It was very secretive. My suspicion is that the government saw families sticking together, continuing to worship Jehovah, and they assumed that, by tearing apart this most basic unit, they could weaken the spirit of our brothers.

"The earliest I remember hearing of it was in the Autumn of '23. The news came through one of our local elders, brother Engel. He had heard that a group of twenty brothers had been taken from their families and had been told they were needed at another factory. No one had heard from them since. Brother Engel told us to not give in to fear, and to be cooperative with the authorities and 'meek like doves'.

"Later I experienced it firsthand. A group of policemen posing as managers from another branch of the company I worked for explained that I needed to move departments. They came to my workplace and forced me to leave immediately with them. When I boarded their van I realized who they were. They handcuffed me, blindfolded me, and drove me to somewhere far out in the countryside, where I boarded a train.

"It was difficult to believe that what was happening was real. I had always thought of modern Germany as progressive, with freedom and human rights guaranteed for its citizens. What was occurring seemed impossible, an atrocity from another time. Part of me wanted to fight, to demand a legal hearing in a court of law, but I remembered Brother Engel's admonition to cooperate and wait on Jehovah.

"Thirteen other brothers and myself were kept on the last carriage of the train. We were loaded on in the middle of a cold night without being told where we were headed or if we would ever return home. Once inside, we were chained to our seats. The handcuffs were never removed. Two guards sat by the door at the front of the cabin. They spoke between themselves with soft voices that we couldn't hear clearly, but the word *zeugen*–witness, in German–could be heard often. We wondered what would become of us.

"That first night was especially cold. Although we shared a compartment with a shipment of blankets and jackets for the German army, our captors denied us their use.

"'Pray for your God to bring the sun early,' one of the guards said mockingly. We spent the first night hungry and shivering. The second day was slightly better. We were fed, and the sunlight warmed the train carriage to a bearable temperature.

"On the evening of the second day, a man dressed in an army uniform entered our carriage. I can still smell the smoke of his cigar. I could tell from the stripes and icons on his chest and shoulders that he was an important man, perhaps some sort of lieutenant or captain. He smiled as he looked us over, a pleased hunter who had finally caught his prized prey.

"'I have read your people's history,' the man said. 'I know, for example, that Adolf Hitler had a vendetta against you during the second World War. Promised to wipe you from the face of the earth, in fact.'

"'It is true,' said the brother closest to the man in uniform. His name was Jens Kissler.

"'Hitler was a sociopath, of course,' the man continued, smiling. 'But when it came to you people, I think he had the right idea.'

No one spoke as the train continued up the slope. Were they taking us to be executed? It seemed possible Then Jens spoke up:

"'Sir, you may do with us as you please. Whether you intend to harm us or kill us matters not. We will never compromise our integrity to our God.'

"'A true martyr,' said the man. He approached Jens slowly, inhaling deeply on his cigar and blowing smoke into our brother's face.

"'You may forget, zeugen, that your people's struggle extends far beyond the confines of this train compartment. Decrees from the highest, most powerful committees in the world have deemed your Organization a menace to all society.' The man knelt, removing his cigar and looking directly into Brother Kissler's eyes.

"'The problem with Hitler, you see, is that he wanted to wipe you people out alone. But we won't make that mistake this time. We have the cooperation of almost every government on earth! Whether we have to freeze you people in the mountains or burn you in desert, we will not give up until our mission is complete.'

"With that, he pressed the glowing embers of his cigar butt into Jens Kissler's thigh. Jens screamed as the sickening smell of burning cloth and flesh filled our small compartment.

"Satisfied, the man rose and walked back to the door. 'If any of you expect to eat in the next three days, one of you must denounce this archaic faith of yours. Otherwise, you have my permission to die together.'

"No one slept on the second night. We did our best to strengthen each other, reminding ourselves that these trials were reasons for joy. After all, they were clear proof that we were on the last dot on the prophetic timeline ending with Jehovah's salvation.

"It snowed hard on the third day, forcing the train to slow its ascent into the mountains. Two of our brothers were now showing signs of sickness. The burn on Jens's leg was causing him terrible pain. And we were hungry. But all of these discomforts paled in comparison with what came next.

"At approximately noon on the third day, while the two guards at the front door taunted us with their lunch, we heard a massive, terrifying sound. Then it came again, louder and closer, and again, and again, in sharp succession, causing our carriage to jostle and pitch in the air.

"As the sounds neared, they became more distinct. Metal rending into pieces. Glass shattering and scattering. Soft bodies being thrown violently against walls and breaking from the impact. Screams.

"Somehow, our train had crashed, and the forward carriages were tumbling down the side of the mountain one by one. We knew it was only a matter of seconds before our cabin, at the very rear, was pulled down with the others. I looked around at my brothers and offered a prayer for the group.

"'Jehovah,' I said, trying to keep the fear from strangling my voice. 'We are here because we served you until the end. Please remember us. And please, Jehovah, forgive these men...'

"My final words were cut by silence. The awful crashing noises had ceased. The sound of our certain death had been replaced by the howling of wind and snow.

"One of our guards, who we later learned was named Lukas, inspected the outside of the train and discovered how we had been saved: the final coupling linking our carriage and the one ahead had come loose during the crash. This had allowed us to break free, sparing our lives. All of the other cars, including the main engine, had fallen from the cliff and into the deep gorge below. Lukas applied the manual brake to prevent us from sliding back down the slope and returned with a serious look on his face.

"'Free them,' he said to Uwe, the second guard. 'We cannot afford to be on the wrong side of this battle again.'

"As it turned out, we were stuck in an ideal carriage; besides blankets, the army supplies included ready-to-eat meals, heat packs, medical supplies to dress Brother Kissler's leg wound, and just about everything else we needed to survive.

"Our captors-turned-comrades asked many questions that night, wanting to understand all they could about our Organization and why we were being persecuted so thoroughly in the world. Between the fourteen of us, we were able to provide answers based firmly on the scriptures. We even taught them one of our kingdom melodies–number 132, *A Victory Song*.

"We slept well on the third night. That is, until we heard a loud banging coming from outside the train wall. We scrambled to our feet, partly afraid and partly in expectation of how Jehovah would save us, if needed, again.

"'Who is it?' Lukas yelled, gripping his rifle and keeping his back to the wall.

"'Your brothers!' Came a voice on the other side. Lukas was confused, and even more so when he noticed the fourteen of us begin to leap and cry with joy.

"'Open the door! Open the door!' I yelled.

"Lukas obeyed, and in flooded a group of men in heavy fur coats with lanterns in their hands.

"'You were supposed to arrive yesterday, we were all waiting for you,' said one of our brothers. I could tell from his accent that he wasn't German.

"'What?' One of our brothers asked. 'I don't understand. How could you know we were coming?'

"'The serial number on your train car. We had your train diverted a few days ago by a brother near the border. You were supposed to arrive safely in Switzerland at seven o'clock last night, but when your train went missing we came looking for you!'

"'But how could that be?' I asked. 'Our train was full of other passengers and policemen. How could you expect to welcome us?'

"'He hasn't heard,' said one of the other Brothers.

"'Heard what?' I asked, suddenly full of excitement.

"'It's over. Yesterday was the Day of Jehovah. Our enemies are gone. It's just us.'

It was all too much to take in. The thirteen German brothers and myself collapsed against each other, unbelieving, sobbing with relief. It was over. Over!

"'But who are *they*, then?' Asked one of the brothers, moving his lantern towards Lukas and Uwe, who were still in police uniforms and holding guns.

"'They are with us,' I said. And that was how it was, for me, in the end."

After spending a week or so with Otto in his crooked cabin in the woods I moved on to my final destination, Los Angeles. I was expected for work on Monday and wanted to get in a little early to get accustomed to my surroundings and meet some of the other volunteers. By this time, almost four years into the New World, more and more foreign brothers and sisters were arriving from other parts of the world.

Mark & Elise Raven

I had known Mark since we were children. We had grown up in the same congregation–West Fremont–and we were close friends through our teens. Mark had helped me out a lot in school; he was a better student and a better Witness. After graduation we went our separate ways–Mark pioneered and I went off to college.

When I graduated and began my career, Mark was starting his fifth year in full time service and was a temporary Bethelite working on the Warwick project in New York. We'd email from time to time, but our friendship began to fade. Mark knew nothing of selling insurance, saving for a house, and wanting to start a family, and I knew nothing of Bethel life. It sounded exciting, but I'd made my choices and was happy as a publisher in my congregation. The ministry was difficult in our area, but I was doing my best.

It was ironic, now, to be standing on the lawn of the mansion Mark was living in, a home in Beverly Hills with floor-to-ceiling glass windows and granite fountains. A swimming pool wrapped itself around the south side of the house, overlooking the valley below.

I parked my Yamaha next to the lawn and rapped my knuckles against the thick wooden doors which appeared to be twice my height.

Mark flung the door open and gave me a warm hug, friends reunited at last. It felt good.

"I can't tell you how glad I am to see you," Mark said with misty eyes. I felt similarly, and was surprised to be tearing up as well.

Mark let me take a shower in one of their bathrooms upstairs. The water pipes were fed directly from solar-heated reservoirs on the roof, meaning hot water. It felt incredible. I walked back downstairs via a marble staircase that swooped down from a the second story walkway to the foyer.

"This house is something else," I said, drying my hair with a towel.

"Yeah, it's ok. A little too gaudy for us, though." Mark's wife, Elise, came from the kitchen with two beers. I was thrilled to find that they were cold.

"Generator?" I asked, staring in disbelief before prying the cap off.

"No, all the generators go towards the clean up effort. This is the result of a chemical ice pack, a mix of water and ammonium chloride. Throw a few in a cooler with beers and a few hours later–" he held the bottle up.

"It's fantastic."

We swigged at the beer in silence, gazing out at the valley below. Only a few scattered lights could be seen as the sun went down.

"LA sure took a beating," I said, whistling. "Were you here, during Armageddon?"

"No. Elise and I were still in Warwick at the time."

"What was it like there?"

"The move upstate was definitely Jehovah's direction. Brooklyn was a warzone at the peak of the Tribulation. I imagine that Bethel would've had to shut its doors much earlier if the headquarters had still been there in the city. Warwick managed to stay open up until the very end, up until the government came in and shut us down.

"They stopped the printing presses and cordoned off the shipping areas to prevent us from sending literature out, and harassed many of the Bethelites, even arresting some under charges of sedition and treason to overthrow the government."

"Because of the *Armageddon* tract?" I asked.

"Yes."

I recalled first seeing the tract when it was passed out at one of our home meetings during the Tribulation. The cover artwork had caused quite a stir: a mass of military troops carrying the nations' flags, surrounded by a heavenly force of angels ready to strike. It had been the last worldwide preaching campaign of Jehovah's Witnesses.

"How long was Bethel shut down?" I asked.

"Less than a month. The Great Day ended that."

"And what was the reaction of the Bethel family?"

"We were happy, as everyone was, but we knew we had a lot of work to do. The friends needed spiritual food badly. So the brothers organized the Super Conventions and sent delegates from headquarters on foot, motorcycle, car, boat, or whatever else was available to all the branches around the world. The material had to be translated, then prepared, and invitations had to be given to every person on the planet.

"The result was a special five-day convention that took place during the same week worldwide, less than a year after Armageddon. It was the first time since before Adam and Eve sinned that every human on Earth was united in worshipping Jehovah."

I thought back to the convention I attended in Atlanta. I

remember goose bumps prickling my arms when instructions were given on the tasks that lay ahead to prepare for the resurrection.

"So how are things progressing, then? Are we on schedule for everything?" I asked.

"I assume so, but I'm no longer in close contact with headquarters. My wife and I were assigned here last year to care for the Los Angeles area. The Organization wants to turn this into a major hub for those sailing in from South America, Asia, and Australia. We're here to look after cleanup and start the slow rebuilding process."

"And the Beverly Hills mansion?" I asked, noticing for the first time a giant crystal chandelier hanging from the vaulted ceiling above my head.

"Not our choice. The local friends found it during a Salvaging operation. It was one of the few places that hadn't been completely ransacked during the Tribulation. They insisted we stay here when we flew in."

"*Flew?*"

"Yeah, a brother with a private jet brought us in from Pennsylvania. The Organization is looking for more brothers and sisters with flying experience, by the way. If you know of any, I can provide you with the radio frequency for Warwick. They're building a runway and hangar there now, actually."

"Living in a mansion and taking private jets," I said wryly. "Looks like Jehovah took care of you two real well!"

"Again, not our choice. We were happy in our little Bethel cubbyhole."

"Don't believe a word he says," came Elise's voice from the kitchen. "He loves it."

Even with the luxury of a giant bed and a plush comforter, it took a long time to fall asleep that night. I was tired, but my mind was still somersaulting through everything I'd experienced in the previous months. Looking back, it was all a blur.

And maybe it was *too* comfortable. In all the time I'd spent in the New World up to this point, only a few months' worth of nights were spent indoors, and only when it was too cold to be outside. It was strange, now, to realize that my body had gotten so used to cots and sleeping bags, and that the sprawling oversized bed in Mark and Elise's mansion was simply too big for me. I finally lugged the pillows and comforter to one of the guest bathrooms, where I slept soundly in the Jacuzzi.

Abdel Yassin

The man made his way cautiously around the cement pylons, each step placed carefully before the next. With a fortuitous full moon in the sky he didn't need his flashlight; besides, his night vision was keener than ever. His hand paused at each pillar, making sure that the connections between the fuses and plastic explosives were secure. When he was certain all was in order, he materialized from the shadows and took his place behind a van filled with sandbags and lined with a wall of cinderblocks.

"Are we good to go?"

"Yes," said the man. "Let's bring her down."

Indistinct voices mixed with static echoed from one station to the next. A red plastic cover swung open on a hinge and the countdown began.

At zero, a button was pressed, sending an instantaneous electrical pulse through the complex web of fuses and into a series of carefully placed blasting caps. Brilliant light erupted outward, as if dawn had come seven hours early with the sun rising oddly in the basement of a high rise instead of the horizon.

The shockwave exhaled a ring of dust from the epicenter of the explosion along with chips of concrete and metal. The men leaned from their cover in time to watch the ground swallow the fifty-story complex whole.

"Bird's Eye, how's it look?" Asked the man into a walkie talkie. A pause.

"Right on the line. Good blast, Abdel," came the response from a rooftop somewhere overhead.

The man looked at me and smiled.

It was my first night on the Demolition crew (or Blast Crew, as they preferred), and it was unlike any of the other crews I'd been a part of. Many of the volunteers seemed to be ex-military, with their buzzed haircuts, rugged faces, and no-nonsense demeanors.

I was eager to meet one of the workers in particular, Abdel Yassin, who had ferried over recently from Europe. Like many I would come to meet during my journeys, I had already heard bits and pieces of his remarkable story but wanted to hear the rest of the details firsthand.

We talked the next morning after a late brunch. Because of the dust clouds caused by their work, Blast Crews usually worked late into the night, allowing the air to clear while they slept. This meant they got up a little later than most, and I wasn't complaining.

"So how did you like your first blast?" Abdel asked me as he finished a sesame bagel.

"It was...exciting," I said.

"Were you scared?"

"Uh, a little, yeah. No one has ever been hurt doing this?"

"Not yet, that I know of. We are very careful. We check everything half a dozen times and take many other precautions. It is safer than it looks."

"So what was that building we took down last night?" I asked.

"Another old residence. Inspection crews went through this area earlier this year, before the rains, and said it was hazardous. When we checked again on Monday it had gotten worse. There are probably twenty other buildings in this area just like it. We'll be here another few weeks making sure to get them all."

"What happens after your crew is done with an area?"

"In areas like this, so close to a seaport, cleanup crews come in right after us, sometimes as soon as the next day to deal with the rubble. Since they're expecting lots of foot traffic here, we need to be sure it's cleared and safe. In other less populated areas, we just leave the rubble where it falls, since it'll probably be decades before anyone decides to return. By then this will all be overgrown and safe to walk."

Abdel sipped at his coffee, looking over his shoulder at the ruins of the previous night's detonation. His skin was a caramel brown and streaked with black hair. Deep-set eyes and a ridged nose were chiseled into his stony face.

"I imagine that's a tricky thing to do, setting up the charges to bring a building straight down like that," I offered.

"Indeed. The timing and placement have to be precise. If the building goes down crooked, or fails to collapse completely, then you have a *big* problem." Abdel lifted his eyebrows to emphasize the danger.

"How long have you been with Demolition?"

"Only a couple of months. I heard there was a need for brothers with demolition experience while I was in France–have you been?"

I shook my head.

"Not recently, no." It had been nearly six years since the Great

Day and I was still on the continent of my birth. There had been so much to do and see here that I'd barely given a thought to migrating.

"You should visit sometime. The brothers and sisters there are working on this incredible museum in Normandy."

I thought back to the several trips I'd taken to France before the Tribulation. I'd always enjoyed touring through Paris, the only place I ever had time to explore in the day or two between business meetings. The cuisine, those romantic scenic spots. Even its tackier tourist traps were still elegant and quaint when compared to anything in America.

"Whatever happened to Paris? Was it ever rebuilt?" I asked.

"I heard it was one of the earliest demolition projects in Western Europe," Abdel said. "The fire storms had taken down most of the city, but cleanup crews were sent in afterwards to bring down the remains. As far as I know, it's still just ruins. Too far from the coast, I think, to be useful. For now, anyway."

"Tell me about your past, Adbel. How did you end up here?"

"I was born in Pakistan in 2001. My earliest memories are of living with my uncle, Hassan. He was a stern man driven by a strong sense of duty, and I respected him although we were never close. Hassan was a protective uncle, and the closest thing I had to a father. He was a quiet and private man, but did his best to provide me with a good education and food each day. He would often return home late in the evening, make me some bean stew and bread for supper, and head off to bed while I watched American cartoons–I loved *Tom & Jerry*."

"What was it like growing up in Pakistan?"

"The Pakistan of my childhood was an exciting place to be. The country's scientists had put a rocket and a satellite into space and were developing nuclear weapons–only the seventh nation in the world to do so, they liked to boast. You can imagine why, years later, I was puzzled to learn that Western countries had thought of Pakistan as a barren desert full of bazooka-toting jihads in caves. Terrorism was only a small part of modern Pakistani life, and it was nothing when compared with the leaps and bounds the country was making in so many areas.

"My uncle taught me to be proud to be Pakistani, and prouder still to be a Muslim. A Sunni Muslim, that is.

"'Be thankful you are not a Shia,' my uncle sometimes would tell me when we finished our prayers, referring to the other Muslim sect, which was a minority in our area. When I asked why, he'd simply say:

"'They are not true to Allah. Allah knows all.'

"I never understood what this meant but was thankful all the same. "Thank you Allah, for not making me a Shia," I would pray sometimes alone at night. No one taught me to pray like this, but it felt right to express myself freely that way.

"When I was eighteen, I was thrilled to receive an acceptance letter from the university of my dreams, a technical institute where I would pursue a double major in engineering and aeronautics. I felt like I was riding a wave into the future. I could tell my uncle was proud, too, and this meant a lot to me.

"During my first year at university, a form of the Liberation Act was passed by the Pakistani government, sending shockwaves through the Muslim community. The mosques were closed and worshippers were told to keep their religious activities confined to their homes. Pakistanis could not understand how the government, supposedly run by good Muslims, could commit such a sin against Islam.

"And with the confusion came frustration and then retaliation.

"Average people became extremists. Students blew themselves up near the capitol. Bullets were fired into the windows of houses thought to be occupied by government officials and politicians. Thousands of innocent people were killed.

"One day, while sitting in the school cafeteria and watching the latest news coverage of another suicide bombing, I could feel that I had finally had enough. I broke down, sobbing into my lunch tray. I clasped my hands together and prayed, as I had when I was a child:

"'If you are really there, God, why are you letting this happen? Good Muslims are killing each other. How can this be your great will?'

"When I finished praying I wiped my face on my sleeve and looked at the plate in front of me. I didn't have an appetite. Then came a voice, a foreigner speaking English:

"'I've never seen a Muslim pray like that,' he said. I felt very embarrassed. But the man's look wasn't accusatory, just curious.

"'An old habit,' I replied. The man sat down across from me and glanced over to the screen mounted from the ceiling. He was a Westerner and looked to be in his forties. He definitely wasn't military, though, and didn't dress like a teacher either.

"'Are you a tourist?' I asked.

"'I was living in Ürümqi, but it got a little dangerous for foreigners there so I decided to try life here for a while.'

"'China?' I asked, shocked. Ürümqi was part of Xinjiang province at the farthest western point of China, not far from the eastern boundary of Pakistan, where we were.

"'What were you doing in China?'

"'Living, teaching, exploring. What about you? Are you a

student?' I explained that I was, and what my majors were.

"'Sounds like a full curriculum,' said the man. His name was Thom Sorensen, and he was living near the campus with his wife, he explained. They had originally moved to China from Denmark and had enjoyed their lives there until a political uprising forced them to evacuate.

"'I'm sorry you have to see Pakistan like this,' I said. 'It's usually a wonderful place to be. But lately...'

"'You don't have to apologize,' Thom said. 'The whole world is like this. In my hometown they've closed dozens of churches.'

"'What do you think is going to happen to this world?' I asked. My words surprised me. Speaking of these things was very uncustomary, especially when talking with a foreigner. Thom Sorensen took awhile to reply. He seemed to be studying me.

"'Let me ask you, Abdel, what does the Quran say about the future?' Another wave of embarrassment. I didn't really know. Some Islamic scholars said the scriptures indicated that the world would be swallowed by a black hole in space; others said it would be burned with fire.

"'It says the Earth will be destroyed, and the good people will be saved.'

"'I see. You know, a lot of Western religions teach the same thing.' This was true. I'd recently read a book on the history of Christianity and knew that there were many parallels to Islam.

"'What's always been funny to me, though,' Thom went on, 'is that those Western religions claim to be based on the Bible, and yet the Bible disagrees with them almost entirely.' That was true too. I knew that Jesus had said to *love thy enemy*, and yet many wars were backed by Christian nations. The Bible also condemned adultery and fornication, while modern churches condoned it.

"'One thing that I've always found very interesting about the Bible is what it says in the Psalms about the Earth.' Thom pulled out his smartphone and selected an application. He typed in 'Psalm 37:10, 11' and showed me the screen. In the top box, the verse appeared in modern English. I read through it, but it didn't finally register until I saw the script in the bottom box, the same verse displayed in Urdu, my mother tongue.

"'You see, the Bible actually says that we'll get to live here on the Earth.'

"I admired Thom's familiarity with his scriptures, but wasn't convinced. I had been taught that the Bible, while originally inspired of God, had been changed thousands of times over the centuries to suit the needs of the church. Only the Quran was truly reliable. I explained my background as a Muslim. Thom just nodded respectfully.

"'Forgive me if this is intrusive, but just now, when you were praying, you seemed...disturbed. Can I ask why?' Thom asked.

"'I think I just need more faith to help me understand what is going on with this world. I mean, didn't you feel that way, when you heard about your church closing?' I asked.

"'Actually,' Tom said, drawing in a slow breath, 'it's pretty exciting for me.'

"'Exciting?'

"Thom nodded.

"'Why would you be excited? I find all this news depressing. I feel sick in my stomach,' I said.

"'Well,' Thom said, 'the answer to your question is in the Bible. If you're willing to hear it, maybe we can meet again soon. My wife is waiting for me at the grocery store.'

"My curiosity peaked, I agreed, and became Thom's first Pakistani return visit. Thom and his wife Halle, I later learned, were helping local Chinese to study the Bible. Many Chinese had emigrated to Pakistan in recent years. When I learned that Thom and his wife had chosen this difficult and dangerous life over returning to their homeland, I was deeply impressed. I could see that they really wanted to help other people learn about their beliefs. Would a Muslim do that?

"Over the next six months, my discussions with Thom brought me more satisfying answers than anything I had learned in the Quran, and I could hear the ring of truth clearly. But because of tensions between nations in the UN and increased anti-religious propaganda, Thom and Halle were forced to return to Denmark and we lost contact.

"Although I had met some of the local Pakistani brothers, I lost contact with them, too. I tried calling their cellphones, but their numbers had all changed. I felt very alone then, and unsure of what to do next. Around that same time, something horrific happened at my school.

"One of my classmates, angered by the religious bans, built a homemade explosive in his dormitory. As he was assembling it, the device detonated in his hands, killing himself and thirty-four others, including the six-year-old daughter of one of the faculty who had come to work that day with her father. The university was closed temporarily and I was sent home, shaken and needing Jehovah more than ever. But I had one more trial to face."

Adbel broke off for a moment, and I could see that the memories were difficult for him.

"You would think that I'd be able to do better than this," he said, shaking his head. "I guess these wounds need time."

One of the volunteers from the kitchen whisked by and offered to warm our coffees. Abdel nodded, took a sip and continued.

"When I returned home, I was happy to see my uncle. I'd only been back home once before since leaving for university, and that was before the Act had been passed, before the chaos. But the home I returned to was not as I had remembered. The neatly arranged frames on the walls were crooked and covered in dust. The place reeked of garbage and rodent droppings. Nothing had been cleaned in months, it seemed. And my uncle was nowhere to be found.

"I approached his bedroom door and knocked gently. 'I'm home, uncle,' I said quietly.

"'Abdel, wait outside.' The words were cold and distant. I wondered what had happened to him. I sat down on the dirty couch in the living room. Next to me lay a pile of pamphlets. They bore different insignias on their covers, but the content was the same. They were extremist literature, encouraging average citizens to take action in the name of Allah and eradicate all enemies of Islam. I had heard about these types of pamphlets but had never seen one: universities were careful to keep this type of literature away from students.

"When my uncle finally emerged from his room, he looked unwell. Sweat lined his brow and jaw. There were grey smudges on his face and clothes.

"'Are you ok uncle?' I asked.

"'Are you?' He said. There was a kind of wildness in his eyes that frightened me. 'Can any Muslim be ok? Is Allah ok? What do you think? Did your university teach you?'

"'Uncle, I am sorry if I made you upset. I just came home to see you. Our school had to close–'

"'It is a Shia plot, Abdel. I should have known this earlier, but my eyes were blinded with sin. But now, now I can understand clearly."

"'Shia plot?'

"'Yes, of course. Their way of amassing power in parliament! They must be working with those Hindus to stop our religion. Once they have silenced the Sunnis they will take this country and divide it with India, like a slaughtered animal at a feast. We must be smart, Abdel.'

"'That doesn't make sense, uncle. Think about it: all the mosques are closed, both Sunni and Shia. This is not conspiracy. Please, you must think clearly!' There was something, perhaps the insidious look in his eyes, that made me feel very desperate and threatened.

"'You do not see now, my nephew, but you will soon. Just watch! Those Shia dogs were clever this time, but we Sunnis will prevail! We must pray to Allah to bless our mission!'

"'What mission, uncle? What are you talking about?'

"'*Istishhad*, my nephew. This is our time!'

"The word was like a bucket of ice dumped onto my body. My muscles froze. Electric tension shot through my nerves and bones. *Istishhad* was the Arabic word for martyrdom, a term made infamous by Islamic extremists. My uncle, I now realized, was about to do something terrible.

"'Please,' I begged him. 'Do not do this. There is no good that can come of it.' I was on the brink of panic now, but it was too little too late.

"'It is as good as done, my nephew. And you are wrong, there are many blessings waiting for me. This is the will of god, Abdel. Others will see that, just as I have, and they will follow in my footsteps, just as I follow in the steps of prophets before me.'

"'What prophets killed innocent people?' I tried to reason.

"'Prophets were the messengers of God, my nephew. Those messages were often ones of destruction for the unrepentant. This is the will of Allah. You must see it clearly.'

"'And what if you're wrong about this? What happens to those that are killed?'

"'If they are truly innocent, they will become martyrs too, a reward directly from god. Come with me, my nephew. Let us fight together.'

"'No, uncle. You are wrong. All of this is wrong. Please listen to me. Please.'

"But my words were useless. He had knelt on his prayer mat and had begun his ritualistic chanting. I stayed for a few moments, watching him rock back and forth on his knees, petitioning his god. There was a certain quality that had not been there before, when I was a child. It was frenzied and unthinking, like a rabid dog restrained by a tensile leash.

"*This is not my uncle anymore*, I thought.

"That night, when he'd gone to sleep on the couch, I snuck into his bedroom. Diagrams and computer printouts were taped to the walls and windows, empty tubes and boxes were littered on the floor. A few spools of wire sat next to the desk, atop which rested a soldering iron it its stand. It didn't take long to finally locate the item that all these pieces had come together to build. I found it when I reached under the

72

old spring mattress: a black hunting vest laced in wires and plastic explosives.

"I hadn't expected the device to be so complete. My uncle was a chef by trade, not an electrician, and certainly no extremist. I realized that it must've taken him months to learn the skills and collect the materials needed to build it.

"I pored over the charts on his walls, trying to understand how the device worked. I located the power supply that would send the electrical charge, the wiring that connected each of the blasting caps, and the connector to the hand-operated detonator. I carefully placed the vest on the table and inspected each component, looking for something I could disconnect inconspicuously. I finally decided that the detonator was the best choice, and after screwing it open, I carefully disconnected the wires. After reassembling everything, I slid it back under the bed, leaving the room exactly as I had found it.

"But as I laid in my bed that night, I realized that my sabotage meant nothing. If he took the vest out in public and tried to detonate it, he would be arrested and tried, likely even being sentenced to death as many other failed suicide bombers had been in the past. I had saved a lot of lives, but not his.

"The next morning, after a restless night, I felt my uncle's hand on my shoulder. 'It is time, Abdel,' he said. And then, putting his keys in my hand, 'you will drive.'

"It made sense for me to go with him. If I was to protect him, I had to be with him. But this didn't make the drive any less excruciating, nor the knowledge of what was coming any less haunting. I sat there, moving the steering wheel in a kind of mindless abandon, wondering what I could say to change his mind, but there were no words.

"I watched as he slipped into the vest and draped a tunic over himself to conceal it.

"'Uncle,' I finally said, 'there has to be another way.'

"'Take me here,' he said, spreading a map out on the dashboard and pointing to a spot he'd circled in red. He pulled a small device from his pocket and plugged it into a socket in the vest.

"'What's that?' I asked.

"'A failsafe. If I am stopped, or shot, or for any reason unable to trigger the explosion, it will detonate automatically in twenty minutes. Enough for you to leave safely, if you so choose.'

"A sickly horror washed over me. The sounds around me were dull and hollow, like noises heard under water. My mind was hazy and unfeeling. And before I realized it, we were there.

"My uncle embraced me, said something about Allah, and exited the car.

"I knew that I needed to leave, but I couldn't. My body felt too heavy, like the paralysis you feel in a nightmare. I could only watch.

"My uncle approached the building and scaled the iron fence. I watched the guards in military fatigues run towards him, shouting. I watched him pull the tunic from his body, throwing the guards and several pedestrians into a panic.

"My uncle lifted the detonator in his right hand.

"And at that very moment, it began. It came from all sides at once, echoing off of buildings and shattering glass windows. It was an un-human sound, I recall. It was mechanical, in a way, like a foghorn or a train whistle, but there was more to it than that. You could feel the life behind it.

"I raised my eyes skyward, and there they were: countless figures of glowing men, each with a trumpet to his mouth."

"The Great Day started right then and there?" I asked.

"Yes. The timing was simply... unreal."

"And what about your uncle?"

"He survived. As you can imagine, at first he believed it was Allah's smile of approval for his act of martyrdom, but was shaken to his senses when the angelic proclamations began."

"I think that shook a lot of people up," I said, remembering the way many Americans reacted on that Day.

Abdel glanced at his watch. The blast crew would be starting their morning shift soon.

"Just one more question before you go," I said. Abdel nodded obligingly as he slipped into his bright orange safety vest.

"How did you learn about explosives? Was it just from studying the diagrams that one night?"

Abdel thought this was funny and let out a hearty laugh. "No, I was never that clever. Actually, my uncle taught me."

"Oh, that makes sense," I said, satisfied.

"You met him last night, actually. We usually call him by his nickname, Bird's Eye."

Gazini Itowale

The man at the ledge was stolid, motionless. His spindly fingers were interlocked behind his back as he looked down on the valley. A light breeze stirred over the precipice, gently tossing his sheer cotton pants and cloak. I had seen him do this many times before, usually right before breakfast. I had never talked to him, though. As the crews in L.A. continued to grow, it was becoming more and more difficult to keep track of new faces, especially with my unusual work hours.

Now, however, with my transfer from Demolition to Parks, I'd have more time to socialize with the others in the morning, and I decided that I'd start with the man at the ledge. I approached him quietly, not wanting to disturb what I suspected might be his personal prayer or meditation time.

As my feet stepped into the dewy grass, leaving dark dapples in the lawn, he spoke:

"Brother Mitch Hanson, I presume?"

I froze.

"It's your scent that gave you away."

"Oh," I said, suddenly very self-conscious.

"It's not a bad scent. It's the scent of almonds."

"Almonds? That's odd. I can't remember the last time I had any."

"Yes, the smell is a puzzle. But then I remembered that certain explosives have that same smell, meaning that you must be on a Demolitions crew. But since the men from Demolitions are never up this early, you must've recently switched assignments. So far as I know, only *Mitch Hanson* has recently switched from Demolitions. Transferred to..."

"Parks."

"Right, parks. Quite a change from blowing things up, yes?"

"Yeah, it'll be a welcome adjustment," I said, not knowing what to make of my curious new friend. "Were you really able to deduce all that from just a scent?"

"Yes. I hope it hasn't offended you. Some misunderstand me..."

"No, not at all. It was just a little... unexpected. Like something out of an old detective novel."

The man threw his head back and let out a resonating laugh that I imagined could be heard in all of the valley below. Two rows of brilliantly white teeth glistened in the morning light. "I laugh, you see, because it is not the first time I have heard the comparison. My name is Gazini Itowale. It's a pleasure to meet you, Brother Hanson." He shook my hand with a winning smile.

"Mitch is fine. Nice to meet you too. Where are you from?" I asked.

"Lagos, Old Nigeria."

"Africa? How did you make it all the way out to California?"

"Ah, I came to America during the Great Tribulation. I was working at the Center for Disease Control in Atlanta."

"No kidding, I'm originally from Atlanta, too."

"A small world. And now, a lot *smaller*."

"What were you doing at the CDC?" I asked.

"Do you remember the 'Nile Death'?"

I nodded, recalling the epidemic that had begun sweeping through Africa and into Central Europe during the Tribulation. It had been likened to Ebola: highly contagious, with a fifty percent fatality rate and a grisly end. It had been one of the final epidemics in an Old World that had already been brought to its knees from a plethora of conflicts and disasters.

"I was assigned to help one of the research teams in an effort to find a cure."

"If I remember correctly, that cure was never found..."

"That is correct. Armageddon came before a cure could be discovered, which was fortunate; after months of research we still knew very little about the disease, where it had come from, and how it could jump so quickly. I shudder to think what would have happened had Jehovah not intervened when he did."

Gazini's sentiments were similar to most members of the Great Crowd. Armageddon had come at exactly the right moment. Mankind had been on the brink.

"How severely were our friends affected by the Nile Death?"

"Although the infection and death tolls among the friends were significant, it was small in proportion to the total number of Witnesses."

"Why?"

"The simple answer is: Jehovah's people are more hygienic and live clean moral lives. It was similar with AIDS. Jehovah's people didn't engage in casual sex or use hypodermic needles by way of drug addiction. Thus, very few Witnesses contracted the disease.

"Of course, an airborne pathogen such as the Nile Death is

different: it's contracted much more easily. However, because our friends were careful with their drinking water and kept their homes and bodies clean, the rate of infection among the brothers stayed comparatively low. Still, there were casualties."

"And you stayed in Old America after Armageddon. Why?"

"I had come with my wife and two sons. The rest of my family in Lagos had always opposed the Truth. There was no reason for us to return."

"So what happened to you and your family after Armageddon?"

"We moved to Florida. Atlanta was a little too cold for us."

"Too *cold*?"

"Lagos is warm and dry all year round. Anything above 28 Celsius–that's 80 Fahrenheit to you–is simply too cold for us."

"And what was Florida like?"

"When I think of Florida, I think of the smell of damp grass and sunscreen."

"You really have a thing for smell, huh?"

"A learned skill. When I first left college, I worked as a doctor in a poor and remote village in the south-east part of the country. The hospital was a small, dirty building with barely enough government funding to keep the doors open. Many of the nurses were untrained. And the equipment, if it worked at all, was usually outdated and faulty. So I learned to rely on my senses, including smell.

"You see, a healthy body and sickly body produce different odors. Sometimes it is an obvious difference, sometimes it is subtle. This could be due to a compound released by the body's sweat glands, or by a change in blood composition, or acids secreted into the mouth. In fact, a person's breath is usually one of the easiest ways to detect the conditions of his or her lungs, kidney, and liver. I learned, over time, to diagnose patients partly based on their odor."

"Interesting," I said. "So, how does everyone smell now?"

"Healthy! And not just because we not have perfect bodies without blood, stomach, or lung deficiencies. We are enjoying a perfect, New World diet. For example, by my estimate, we're drinking three times as much water as we did in the Old World."

"Because of all the physical labor?"

"No doubt that plays a part, but also because it's practically the only thing left to drink. The fructose sodas and pseudo-juices have mostly all been consumed. We don't really have a choice, at this point."

"And drinking more water leads to a healthier body, and less odor..."

"Also, we're all strict vegetarians now. That plays a huge part in attaining a neutral body odor. Add on top of that the absence of saturated fats and preservatives, and you begin to see why we smell so much better. And that, of course, is just one small benefit of many. Our skin has cleared up, we feel much more energetic, we have less muscle pain, and on and on the list goes."

"I always thought that was just perfection doing its job."

"I'm sure it is. But what we put into our bodies has a definite impact on our overall health, too. Put all that Old World junk food into a perfect body and deprive it of sufficient water and I would be surprised if it would function as well as yours and mine."

"That makes sense. As a doctor, have you been able to tell any major physical differences between our current perfect bodies and the ones we had in the Old World?"

"Well, there are the obvious changes that we all went through: the muscle growth, the slight facial restructuring, fading scar tissue, fuller hair, and minor spinal growth, that sort of thing. Of course, all those were apparently just our bodies rejecting slight genetic imperfections.

"Some of the other changes are less evident. Our bones, for instance, are stronger than they used to be. It's difficult to test, of course, but you can call it an ex-doctor's intuition. If this is true, it would be another instance of our bodies returning to a perfect condition."

"But we can still get hurt."

"Oh yes. Have you?"

"I've cut myself a few times shaving, and cut my finger once or twice," I said.

"Yes. It is my suspicion that those kinds of minor injuries will be with us on into eternity. A body that can't get injured doesn't need the ability to heal itself, as ours have. Our blood clots, cuts scab over, and so on. Have you noticed, though, that the healing process is faster?"

This was true. Razor cuts left on my face were usually invisible a few hours later. Even the one time I'd sliced into my finger with a piece of glass shortly after Armageddon, the healing process seemed to pass unusually fast. In about four days, the wound was invisible.

"Have you seen any serious injuries in the New World?"

"Yes, but only in the few months after Armageddon, and usually just among smaller children. Even then, it was nothing life-threatening. One eleven-year-old girl needed stitches when she cut her arm on some wreckage and a teenager broke his leg when he fell from a scaffold. I suspect these injuries happened because they were inexperienced, and had just begun the process towards perfection. In any case, it was a warning to all of us, a reminder that we aren't invincible."

A voice echoed out from the tent behind us, signaling the start of morning worship. Gazini and I trudged back through the dewy grass in silence.

I thought about what an incredible thing bodily perfection was. I felt stronger, faster, healthier, and even a little smarter than I had been in the Old World, and it had been only nine years since the Great Day. There was no denying that we were already we were a changed mankind.

And yet, we had really only just begun.

Kevin MacDarmid

In the span of eight years and two months, I had seen Los Angeles transform from a smoky pile of debris to a verdant landscape. Several large parks had been built, which were quickly being claimed by the natural wildlife which seemed as curious about the future as we were. When I left, the Long Beach harbor was nearly at full capacity, with ships from as far away as India and Russia lining the docks.

The ship I would be boarding was the *Abrigol*, an 80-ft yacht that had been built in Panama. With an international crew of eleven and thirty-four passengers including myself, I eagerly awaited the experiences I'd have (and hear of) during the next twenty days.

On the cool, crisp morning that our ship was scheduled to depart, I noticed a man sitting on a crate at the edge of the pier. What caught my eye was his silver head of hair and beard. With the Old World so far behind us, grey-headedness had all but completely disappeared. Still, I resisted my impulse to stare and boarded my boat, finding my small cabin quarters and settling in.

To my surprise, the man boarded the same boat and was, in fact, my Captain! After most of the crew and passengers had gone to sleep on the first night, I spotted him reclining on the upper deck, gazing at the vast web of stars stretched above our sea. I took a nearby seat, and was soon hearing all about Brother Kevin MacDarmid's story.

"In the 1980's, my wife and I were invited to attend Gilead, where we were trained to serve as missionaries in a foreign land. Months later, after graduation, that foreign land turned out to be Mexico. It was a difficult assignment for my wife and I, given the culture, language, and climate, but we served there faithfully for almost four decades, eventually learning not only to speak Spanish, but also Chinese, which was a big need after the North Korean nuclear incident, forcing many Chinese to emigrate to our area."

"So if you went to Gilead in the 1980's, you should be in your 80's or so."

"86 this month, but who's counting?" Kevin jabbed me with an elbow. "Or could you be referring to this?" He pointed to his hair and beard.

I half nodded, and he smiled.

"My 'crown of beauty'. Well, I greyed very early. I had the hair of a senior citizen when I was only twenty-eight. In Gilead, I had more grey than our instructors! With the reversal process, I expect it'll be one of the last things to go." Kevin MacDarmid returned his glance to the night sky just in time to spot a yellow comet burn into the atmosphere.

"So how does it feel to be an eighty-six year old in a twenty-year-old's body?" I asked.

"Well I don't *feel* old, if that's what you're asking. The wrinkles and liver spots have all disappeared, my teeth have realigned themselves, I can swim, and run, and *think* as I did when I was young. But I do feel that life has slowed down in some ways. Perhaps that's what many of us are feeling now. In the Old System, when could we ever do *this*–sit on the deck of a boat, drifting through crystal clean water, listening to the calls of these majestic creatures..."

Kevin motioned to the family of humpback whales gracefully flanking our ship, lifting their sail-like fins out of the water as if to mimic the boat.

"We can truly see now, as life returns to the way it was in the beginning, how Satan had manipulated people into this *strangled* existence on Jehovah's once-beautiful planet." Kevin returned his glance to meet mine, his dark and intense eyes glistening where the moonlight danced.

"In so many ways, the system had been designed to hide the Creator from mankind. In a race to become their own gods, these frantic people, small and insignificant as ants, spent up their lives. And as much as we tried to avoid worldly ways of thinking, as much as we knew it was there, it was impossible to be free of it completely. Little ants, moving pieces of dirt from here to there, hoping to build the biggest hill before the rain."

Kevin and I sat there in silence for several minutes, listening to the coos and bays of the black whales rolling with the current. The sound gradually diminished as the pod departed and the *Abrigol* continued on alone.

I asked what the Tribulation was like for Witnesses in Mexico. Kevin paused for a few moments, collecting his thoughts.

"Mexico, before the Tribulation, was very religious. The Catholic Church had a strong hold on the people there. When the Liberation Act in America was passed, church attendance actually rose, for a time, at least. Mexicans wanted to show they were 'fiel a dios', or 'loyal to their Lord', as the saying went.

"But as anti-church and anti-religious sentiment mounted, the true quality of their faith was exposes. That was a particularly difficult time for the Witnesses. Churchgoers–or ex-churchgoers, I should say–could not understand why *we* were different, where our faith was coming from, and how, despite everything, we continued with our ministry. It was, in fact, many of these embittered men and women who began to directly persecute our friends there.

"In one area, a remote village near Oaxaca, our brothers and sisters were accosted while working at a Kingdom Hall building site. There were about forty of us there at the time, taking a siesta after lunch. Suddenly, a fleet of old pickup trucks came barreling up the dirt hill. The brothers quickly gathered the sisters and younger ones into the kitchen area, which was really just a frame of metal poles covered in plastic tarps. Then the largest, strongest brothers formed a line, shoulder to shoulder, and walked down to meet the threat.

"It was clear that the men in the pickups had been drinking, evidenced by their odor and the beer bottles and cans clanking around in the backs of their trucks. It was also clear that they meant us harm. Once the trucks had skidded to a stop in a cloud of dust, dozens of men piled out with clubs, machetes, and axes. The same look contorted each man's face: Belligerence. Anger. Malice.

"The leader of the pack, as it seemed, exited the driver's side of one of the trucks and approached the line of brothers. He held a crumpled beer can one hand and a machete in the other. On his head, he wore a tattered baseball cap. He glared into each of the brothers' eyes, going from one to the next, just inches from their faces.

"'Are you *testigos*?' He finally asked, using the Spanish word for *witnesses*.

"'We are,' said one of our overseers, stepping forward. His name was Jose Ruiz. He had moved recently to the area to help with the construction of Halls and encourage the locals, many of whom had been intimidated by gangs of thugs like these. The friends were happy to have him. Aside from being an outstanding elder and shepherd, Brother Ruiz was six-foot-seven, weighed nearly three hundred pounds, and lifted weights every day.

"'You know what we do to *testigos* in Oaxaca?' The man asked.

"'I do. You bring them trouble.'

"'And what will you do about that?' The man jabbed the can into Ruiz' chest.

"'The question you should be asking,' Ruiz responded with slow, measured words, 'is not what I will do about it. But what our God, *Yehova* will do.'

"This seemed to startle the man a little, who took a half step back. When, after a few moments, he still said nothing, one of the men from behind began to shout: *'The machete! The machete!'*

"Our brothers were now feeling very anxious, you can imagine. They shifted uneasily in their line, glancing at each other and wondering what ought to be done next. What about all our friends in the kitchen? Many of them were their wives. One was pregnant.

"But the man in the ragged hat still said nothing. Another step back. Then, he dropped the machete. The brothers jumped a bit as it clanged on the ground. With his free hand, the man clutched his chest, winced in agony, and collapsed.

"No one moved. The gang of men stared at the body unbelievingly. Our brothers, the same. Even Ruiz couldn't quite understand what had happened.

"Finally, one of our brothers stepped forward and knelt down, pressing two fingers to the man's throat.

"'He's alive,' the brother said, 'but needs to see a doctor right away.'

"Jose Ruiz ran to the man's pickup, which sent the other gangsters in a panic, dropping their weapons and hiding for cover.

"'My God, my God, save me!' Wailed one of the fleeing men.

"Taking a look in the cabin of the pickup, Ruiz shouted back: 'His keys are here. I'll take him.'

"The brothers who had been in the line moved forward and picked the man up, placing him gently in the passenger seat and strapping him in. The rest of the men, the ones who hadn't fled, looked on in amazement. Some were praying.

"Jose drove the man–Esteban was his name–to the hospital, where he stayed the night and was released the next morning. He'd had a heart attack."

"Did the project run into any more interruptions after that?" I asked.

"Just one. About a month later, also during a lunch break, the same fleet of pickup cars drove up to the site. Again, the brothers sent the sisters behind the tarp and formed a line. Everyone was a little nervous. Were the men back for revenge? Maybe the man had died and they blamed us?

"But when the trucks reached us, the men that piled out were sober, calm, and even... Respectful. Esteban was still in charge, and he barked orders to the others in a dialect I couldn't understand.

"The men followed his orders, unloading several large crates wrapped in green tarps. When the men had set them in front of the brothers, Esteban walked up to Brother Ruiz, removed his hat, and extended his right hand.

"After they had shook hands, Esteban said, 'A man who is willing to help his friends is nothing great. But a man who helps his enemies is something special. If you are God's people, I will not, I cannot fight you.'

"He then stepped to the crates and unlatched the canvas covers, revealing cages full of live chickens!

"As it turned out, Esteban ran a chicken farm not far from the Kingdom Hall site. When he had heard the Witnesses were building a Kingdom Hall nearby, he had been angry and afraid, since his former church pastor had told parishioners that the witnesses were thieves and zealots. But after our encounter the previous week, he had changed his mind.

"The brothers thanked him warmly and welcomed him to meetings once the Kingdom Hall was finished."

"Did he ever accept the invitation?"

"I'm not sure. Sadly, the Kingdom Hall was never completed. The Mexican government banned us soon after our encounter with Esteban, and construction work halted."

"How did our activities continue there after the ban?"

"As in other areas, our activities continued although the methods changed. We wore casual clothes in the ministry and stopped going door-to-door. We were cautious about mentioning what Organization we belonged to, and some of our publication covers were redesigned to be less conspicuous. But the work moved forward, and many more came to know the truth. It was as if the ban had done little to nothing to stop the "desirable" things from being shaken from the world.

"However, once the persecution became more direct, more intense, we did have our share of disappointments. Some of our students and even brothers and sisters stopped associating. The Mexican government imposed heavy fines on our friends, confiscating many of their belongings. They especially targeted the wealthy ones in the congregation, hoping that these would compromise sooner than those with fewer belongings. Sadly, this tactic sometimes did work.

"But in the end, the majority stayed faithful and are here with us today."

Dev, Sadra, & Avin

"All I'm saying is, the process has surprised me. I guess I was expecting something a little more... immediate, I guess." A man with crossed arms shrugged and leaned forward against the table.

"Remember, Avin, every detail of every process contains a valuable lesson," said another man. He looked to be the same age as the first, but I could hear age in his words.

"And not one promise has failed. That's important to keep in mind, too. Things may not have gone according to our expected timetable, but what does that matter?" A third voice said. It was a woman with rusty blonde hair tied back in a green ribbon.

"So what about you,? What were you expecting, when you thought of being perfect?" The young man asked.

"Well for starters, we were really hoping for a set of wings and the ability to see through walls," said the woman with a wink. The three of them chuckled and so did I, but was embarrassed when they caught me eavesdropping.

"Sorry," I whispered. "Couldn't help but overhear your conversation."

"Not at all," said the man. He invited me to join them and I sauntered over, still feeling a little shy.

"My name is Dev Carlton. This is my wife Sadra. And this is Sadra's nephew, Avin." I shook their hands and introduced myself.

"So where are you headed, brother Hanson?" Dev asked.

"La Unión, El Salvador," I said.

"There are some amazing things happening there," said Hal, nodding excitedly. "I've never been, though. Where're you from, I mean, originally?"

"Atlanta."

"Small world!" Exclaimed Sadra. "We were in Savannah a couple of summers ago. That area is just gorgeous now."

"I wouldn't know," I said. "I left right after the Great Day and never went back."

"Are you on your own then?" asked Dev.

I nodded.

"What about you all? Where are you going?" I asked.

"Actually, our final destination is Manila, by way of Honolulu."

"After all these years of wanting to visit Paradise, and finally we just had to wait for Paradise to come to us," Sadra said.

"We were just discussing the latest magazine on perfection," said Dev.

"Ah, yes, I guessed as much. Great articles." I said.

"How far back do you go?" asked Avin. It took me a few moments to realize he was asking my age.

"Born in '92, Old World."

"Oh," he nodded. "I had a friend in Atlanta. He was there during the Great Day. Well he moved from Pennsylvania to Atlanta. I haven't heard from him or his family since before. They weren't doing great, you know, spiritually. But I sure hope they made it."

We were silent as Hal seemed to wrestle his thoughts. "I mean, there were others that made it that didn't seem so spiritual, right? When we had our first post-Trib meeting, I remember seeing some folks who had been completely *MIA* for awhile during the Tribulation, and I was like, 'huh?'."

I had the same recollections and chuckled.

"Well that's why I'm glad we didn't do the judging. Clearly Jehovah saw something in those friends' hearts that warranted salvation. Had it been our decision, we may have judged wrongly," said Dev.

"Yeah, I guess that's true." Avin bit his lip.

"Remember, too, that endurance under trial has always counted a lot to Jehovah. Those that just squeezed through the narrow door will need to work hard to build themselves up, because there are more trials ahead of us."

"Ugh, don't remind me," Hal said, covering his face with his hands. "The last one was hard enough."

"But you were faithful, which gives you the advantage in any future trials."

"And it's not worth worrying about too much now. We've got another what, nine hundred and eighty-seven years?" Said Sadra.

"Something tells me it'll be here sooner than it sounds," I said.

"True. I can't imagine how time will fly when we've been doing this for hundreds of years. And I still can't imagine it ever getting boring," Sadra said.

"So what about you, Brother Hanson? How did you imagine things would be on this side of Armageddon? Anything surprise you?" Asked the young man.

"Oh sure, lots. I figured the resurrection would be one of the first things we'd have to look forward to in the New World, and that we'd all be building our own mansions and vineyards within the first few years. I hadn't taken into account how much reorganization and rebuilding would be involved. And yet, now that I've experienced it, I've realized this was the best thing for us."

"Why do you say that?" Dev asked.

"Well, it gave us a job to do together. After everything we'd been through during the Tribulation, I feel like we needed a project like this. And I've learned a lot of practical skills, working with brothers and sisters from all over the world."

The others nodded thoughtfully, and Dev added: "I agree. And I feel the encouragement we were given to travel in the volunteer work was insightful, too. Like you say, there's much to be learned from serving with people of other cultures and backgrounds."

"I've still got a long way to go with that one," Sadra said wryly with a wave of her hand. "I didn't expect it to be so hard. I guess sometimes I just miss our old culture, foods, and so on, from America."

"I'm sure that, like everything else, it'll get easier with time," I said.

"I'm sure it will," said Dev. "By the way, have you noticed how our memories are improving? I was just telling Sadra this morning that my ability to recall names, figures, detailed instructions, and even minute details from long ago has all gotten much better."

"Same here," said Sadra. "Recently I've actually been able to recall conversations I've had with other people from decades ago. The brain is an amazing creation, isn't it? All that information was stowed away up there, it just needed something to clear away the cobwebs and dust it off."

Suddenly a burst of static blew in from the dining room speaker. A scratchy voice: "Brothers and sisters, this is your captain speaking. An interesting phenomenon can be seen from the port-side deck. That's the *left side*, for all you landlubbers, heh." Another burp of static and the PA went dead.

Dev, Sadra, Avin and myself, along with a handful of other dining passengers, cleared our trays and clambered onto the deck. A few of the crew were already there, pointing and taking pictures.

Roughly one hundred meters beyond our boat, the water was beginning to churn. It appeared to be a wave at first, but it didn't move laterally. Instead, it seemed to be circling. I had read about whales creating whirlpools to trap plankton before, and wondered if that's what I was witnessing. But no, the water wasn't swirling downward, into the depths, but rather *outward. Upward.*

Then came a wind, knocking against the sails.

"Rig 'em," shouted the captain from the upper deck. The sailors scrambled to their posts, winding gears, gathering rope, and soon the sails had disappeared.

"What is it?" One of the passengers asked.

"We just call them spouts," said one of the crew, a sturdy man with a bundle of rope on his shoulder. "I think that's the fifth one I've seen this year. I hear they're more common in deeper waters."

"What is it doing?" I asked.

"No one's sure yet, but if it keeps up, I might need to find a new assignment." The sailor smiled.

"What do you mean?" I asked.

"Can't sail a ship without a sea." A wink.

Miguel, the Innkeeper

We arrived in La Unión, El Salvador, on a warm spring evening just as the sun was dipping into a red sea. A handful of local brothers helped us tie *The Abrigol* to the pier and welcomed us with paper bags of freshly ground coffee and cool sticks of sugar cane. Captain MacDarmid had prepared for this gift exchange, and had a few of his crew unload several cases of Californian red wine to our hosts' wide-eyed delight.

After we'd all checked in with the lodging department we headed to our individual rooms and slept. The others had looked forward to a bed that didn't sway with the sea during the night, but as for me, well, I kind of missed it. Nights on the ocean had been wholly tranquil and reassuring, as if each wave that passed beneath our hull did its part to heal the wounds of the past. I missed staring out of my porthole into the bluish-purple haze of a starry night and talking with my Creator.

Of course, a steamy, hot shower and a full-size bed with smooth, clean sheets did have a certain appeal, too.

I was energetic and ready to work as I climbed down the oak staircase into the dining room the next morning. The air was thick with the aroma of coffee and fresh fruit. The large wooden table was lined by many of the faces that had been with me on our voyage from Long Beach, but there were new friends I didn't recognize, too: a young (maybe?) Asian couple reading a daily text, a family of five almost finished with their breakfast of eggs and fruit, and next to me, a brother I had seen the night before. He'd helped us get settled in our rooms and shown us how to operate the lanterns in case we wanted we get up during the night. His name was Miguel, and he was the innkeeper.

"How did you sleep?" He asked as he poured me a cup of coffee. The inn roasted their own locally-grown beans.

"Well, thanks. The room was very comfortable," I said, letting the fragrant liquid drizzle slowly onto my palate. It was the best coffee I'd had in my life.

"Well that's good. Sometimes, after being out there for so long,

91

it's difficult to get used to a stationary bed. Or room, for that matter," Miguel said with a smile.

"Sounds like you've spent some time out there yourself," I suggested.

"Only a couple of months. Many of the friends who come here have spent most of their time on this side of Armageddon at sea."

"Why so much sea travel?" I asked.

"After the Great Day it was the only way that many could travel into North America. Many of the major roads and highways inland had been destroyed on the South American continent. Many brothers and sisters would ferry the friends from those areas into La Unión, and from here they would travel North. Some stayed."

"What destroyed the roads there?"

"Flooding, landslides, earthquakes, you name it. A lot of those areas are still in ruins. And with so few living people left, I doubt there will be any impetus to restore those areas anytime soon. But we'll see."

I took another sip of coffee and imagined those brothers going back and forth from this area to South America, bringing hundreds of friends to the North.

"You have a beautiful town here, La Unión," I said.

"Yes, we enjoy it."

"What did it look like during the Tribulation?"

"Some things haven't changed. The ocean is still in that direction and the buildings are in that," he smiled. "But everything else. Well, that's a different story. Have you heard of Enlightenment Centers?"

"No."

"They were a clever tactic the local government used to lessen mob violence when they started banning religions. El Salvador was one of the last countries in the area to enforce religious bans, so they had the benefit of seeing how other governments had done it before them. In areas like Mexico and Brazil, pro-church riots caused much damage and expense. So the government here disguised their bans as a kind of educational reform.

"They would let the churches exist, but their preachers had to include information in their sermons designed to subtly turn their parishioners from the church. For example, they had to explain the problems that religion had caused in other areas, or why supporting local government reforms was good for the people, or why evolution was a trustworthy explanation for the origin of life.

"To the untrained ear of Babylon the Great, these teachings seemed harmless. The churches were willing to do anything to be spared the fate of total bans, which would mean closed doors and empty coffers.

"Jehovah's people, on the other hand, saw right through this tactic. Of course, aside from teaching evolution at the meetings, their other requests weren't incompatible with what we were already teaching from the platform: false religion *had* created many problems, and obeying one's government *was* a positive thing, to a point.

"But for churchgoers, the gradual change of the message they were hearing began to produce the results the government had hoped for. Religion seemed less appealing, less important, less necessary than it had before. *After all*, people thought, *we have our wonderful government and we have science.* And so, in the span of less than a year, church attendance had all but dried up. This meant that when taxes were imposed suddenly on all religious organizations, the churches had no way to pay them and keep their luxurious buildings kept up.

"The government then went back and made a deal with the churches. If they wanted to keep their jobs and their buildings, they could; they just had to remove *all* religious topics from their sermons and stick to the government-provided agenda: pro-government, pro-science, anti-religion. Unsurprisingly, most of the churches accepted this bargain. The buildings were renamed Enlightenment Centers, and the religious iconography was gradually removed.

"And that was how, the little wild beast of El Salvador gobbled up a chunk of the Great Harlot."

"What about the Witnesses, though? What happened with the Kingdom Halls?"

"They were confiscated, but not until much later. What the government really wanted was the *churches'* money. After establishing the Enlightenment Centers, they were able to take over the churches' finances and drain them dry. The Witnesses, on the other hand, weren't much of an appealing target. Our buildings were simple and modest, without stained glass windows, marble statues, or gold ornaments. So they were left alone, until the very end."

"And how was the end?"

"Difficult, as it was everywhere else. The government's first attack had been cunning and indirect, but its final tactic was fierce and unmistakable. Many of the brothers were imprisoned and beaten, myself included. This, of course, was all supported by the public, who now generally viewed any religion as a negative thing."

"What was it like, when Jehovah stepped in?"

"First were the trumpets. I've asked a lot of our guests about this, and it seems that this first phase of Jehovah's Day was the same everywhere. Those marvelous, reverberating trumpet blasts. They still ring in my ears."

I could hear the blast in my ears, too, when I tried to remember it. It had had a unique ability to resonate within one's whole body, in the bones and heart. For Jehovah's people, it brought a kind of peace and relief, for his enemies, a frenzied terror.

"You had the angelic announcement next, too?"

"Yes, we did. I remember being so happy when I heard the angel speaking, repeating those words over and over. Finally, Jehovah's name was being vindicated! Yes, he existed! Yes, he cared about us! Yes, we were his people! I was so proud that day."

"Were you still in prison at the time?"

"I was. The cell was small, but those noises penetrated the walls and brought me and the other four brothers in the cell great comfort. We immediately prayed to Jehovah, thanking him, and expressed our readiness for whatever came next. When we opened our eyes, a sixth man had entered our cell. He wore a white shirt and cleanly-pressed khakis and had a look of determination on his face.

"Thinking he was one of the prison guards, one of the brothers asked, 'Are you here to kill us?'

"'No,' said the man. 'We are on the same side. Go, quickly, and gather all of our friends to the coast. Deliverance is near.'

"And with those words, he walked through the prison wall. We were frozen with disbelief. We had just spoken with an angel of Jehovah!

"Finally, someone tried the cell door, swinging it open on its hinge. We were free! We called the brothers and sisters in our congregation and instructed everyone to make their way to the coast. Then we called the circuit overseer to let him know what had happened and what we had to do.

"'I know, I know,' he said impatiently, 'he visited me, too–' and hung up.

"Within two hours, we had done exactly as the messenger had instructed, standing on the shore of La Unión, watching with anticipation..."

"And then?" I asked.

"Well, go see the museum for yourself."

I didn't know what that meant, so Miguel explained how to get there from the inn, and that all my questions would be answered.

"It's best to see it for yourself," he said as he cleared plates from the tables.

Sameer Sengupta

After Armageddon, most cities had climbed slowly from the wreckage. La Unión wasn't one of them. The Salvaging and Demolition teams had long since completed their work and moved on to Colombia, Venezuela, Ecuador, and other areas in the South American continent, clearing the roads as they went.

La Unión was clean, developed, and efficient. And its lush location against a sprawling beach didn't hurt, either. Walking around the town, I noted that many of the buildings felt native to the area. Although most had clearly been constructed post-Armageddon, they had been designed and built to keep with the local style: stark white exteriors accented with sky blue trim, tall rectangular windows flanked by ornate iron railings, and red terra cotta rooftops. It was the first of many places that I could imagine myself settling in, once I was ready. Once I was with my family again.

It's worth noting that at this point that I was forty-seven years old, but felt much more energetic than I had coming out of the Old World in my thirties. Recent environmental studies had shown a decrease in carbon monoxide (the primary pollutant caused by petrol-burning automobiles) of 98.9%. The seas, rivers, and lakes had shown similar improvement, many once-barren areas now teeming with life. Little by little, everything was getting better, and we were feeling healthier.

But there was still work left to do, and I was happy to be busy.

At this point, the foremost task facing mankind was agricultural education. Before we could fulfill Jehovah's purpose to cultivate the earth (and before anyone could be resurrected), we had to learn to grow and store our own food. This, I found, was harder than it sounded. The ultra-convenience of the Old System had been a way of life, but it hadn't been normal. In the Real World, having an assortment of fruits and vegetables meant months tilling, planting, and waiting on a plot of land to yield produce, not a half-hour errand to the local grocery store.

What we were learning, among so many other things, was patience. We had *forever*, for goodness' sake. We could wait a season for tomatoes.

"In the Old World, growing food was actually more difficult than it is now," said our instructor, Yeasa, a sister who appeared to have both Asian and Hispanic roots.

"In those days, you really had to know what to plant when. For instance, some vegetables had to be planted before the last frost of winter, and some after, and so on. It was a tricky task." She pulled the shed door open with gloved hands and handed the half dozen of us hoes, pickaxes, and small toolkits.

"What we're finding now, though, is that plants are a bit hardier, and the weather is certainly better, and cleaner. This means we can be less concerned with remembering all that stuff. We're still rotating crops, of course, and letting the land rest every few years, but for the most part..." she put her hands on her hips and wiped her brow, "well for the most part things just grow themselves."

That seemed to relieve us all a little, and Yeasa smiled. "We still have to help them along, of course," she said. She led us around the side of the shed behind a line of pine saplings. "Especially when the land starts like this."

The relief drained from our faces as we got our first look at the plot we'd be cultivating: it was nearly five acres of gravelly terrain with patches of grass and debris from the Old World.

"Can't this just be bulldozed?" Asked a voice from behind me.

"All the bulldozers already headed out with the demo crews last Fall," said Yeasa with a hint of sympathy. "Besides, heavy machines like that tend to pack the soil down. After a rain, that soil hardens and is even more difficult than this to till."

A wave of resigned nods went through the group. Yeasa gave us a few more pointers, told us where lunch would be served, and headed back towards the ranch house on the hill. We looked at each other, shrugged, and got to work.

We had been assigned to work in pairs, and our first task was relatively simple: till up the soil, remove the rocks and debris, and even out the topography. My partner was Sameer Sengupta, a brother from India who'd made his way over to El Salvador only a few months before myself. We chatted as we worked.

"Where were you when the Great Day began?" I asked while excavating a chunk of concrete.

"On a cargo liner in the South China Sea," he replied.

"What brought you there?" I had nearly completely dug the slab of stone from the ground when I realized it was connected to a larger piece of concrete by several cords of rebar.

"Youthful rebellion," Sameer said with a smile. He opened his toolkit and handed me a hacksaw.

"Were your parents Witnesses?"

"No. Hindus. I often wonder what I would have become if my parents had been Witnesses, though. It is a troubling thought."

"So I take it you and your parents didn't always see eye to eye?" I asked.

"My parents were very traditional. They had arranged most of the details of my future before I had turned thirteen, even picking out the girl I would marry. They expected me to study engineering, go to college, marry, and have children, all according to their timetable."

"And you didn't agree."

"I wanted to make my own decisions, live my own life, and so forth. A lot of young Indians in my generation were doing the same, much to our parents' dismay. When I was just seventeen years old I secretly left school and took a train to Visakhapatnam, a large port city on the east coast. I found a job in a shipyard there, thinking that this life would allow me to see the world and be a free man."

"Did it?"

"It did afford me the chance to see new parts of the world, and I didn't mind life at sea. But it wasn't freedom. We often worked long shifts without breaks, sometimes double shifts when the crew was slim. This was dangerous, especially when the seas were rough. I remember one stormy night when one of my shipmates, a young man from Sri Lanka, had his leg caught in a rigging line and was flung into the waves. His harness somehow came loose, and we never saw him again. I was especially angry when the captain refused to report the death to our port of origin, saying that he'd call it in when we made harbor the next week. It was the first time that I realized that in my quest for freedom, I had ended up becoming a kind of slave."

"When did you finally learn the truth?"

"I had been working on the shipping lines for about three years when I first came in contact with Jehovah's Witnesses. I had picked up smoking, drinking, and gambling in that time and was more miserable than ever. I was still too proud to return home, though, and felt resigned to my life as a sailor. But then one day we docked in Tokyo and some Japanese men came onto our ship with a box full of books and magazines. We communicated in English, and I was surprised to learn they were Christians. I challenged them with questions about God, religious corruption, and the nature of the soul, and they answered each one from the Bible.

"As a child, my parents had spoken often of the gods and saints of Hindu, but I always had the feeling that they didn't fully understand

97

it themselves, that it was more of a tradition than an actual, comprehensible belief. This is how most religions appeared to me: confusing, traditional, and illogical. Still, I believed in the existence of a God, and for the first time I felt I was learning who He might actually be. The two Japanese brothers came back again the next day and brought me a small bag of books, DVDs, and even a few small gifts from Japan. I was very touched by this act of kindness, and strongly felt that these were God's people.

"I read the books they gave me at every chance I could, especially the small Bible, which was in my mother tongue. The more I read, the more I wanted to become one of Jehovah's people. After reading through chapter fourteen of the *Bible Teach* book, I decided to quit smoking, although the drinking would take a little longer. I also began to think about reconciling with my parents."

I'd finally cut through the thick strands of rebar and Sameer helped me to pry the smaller piece of concrete from the ground and into our wheelbarrow.

"So did you return home?"

"I called. I'd written them a letter when I'd boarded my first ship in Visakhapatnam, so they knew where I was, but that phone call was the first time we had spoken in years. I expected them to be very angry with me, but they were just happy I was safe. I felt very guilty, hearing my mother cry on the phone like that. I realized how selfish I had been, and for what? I promised my parents I would return as soon as I could, and that I had wonderful news to tell them upon my arrival. Unfortunately, I never had the chance."

"What happened?"

"That year, a nuclear plant went unstable, sending radioactive waste into nearby villages and killing thousands of people. My parents were among those."

"I'm sorry," I said, stopping my work.

"It's ok," Sameer said. "I have a strong hope that I will see them shortly. We have so much to talk about."

Sameer walked to the edge of the field and returned with the emptied wheelbarrow.

"The next couple of years were very difficult on that ship. When my shipmates discovered that I was reading religious material, they criticized me and threatened to beat me up if I didn't throw my books overboard. My faith was not very strong then, so I complied with their wishes, though I hid some of my favorite books in a small compartment below my bunk.

"Whenever we docked, I would search the town for the

Witnesses, but could never find them. I was told that they had been completely disbanded, just like the other churches and mosques. Finally, during one of our trips to Sydney, I heard a different answer. I was told the Witnesses could be found at their 'church hall' not far from the shipyard where we were docked. I ran, stopping only to ask for directions, for seven kilometers. Finally I found it: an old building on a small road. But the doors were chained shut and the windows had been pasted over.

"I went around the back of the building, hoping to find someone, but the street was empty apart from a few dumpsters and empty boxes. I peeked in one of the dumpsters and realized that something had been burned inside; there were black and grey flecks of ash in a large pile of soot. I rocked the dumpster back and forth to get a look at what had been burned and realized it was Witness literature.

"Excitedly, I jumped into the dumpster and began sifting through the ash, looking for something that hadn't been consumed in the fire. In the farthest corner in a shadow, I found it: a large red book called *Revelation*. The edges of the pages were charred and the back cover was missing, but the words were legible. I was so happy to have something new to read! I stuffed it into my jumper and walked back to the ship.

"The book was a gift from Jehovah, exactly the spiritual food that I needed at that time. It explained in detail all the events that had been happening around the world, from the fall of false religion to the attack on God's people. I knew now, without a doubt, that I had found the truth. I vowed to stay loyal to Jehovah and help my shipmates learn about Him."

"Did any of them accept the truth?"

"A couple of them were willing to talk about spiritual things, but they were scared. Many of the men on our ship were glad that religion was a thing of the past, and were militant towards anyone who hadn't adopted this view. Still, over the next few weeks, we continued to discuss the things I had learned from the Witnesses' publications.

"And the Great Day happened shortly after that?"

"Yes. We were on our way to Shenzhen, China, from the Philippines. It was around noontime when the trumpet blasts began. Though the sky had been bright and clear that day, everything went dark when the trumpets began. A dense fog set in and the sky turned black with thick, inky clouds swirling above us. The waves dissipated beneath the boat. Many of the sailors came out from their cabins to see what was happening. Some of the men thought it was a kind of natural phenomenon. One insisted we were being attacked by aliens. But when we saw the glowing figures in the sky and heard the angelic announcement, it was clear that this was something else.

"I remember, also, being surprised that the announcement was in Hindi. When I tried to translate it to English so that the other sailors could understand, I discovered that each man was hearing it in his native language."

"How did the sailors react to hearing the angel's message?" I asked.

"It was a little different for each person. Some of the men just stood there, frozen in awe. The few that I had been witnessing to were excited, as was I. But others were terrified, including the captain. This terror quickly spread through the crew. Words were screamed in a panic. Some of the men went below deck and brought back guns, firing them into the clouds. Of course, this was useless. The fired rounds simply disappeared into the sky. One of the men threw a grenade.

"These men, the ones who fought back, were the first to go. An angelic figure holding a sword passed over and through the ship's walls. The men it touched would stand still for a moment, with a puzzled look of terror on their face, and then turn into a brilliant red light and vanish. Only a fine grey mist would remain of them, which would settle to the deck and become a thin layer of dust.

"It took only a few minutes for the angel to finish. It then returned to the deck where we were standing and addressed us directly. 'Fear the true God, Jehovah,' he said. Then it became a beam of light that shot into the dark sky above. The clouds and fog cleared, and our ship continued to its destination."

"What was it like when you arrived?"

"There weren't enough of us to dock such a large ship, so we had to stop before we reached the pier and take one of the rafts to shore."

We finally managed to free the second, larger piece of concrete from the ground and into the wheelbarrow.

"Shenzhen was...surreal. I had been there many times before. It had been this hive of activity, even in the middle of the night, with thousands of people zipping around the streets, riding motorcycles, driving cars and tractors, towing shipments to and from the harbor. But now it was completely silent. The ground was covered in that same grey dust, and the air was acrid. In the distance, I could see that many buildings were still smoking. A few Chinese men and women were sitting on a pile of crushed cardboard, but no one was speaking. They barely noticed us when we climbed onto the dock.

"There were no police, no security checks, no papers to sign. So we wandered into Shenzhen, wondering what would happen next. We would occasionally run into other people in the streets, but we couldn't communicate with anyone, until about a week later.

"We were eating dried noodles that we'd found on the back of a truck when a man on a moped stopped us.

"'You speak English?' the driver asked. He wore sunglasses and a handkerchief was wrapped around his face.

"'We do,' I said, a little warily.

"'Are you Witnesses?'

"'Yes!' I said, not really realizing what I was saying.

"'I am brother Hirigara,' the man said. He removed his handkerchief and glasses and revealed a warm smile.

"I looked at the man and could not believe my eyes. It was the same brother that had first introduced me to the truth in Tokyo! I wrapped my arms around him and began to cry. When he realized who I was, he could not quite understand how I had gotten to China. I briefly explained and thanked him over and over for helping me to learn about Jehovah.

"As it turned out, Brother Hirigara had moved to China with his wife shortly after we had met in Tokyo. He'd been in an English congregation at the time but was also studying Mandarin and was asked to assist the brothers in Shenzhen. The Tribulation had begun shortly after his move there, and he'd been there up through the Great Day. In a way that only Jehovah could arrange, we had been reunited at last.

"We found bicycles nearby and followed Brother Hirigara to an empty factory a few kilometers away where the English-speaking Witnesses had gathered. A few brothers from the Hong Kong branch had come over immediately after the Great Day to encourage the friends and give basic instructions on how to care for each other before the next phase began.

"It was, up to that point, the happiest moment of my life."

Over the next few years, Sameer and I would spend many more days like this, tilling the soil, planting crops, and harvesting fruit. He had many more stories from his time spent in China, and I decided that someday I would have to travel there to experience it for myself.

Yeasa Valdez

"So how are you enjoying your first few weeks?" The girl asked.

"It's been...rewarding," I said. "I haven't been in this kind of physical shape since, well, ever." Some of the others at the table chuckled. Obviously I wasn't the only one.

The girl turned to face the five acre plot of land we'd been laboriously combing free of wreckage. What had once been a lumpy, unattractive field of debris was slowly transforming into an arable plot of land. The landscape had been evened out and tilled into long, straight rows of puffy brown soil. We were almost ready to plant, though we didn't know yet what it was we'd be putting into the ground.

"I hope you all plan on seeing this project through to completion. I know it's hard work, but trust me, it's worth it."

Everyone seemed to believe her. It was almost six o'clock and we'd just finished our dinner on the second-story patio of the ranch house beside the field. Two horses were grazing on a hill in the diminishing dusk light while a couple of locals kicked around a soccer ball. It had been a long day, and we were kindly assured that it would get easier. The other workers retired to their rooms in various inns around the town, leaving the girl and I to watch the sunset in silence.

"Yeasa is an interesting name," I said. "Where's it from?"

"My parents' imagination, I believe. They were, or are, rather, very creative people. Although ironically I've run into two other Yeasas since I've been here in La Unión. Same spelling too. Don't tell my parents."

"Where are your parents?" I asked.

"Still in Brazil."

"You grew up there?"

"Sort of. It's a long story."

"I'm not tired yet. If you're not, that is."

The girl seemed to be weighing her options, and finally conceded, "Sure, why not."

As the sun finally rolled off the horizon into the sea and a white string of lights flickered on the bannister, Yeasa began her story.

"Our family originally started in Vancouver, Canada, where my parents met. My mom was Canadian-born Japanese and dad was Spanish. Although their backgrounds were pretty different, they were both adventurous, eclectic people, and they enjoyed pioneering together. A few years after getting married, they joined a Spanish congregation, with the goal of one day moving to South America. Unfortunately, a 7-pound 4-ounce surprise threw a bit of a wrench in those plans."

"You."

"Correct. It wasn't an easy adjustment for them, but they did a pretty good job with it, as I can only remember good things from my childhood. Learning to finger paint at the zoo, playing flashlight tag with the kids from the congregation, Bible dress-up parties, and so on. I wasn't an unloved child, in other words." She smiled.

"Still, my parents never forgot their goal, and they kept praying about it. I remember, as a little girl, sitting on Dad's lap as he Googled pictures of South America, explaining to me how the ministry was so exciting there, and wouldn't it be nice if we could all serve Jehovah there one day? It did sound nice, but I liked my life in Vancouver with my friends, and I liked my school, and didn't think we'd ever actually leave.

"But when I was sixteen, during our family study one night, Dad explained that he had found a job in Brazil, had contacted the elders in one of the congregations there, and that, if we all agreed, we could move. Mom was ecstatic. She literally jumped up and down in our living room shouting 'Brazil! Brazil! Brazil!'

"I was a little less enthused, but I knew how much they wanted to go, and Dad promised we would just try it out for a year and we could always come back if it didn't work out. So I agreed, and by the end of the next month, we were chasing roaches out of our kitchen in a small apartment on the edge of São Paulo.

"Dad and Mom decided it would be best (for me, probably) to be part of an English congregation. They did their best to find me friends in our congregation and others nearby, but the move was difficult for me, and I preferred being alone most of the time. I missed everything about my old home, and Mom and Dad were really worried about me.

"They enrolled me in an international school, which meant that I could continue my classes in English. I found that a lot of my classmates were in a similar situation. Their parents had moved from foreign countries for work and had dragged their kids along with them. It seemed that no one wanted to be there, and I found a kind of camaraderie in our despondency. After school the kids would get together and drink and smoke, often complaining about how stupid and selfish their parents were. Although I knew my parents were different, their words struck a chord with me, and before long I was adopting their attitude towards family.

"Dad and Mom noticed the change in me immediately and did their best to help me, but the rift between us just grew larger and larger. Soon I'd picked up all kinds of bad habits, and they had no idea what to do to help me.

"Then, one night, my life changed forever.

"I'd started hanging out with my classmates on the weekends. We'd go into the city, sometimes get a few beers, and drive around aimlessly until nighttime. Somehow my parents never found out about this, though I'm sure they suspected that I was lying about being with witness friends from other congregations.

"But on this particular night, we drank more than usual. One of my classmates, a girl named Nikki, was heading back to France, and we decided to party hard on our last night together. Troy, who was a year older than us, partied especially hard. He was also behind the wheel when we crashed.

"I don't think I'll ever forget the feeling of his Jeep smashing through the guardrail of the bridge and into the river. Shards of glass from the windshield cut into my face and hands, followed by a powerful gush of water that broke four of my ribs and knocked me unconscious.

"And I had it easy. Nikki and the other girl in the backseat were crushed to death when the passenger seat I was in and Troy's driver's seat dislodged from the body of the car and flew backwards with the impact of the water. Only Troy walked away with minor injuries.

"Fortunately, a man driving a minivan saw us go over the bridge, and, along with his teenage son, pulled Troy and I from the wreckage. About an hour later I was in the ER while my parents waited in a nearby room, crying.

"When I opened my eyes four weeks later, everything was different. I couldn't think straight. I kept seeing the car crash in my mind, as if I were stuck in some kind of loop. And my parents' words didn't make sense to me. I could hear them speaking, but didn't understand anything. Even my muscles seemed strange, like I couldn't tell them what to do. My tongue was a useless block of flesh in my mouth. Even the words "mom" and "dad" were impossible to say."

"Why? What had happened to you?"

"I had been unconscious under water for too long. The brain, without having enough oxygen, had been severely damaged. I was mentally handicapped."

"And you knew that, then?"

"It's hard to explain what went through my mind then. There was so much static in my head all the time, and I was so confused and frustrated about not being able to do anything, but I don't think I ever fully realized what had happened. It was a struggle just to remember simple things. And the images of that crash kept coming back, as if they'd been burned into my memory. All I knew was that I had changed from before."

"How did your parents deal with the situation?"

"They..." Yeasa paused to clear a knot in her throat...

"They just kept loving me. So much of what happened in the years after that are a haze, but what I do remember is them getting me ready for each meeting, and for service, and preparing my little bag of books and clipping it to the side of my wheelchair. As much as they must've been hurting all that time, I never saw it, never felt it. I could only feel their love. And I was so angry that I couldn't say thank you, that I couldn't wrap my arms around my dad and mom and say sorry for being such an awful daughter.

"But what I could do was pray. I prayed all the time. I knew that even though I couldn't think straight or speak a clear word, Jehovah could hear my thoughts. I knew, too, that if I tried my best from then on to be a good daughter, he'd forgive me, and he'd bless my family and I. And so, with much effort, I tried to recall all that I could about what I'd studied before the accident, all the scriptures I'd learned as a girl. Gradually they began coming back to me. *Matthew 6:33. John 17:3. Psalms 37:10 and 11. Genesis 3:15.* I would go over these verses again and again in my head.

"I found, over time, that it was easier to sort out the things that were happening internally than those externally. The outside world seemed to be passing by too quickly and too disorderly to fully capture. I would be at a meeting one moment, and then in bed the next, and then someone was giving me a bath, and then I was at the doctor's office. Things just didn't make sense.

"But one thing that always grounded me was the feeling of touch. Whenever my dad or mom would hold my hand, wipe my face, or comb my hair, I could hold on to that moment and put it in my heart. It meant so much to me, being touched like that. It made my whole body warm, as if Jehovah himself were saying, 'Yeasa, I forgive you.' And that helped me to forgive myself.

"And then, one day, the fog cleared.

"I was sitting there, looking out of a large window over a garden, in my wheelchair. My hands uncurled slowly and I ran them over the coarse plastic armrests. I felt the little bumpy stitches in the vinyl seat and the rubbery, grooved tires covered in dust. And then, a little unsteadily, I rose from the seat. A voice, as sweet as spring rain, washed over me from behind:

"'Yeasa!'

"I turned to face my parents, who stood there with open arms and tears in their eyes. And we hugged the greatest, warmest hug in the history of all hugs."

The Armageddon Archives

Nearly a year passed before I finally visited the Armageddon Archives in La Unión that I'd heard so much about. I'd been busy cultivating our plot of land, which we'd named Kainoa, after a suggestion from one of the other workers who was from Hawaii. We were already beginning to see sprouts jutting from the soil, and were now helping them wind their way slowly around the trellises we'd built the previous Spring. We were all a little anxious about how these grapes would turn out, but Yeasa had assured us that the area was fertile, and known for producing healthy, succulent fruit.

When I finally reached the Archives, I was surprised by its modest size. It was only a couple of stories tall and barely occupied the entire block. I had been expecting something much bigger for all its hype. I entered. An attendant behind a curved, bronze desk greeted me. He asked if it was my first time to the Archives and I nodded. He explained that this was a self-guided interactive tour. Any other instructions, he assured me, would be clearly stated on the displays.

The attendant led to me the elevator, pushed a button, and sent me down, deep into the ground, to the level marked "B5".

"Enjoy the tour," he said casually as the doors formed a wall between us.

There was only blackness when the doors opened a few moments later. I wondered if someone had forgotten to turn on the electricity. I took my first step, a little uneasily, into the room, and suddenly a series of bulbs came to life overhead.

On either side of me, tall walls were plastered with large photographs of the Old World. Most were of incidents leading up to Armageddon: the Great California Earthquake, the hurricanes on the Atlantic seaboard, the nuclear incidents in Asia, and a couple of pictures from wars I couldn't distinguish. The two walls met in a doorway a few yards in front of me. Above the doorway, a sign read: The Great Tribulation.

On the other side of the doorway the walls parted to encircle a large room. The ground was covered in thick plated glass, beneath which lay empty ammunition shells, plastic chemical containers, and medical waste. A small engraved sign at my feet explained that these were relics from the Old World. The walls in the room were covered in more diagrams and photographs taken during the Great Tribulation. They were similar to the pictures from the hallway, but these were accompanied by blocks of text explaining each picture. In many of the walls, rectangular holes had been cut to house electronic screens. Embedded into the wall next to each screen was a button with the words "Press Me" etched above it. I pressed one.

On the screen, an array of pictures and newspaper clippings swayed in and out of focus. A narrator briefly explained world conditions during the Tribulation.

It had been a decade and a half since I had lived in the world of these pictures, and I was surprised at how much I had forgotten. To be more precise, the memories were there, but the horrific imagery and the attached feelings of fear and terror had faded. I knew people used to get sick, but I had forgotten what illness looked like. When a picture of a malnourished newborn squirming in an incubation tank flashed onto the screen, I gasped.

It was the same when a video clip of a tank firing a blaze of rockets into a crowded street flashed onscreen; war and violence had been so commonplace in the former world, even inseparable with our entertainment in the Last Days, but now I winced in disbelief.

Was that our world? Had it really been so bad?

The video left me with the weight of regret, not for having participated in any of the former atrocities, but for ever thinking they were normal. I moved from one display to the next, listening to the somber voice define the horrors on the screens. Just when I was beginning to feel that I'd had enough, I noticed another sign dangling from a chain in the middle of the room: Rest area on level B4.

Relieved, I exited through a hallway opposite to the one I'd entered and took the elevator to the level above.

This level was an exhibit of its own. The walls here were made of tall, hollow glass cases that had been filled with multicolored soil and gravel so as to give the impression of sediment layers. Weaving its way through the soil was a complex network of plastic piping that had been cut in half and sealed against the glass wall to allow the viewer a look at what was inside. I pushed a button on the wall, and moments later the pipes gurgled with water.

The top of the wall was covered in a thin layer of green felt and decorated with tiny model houses exactly like the ones found in La Unión. The top of the wall sloped upwards as it approached the entrance to the room where I was standing. At the wall's highest

110

point–a hill, I now realized–a four-legged, unusually tall water tank stood, a tank which I had seen many times, not far from the field we were cultivating.

In the hill beneath the tank, pipes zigzagged through a series of strange mechanisms before finally dissipating into a web of smaller tubes feeding into the buildings downhill. I pressed the button again and watched carefully. The mechanisms, which looked a bit like boomerangs, pivoted on a ball bearing embedded at their bend. Each mechanism jittered back and forth on its bearing as the water passed through the nearest section of pipe. This jittering, I realized after several more button-pressings, was generating an electrical current that powered the lights within the model houses.

Although I didn't fully understand it, I now knew where La Unión's power was coming from. Somehow, they had figured a way to generate electricity using the natural force of water being supplied to their homes. This explained why I hadn't seen or heard any generators in the town. That made me think of Otto and his little cabin laboratory in the woods of California. I wondered if he knew about this technology, and if he was still teasing guests with his crooked house, and when I'd see him again.

Floor B2-3.

Many in La Unión had mentioned "the Red Room" to me in conversation, a nickname for the Armageddon Archives' largest and best-known exhibit. It consumed two whole floors, nearly sixty feet from the floor to the ceiling. There were more display screens in this room than in the Tribulation room, and the walls, as the nickname suggested, were mostly red.

The first block of text explained:

All videos and photographs in this room were recovered from devices found in the wreckage after the Great Day. In some instances, audio streams have been scrubbed to filter foul language and video has been edited for length. Otherwise, the files here are in their original state.

Moving to the first screen, I took a slight breath and pressed the button.

"After summit talks with representatives in the U.N., President Hayes has confirmed that the U.S. will be taking what is now believed to be a global eradication campaign against the sect of Jehovah's Witnesses. This news comes as no surprise after the Witnesses' adamant refusal to accept political mandates within their church doctrine. Worldwide, Jehovah's Witnesses have amassed congregations in over two hundred countries and have often been

labeled as extremist and dangerous..."

The woman with the microphone stood in front of a brick building that was being roped off with caution tape and surrounded by police cars. The camera panned as the reporter pointed to a sign fixed next to the front door of the building.

"Kingdom Halls like these are littered throughout most suburban and urban areas across America. Many have wondered what, exactly, goes on in these windowless, quiet buildings, and with us tonight to help shed some light on the mystery is Cory Haggarty, an ex-Witness. Mr. Haggarty, what can you tell us about this sect?"

"Well, first of all, I have to stress just how dangero–" the man was cut off as the camera jostled to the side suddenly.

The reporter's voice: *"What's happening? Are we still on? Mike? Are we ok?"*

The cameraman: *"Yeah, I think so. Let's keep going."*

The camera steadied itself again and the reporter smiled, apologized, and prodded her guest to continue. But before he could, another jolt shook the camera. This time, the cameraman didn't answer, and the camera fell to the ground.

The reporter was yelling: *"Oh my god oh my god! —— Mike! Mike! Are you ok? Someone call an ambulance! Get your —— phone and call 911!"*

More sounds of panic began to fill the air. Sirens wailed. A woman was screaming. Tires screeched on the pavement. And then a new sound, once I couldn't identify. A dull *THUD. THUD. THUD.* And again. Another. And more. Like rain, but heavier.

Seconds later, the screen cleared as the reporter ran for cover, screaming hysterically and swatting at her head. When the camera auto-focused, I realized that her hair was on fire. In fact, the entire area was dotted with small fires. And when the next THUD came, I realized why. This was a firestorm. But the next bolt of sulfur apparently struck the camera, because the feed went dead and the video ended.

I had heard many stories about these storms, which had been concentrated in the U.S., Britain, France, and South Korea. One family I'd met in Arizona had been locked in a basement by a neighbor who'd turned psychotic during the Tribulation. He had explained to them that he was going to his uncle's house to grab a gun and that he'd be back to "finish them". Shortly after he drove off, however, a fire storm came, burning his house to the ground but leaving the basement miraculously in tact. The family had managed to escape and head to safety. On their way, they found the neighbor's truck overturned on the side of the highway. He'd apparently crashed before he made it to his destination.

In South Korea, a group of brothers had been fleeing in a small raft to an island off the coast when they were surrounded by navy speedboats. After explaining that they were innocent Witnesses simply looking to be reunited with their families, the soldiers' captain ordered his men to draw their weapons and fire on the brothers. Before they could, however, their boats were pelted with fire from the heavens. The brothers' boat was untouched, and a few hours later they made it to safety.

In France, four brothers from the branch office were arrested and flown by police helicopter to a prison camp in Tours. In an effort to dishearten the brothers and sisters present, they requested two fully-armored, weapons-ready military helicopters to escort them, one on either side. Shortly after liftoff, within site of those on the launch pad, the military choppers were shredded in a wave of searing molten rock from the sky, dashing their remains into a line of tanks that had been ordered to escort the others. All military personnel exterminated within sixty seconds. The pilot of the police helicopter, defying orders, returned the four brothers and flew off, never to be seen again.

I walked to the next display.

"Mysterious trumpet-like noises from the skies above: natural phenomenon or an act of god? Worldwide, more than four hundred cities are reporting hearing the same, strange sound. Here are some guesses from our very own streets of London..." The image of the reporter seated behind a desk was replaced by a montage of frightened citizens:

"Definitely a natural phenomenon. I estimate it's something like the northern lights, but instead of light, it's sound..." Said one man.

"Isn't it obvious? This is probably just another secret government weapon being tested. Probably has something to do with all of these earthquakes, too." Said a woman holding a baby.

"I imagine this is ozone-related. Perhaps it's got a hole and that sound is our atmosphere leaking out?" Said a young man in a backpack and glasses.

The reporter continued: *"When asked to comment on the noises, which have now been occurring for nearly two hours, a British team of scientists studying the event urged locals not to worry; although no conclusive causes have been determined, evidence suggests that the noises are completely benign, with an explanation sure to surface soon."*

This clip was followed by a series of others, many taken from low-quality recording devices. In the left lower corner of each video, the location had been superimposed in white letters. The sound was the same everywhere, just as I had remembered in Atlanta: a low, reverberating howl that caused everything to vibrate slightly. It seemed to be the same volume everywhere, too. When voices accompanied the videos, they were often tense and frightened.

"*This can't be good,*" said a voice in a clip from Mexico City.

"*This noise is making the dogs crazy,*" said a man in Tokyo. High-pitched barking could be heard in the background.

"*I really don't like these sounds. When will they stop? It's so... ugh, end-of-the-world-like*" came a voice from New York.

"*I'm not religious, but... I have a feeling I'm going to regret that...*" said a gravelly voice from Rome.

The last video was a little longer, and slightly better quality than the others. It was taken by a teenager with messy hair whose reflection could be seen in the glass window he was filming behind. He was in San Diego.

"*So check this out,*" he said, aiming the camera out the window to the sky above. "*These noises have been going on like this for an hour now, I think. They're saying it's from tectonic plates shifting below the ground or something, but whatever. Somehow I doubt it. Wait. Hold on a sec. What is that?*"

The boy fumbled with the camera, zooming in on the sky, which was beginning to darken as blackish-purple clouds swirled into view.

And then a momentary flicker of lightning as glowing, human forms began descending from the sky. They carried what looked like swords, spears, and bows, and stood twice as tall as a grown human. Giant wings carried them swiftly to the ground.

A hand appeared in the frame, opening the sliding glass door and carrying the camera onto an open patio. "*Are you seeing this!? Is this really happening!?*" Screamed the boy. And then, with a thunderous voice, came the unforgettable angelic announcement:

"*The God of the Universe and Creator of the Earth,*
whose name is Jehovah, has seen your wickedness.
Your acts of injustice have not gone unnoticed.
Your corruption and your bloodshed have not gone unseen.
The Witnesses of Jehovah offered deliverance, but you have taken no heed.
Hear now, you descendants of Adam: the time of reckoning is near.
Prepare to meet your Maker."

The voice behind the screen trembled in fear as the recorder fell to the ground: "*Oh... God...*"

The next few videos in the display documented the climax of the Great Day–the angelic execution of all of Jehovah's enemies, beginning with the governments and their military forces. In one clip, a nuclear warhead was launched from a military submersible flanked by a fleet of battleships and military warships into a line of angelic soldiers above a vast, stormy sea. Two angels flew forth to meet the weapon, halting it in midair. It hung for a few moments in the sky before detonating. The flash of light was brilliant and instantly blanked the screen out, but instead of erupting in a plume of fire and compressed air, the explosion was contained within an invisible sphere. As the light lessened, the two angels could be seen with outstretched arms, shrinking the containment sphere. A few more moments and the explosion was a nothing more than a small cloud of dust and sparkling debris, which the angels released from their protection, falling inertly into the ocean below. The slow, ungainly ships struggled to change course away from their certain destruction, but as the angels passed swiftly overhead, the boats hissed and groaned as their hulls collapsed and crumpled like aluminum cans.

In another clip, taken on a city street in New York, military tanks and troops of soldiers fired weapons frantically at a giant angel. The angel waited, unconcerned, as the bullets tore through his immaterialized body. When the rounds had finished, he rushed forward, and with a single swipe of his blade, the entire regiment lit up in red and exploded into dust. The angel touched his foot to the hull of the tank and it disintegrated.

In the final clip, angels riding on horses dragged sickles through a line of high-rise buildings in Paris, causing them to collapse in a heap of fiery ruins. In a single day, Jehovah's army had exterminated all who stood against Him.

When I emerged back into the natural light of a late afternoon, I found a quiet spot on a bench to sit and sort my thoughts. Seeing those images and videos of the Old World summoned in me a storm of memories and emotions. Foremost, gratitude for having been spared. The looks on those faces in the Archives, that realization of wrong choices and dense regret was unmistakable, unforgettable.

There were other emotions too, emotions that came back stronger than they had in all the years since the day I buried by wife and son. *Emma and Jacob.* The sound their names made as I whispered them into the dusk air was almost too much. Emma would have loved La Unión. Even without closing my eyes, I could see her dancing in the rays of a retreating sunset to the salsa music lilting from somewhere across the valley.

Jacob would've been...twenty-two. A grown man. Perhaps he would've found a sister in La Unión. He'd enjoy all the sailing we were doing in the New World. He certainly would've loved the Archives. I hoped it would still be there when he came back.

How much longer did I have to wait?

Part of me wanted to settle right there, to finally put down roots in the New World as so many others had done. It would be a way to try to put my life on pause until things could go back to what I wished was still normal. And yet, another inclination, an even stronger one, kept pulling me towards the horizon. There was still so much out there. And so long as I kept busy, time would move as fast as it could.

Isabelle & Aria

I had been in La Unión for nearly ten years when intriguing rumors from Asia began trickling our way. It was said, among other things, that technology and architecture had taken impressive leaps, especially near the islands formerly belonging to Japan and Korea. Anyone who'd travelled in or around the area embellished the tales with titillating new details, and I knew I had to investigate for myself. On my behalf, our overseer put a call through to the Tokyo branch office, and by the end of the summer I was sitting on the fourth-story deck of *Jepthah*, a gargantuan, triple-mast sailing vessel.

I would miss many things about La Unión: The little patch of hilly land we'd cultivated into a thriving vineyard. My cabin by the beach full of scrap-wire trinkets I'd learned to make from a once-blind Nicaraguan brother. Miguel's Inn, where I'd spent so many evenings in rapt spiritual discussion with him and others. I'd miss the Archives, too, which were continuing to grow each month as digitized video and audio files were brought in from around the world.

But mostly I'd miss the friends I'd made there. Yeasa, the hardworking vinedresser. Dale and Sharon, the eclectic couple who'd taught me so much about the art of wine aging. Sameer Sengupta, who'd been my close friend in La Unión from the beginning.

The faces bobbed through my consciousness like the waves beneath the *Jepthah*. Not that I felt anything that could be called sorrow, of course. Instead, I felt a tireless urge to keep moving forward. Perhaps it was the knowledge that beyond the prow of our ship and somewhere thousands of miles into the future, more friends like these were waiting to be met. Even among the throng of passengers aboard *Jepthah*, I knew there was so much, right here, to be lived and experienced.

Inhaling one last breath of the sweet, flowery La Unión air, I leaned back in my wooden recliner, propped my legs up, and fell fast asleep.

When I awoke, the day had darkened and the air was cool and dry. A hazy web of stars and planets had stretched itself across a moonless sky above. The water, still and milky but for the even folds rolling from beneath our ship, mirrored the brighter heavenly bodies above. We appeared to be the only souls as far as one could see or imagine, and I remembered why I loved the sea so much.

My stomach, however, was less at peace than my mind, upset at having not been fed since our departure from La Unión. Heading below deck, I decided to see what a search for dinner might yield. I had to consult three different ship directories to locate the nearest dining room, which was on the B Deck, near the back of the ship. It took nearly twenty minutes to locate it, and when I did I was hungrier than ever.

The dining room was simple and elegant. The tables, chairs, and eatery were utilitarian in color and design, chosen for efficiency and cleanliness. I approached a large window that separated the galley and the dining room and asked what was for dinner. The menu was something like: pad thai, ginger cabbage casserole, stir fried tofu, freshly baked sunflower seed bread, and so forth. I pointed to something that looked good on someone else's plate and sat down, famished.

Two dozen other passengers occupied the spacious dining room. Some were studying, a few were playing a board game, a couple were sketching, and the rest were gathered in clusters making quiet conversation. I thought about approaching one of the groups; surely they all had stories worth hearing. But on this particular night I was feeling less than social, and didn't mind observing it all quietly from a distance.

I was taking a bite of a buttered bread roll when the voice spoke.

"Brother Hanson?" It said from over my shoulder. I turned to find the face behind the voice and was startled. Standing behind me stood a tall, olive-skinned woman with wavy, charcoal hair and a crooked smirk. She was gorgeous.

"Yes?" I responded, feeling slightly proud without a specific reason. The long-limbed girl slid into the chair beside me.

"It's really great to meet finally meet you," She said, eyes wide and green.

"Oh? Why is that?"

"You're writing the book, right?"

"I don't know if I'd call it *the* book, but... how did you know?"

"When I was in San Diego, I ran into a few people that knew you. They told me about this brother that was writing a book. A book about the end. And just now, at that table over there, some of the guests mentioned your name, and I put the pieces together."

"Is that so?" I asked, amused.

"Yeah. And I just want to say, I think a book is a great idea."

"Oh? Why's that?" I reached for my Zinfandel and took a sip.

"For us post-Tribbers, of course."

"Ah, I see, so you must be, what, twenty...?"

"Twenty six. I was born during the Tribulation, but I don't remember much of it, so I identify more with the post-Trib generation."

"I see. So why does a book interest you?"

"Well, I guess I just have a lot of unanswered questions... There's a lot I don't know, or don't understand, about the world I was born in."

"What do you want to understand?"

"War. Sickness. Old age. I mean, I've seen pictures, I've heard stories. But it's hard to imagine that it actually happened. It seems so...impossible." I envied her a little. Young, perfect, unable to grasp the evils that consumed our broken society just two and a half short decades ago.

"Thinking back on it all," I finally said, "it's hard for me to believe it, too. But you know, when we were living it, it was sometimes hard to believe that *this* could one day be real."

I watched as a little light went on behind her eyes.

"So what was the hardest, then? About the Old World, for you?" Asked the girl. I mulled it over for a few moments, wondering how others answered in the past.

"To be perfectly honest," I finally said, "as tough at the Tribulation was, it was the small trials, long before, that really took endurance."

Her eyes shone wide, hungry for more.

"Take our ministry, as an example. As I'm sure you've heard, we used to go to people's houses, looking for those who were interested in learning about the Truth..."

A nod.

"And we had a lot of tools to help us: magazines, books, tracts, movies, everything. In almost any language you could imagine. And the information was so good, so practical, and needed. How to cope with different problems, for example, or how to find real happiness in life. These were things that people were dealing with every day. And yet, more often than not, we were refused, and sometimes aggressively."

"Why? Satan?"

"There were a lot of reasons. Some had heard lies about us and thought we were bad people with bad motives. Others were busy. But what it really came down to was that many people didn't want it. They were satisfied with what they had and didn't want to be bothered with anything else."

"Like Noah's time," she said.

"We did our best, but we couldn't force anyone to change. And that took a lot of effort on our part, going to these homes week after week, year after year. Some of our friends couldn't handle it after awhile. They didn't see the point. But, you see, our ministry was so closely linked to our identity, as it always was with Jehovah's people. Without it, we were weak. And that's what happened with those friends who slowed down and stopped. When the Tribulation came, they were defenseless. Their faith had faltered, and it didn't take much to compromise them."

The girl frowned.

"I hope the interrogation hasn't gone on too long," came another voice from behind us. I turned to see a near-mirror image of the girl next to me: young, slender, poised.

"Uh, no. Not at all, not at all, we've just been chatting."

"This is my Mom," said the girl next to me. "Mom, this is Brother Hanson. Remember the one we heard about in California from Liuqin, the one who's writing the book?"

"Nice to meet you both," I said. A handshake.

"I'm Isabelle," said the woman standing. "I apologize for Aria's questions. She's always asking something." Isabelle's skin was a shade darker than her daughters, and her eyes rounder, their green more radiant. I wondered what the girl's father looked like.

"It's really no problem," I said, inviting her to sit. There was a methodical gracefulness to her movements as she slid out the chair across from us and sat, neatly pressing out the wrinkles in her skirt.

"So this book you're writing," said Isabelle. "Is it historical or fictional?"

"I intend on the former, though I can't guarantee none of the latter," I said. "It's my first book, and I'm doing it more as a personal project. For now, I'm trying to collect as many first-hand accounts as I can. I'm not sure how I'll compile them, or how I'll know when it's done. I imagine there are endless stories to be heard out there."

Glancing back at Isabelle, I considered asking her for an interview, but something about her expression dissuaded me.

"I can't wait to read it," Aria beamed. "And what about *your* story, Brother Hanson?"

"My story?"

"Sure. Like where you came from, what you went through during the Trib, how you stayed loyal to Jehovah. You've got to include your story, right?"

It was an honest question, one which had rolled around in my head for years. When I first began compiling the stories, I wanted to be as invisible as possible. This was, after all, not my *memoirs*, but a factual, objective documentation of the events leading up to and following the end.

But with the passage of time, I found my own thoughts and feelings leaking inevitably onto the page. I was understanding more and more about myself now that I was working towards perfection, and I felt a need–to both myself and my family–to make a record of that journey as well. But did my story really belong on these pages? After all, my family would know my story already, or at least, most of it.

So I just said: "I'm not sure my story is suitable for this book, but...We'll see. So where are you two headed?"

"Tokyo. I've always wanted to go. We've got family there, too," Aria explained.

"What about you, Brother Hanson?" asked Isabelle.

"Tokyo too, but first Honolulu. Will this be your first time going to Japan, Isabelle?" I asked.

"No. I spent almost ten years there before the Tribulation."

"Were you with an English congregation? I heard there was quite a need there for awhile."

"No, unfortunately I wasn't doing so well spiritually at the time. I was an exchange student. There was an English congregation near my school, but...I didn't go often."

I noticed Aria had gotten quiet and wondered if I should change the conversation.

"So what was Japan like, in the Last Days?" I asked.

"Like everywhere else, I suppose. Everyone was doing their best to keep up appearances, but the system was collapsing on itself. Of course, I didn't realize it at the time. I was young and naive, and in desperate pursuit of a childhood fantasy. I tried to tune anything out that would discourage me from fulfilling my goal."

"And what goal was that?"

"I wanted to be a professional artist and animator."

"Ah. A study program in Japan would've made sense for that career path," I said, recalling the many animated films Japan had produced in my generation.

"At first, it seemed like I was on track to make those dreams come true. I had designed and written a few short animations, and even had a couple of interviews lined up at animation studios as an entry-level artist."

"But..."

"The Great Tribulation started and it changed everything."

"For the industry or for you personally?"

"Both, actually. The Japanese economy and industry changed a lot then. Some animation studios closed, and the rest weren't looking for animators, especially foreign ones. Foreigners had caused a lot of upheaval after the banning of Christian religions in Japan. A lot of them were expelled from the country, and the rest were sort of shunned by the Japanese. Shortly after all this I headed back to Vancouver to live with my mother."

"Was your mother in the truth?"

"Yes, she was, but she wasn't any stronger than I was. We had to work at it together to come back, but it was what we both wanted. We saw how bad things had gotten, and how little time was left."

"What was the hardest part about the Tribulation for you?"

"Actually that process of coming back to the truth was the most difficult. Well, that and raising a small child on my own."

I glanced back at Aria but had a difficult time deciphering her expression.

"That's really the only thing I remember about the Old World. Mom and Grandma working really hard to take care of me. It's weird, I don't remember anything about the great day. The angelic armies, that Atlantic standoff that was all over the news, that plague, none of it. I just remember my family working really hard to take care of me."

The three of us turned our heads to the end of the room as a small group of men and women entered. They appeared to have walked from the set of a Bible-era drama: One was dressed as a soldier, another as royalty, another as a poor peasant, the fourth as an old man with a staff, and the fifth as a young maiden. They introduced themselves as the ship's traveling performing troupe, specializing in 30-second Bible charades. Using only their gestures and a handful of stage props, they could enact over fifty stories. After each mini-performance, audience members could attempt to guess the characters.

The movements and expressions of the actors were executed with finesse and precision. We watched the first few acts in quiet amusement: David and Goliath, Cain and Abel, and a particularly clever depiction of Moses parting the Red Sea that involved two actors in flowing, blue cloaks simulating the split waters. The next performance seemed to stump the audience, however, until someone correctly guessed Eli and Samuel, triggering muffled noises of revelation from the rest of the audience.

"I can only imagine what that must've been like, Isabelle. Being a parent was difficult for everyone during that time," I said.

"Sounds like you're speaking from experience," she replied.

I was.

James O'Donnell

As the *Jepthah* churned westward in the Pacific, news of my book began to circulate. This was equally flattering and surprising. Up to that point, I had assumed that I couldn't possibly be the only one working on such a project. I had, after all, ran into others who had made extensive notes of the experienced they'd heard. Although I had never read these stories published together in a book, I figured it was just a matter of time. Anyway, up until that voyage, no one had seemed especially interested in my project.

Now, though, things had changed. People were asking when it'd be done, and could I contact them when it was available to read. The benefit of this, I quickly noted, was that interesting interview subjects were seeking me out instead of the other way around, and many others were able to refer me to those whose stories seemed especially worth hearing and retelling.

This is exactly how I met James O'Donnell, a broad-shouldered man with stubby fingers jutting from stone hands that now rested on the table between us. He seemed eager to tell his story when I entered his cabin, and while pouring me a glass of scotch, he began:

"My father was an American soldier during the second World War. He never saw combat, but I didn't know this until years later. From the stories he used to tell me and my little brothers, you'd think he was on the front lines of every major battle fought. There were tales of brave soldiers rescuing their buddies from the clutches of evil Nazis and great, sprawling epics of American pilots being captured, tortured, and later escaping from German prisons. There were dogfights in the sky and romances on the shores. The message was loud and clear, and it left an indelible impression on us kids: if we wanted a life worth living, full of adventure and excitement, we could do nothing better than fight for our country. Unsurprisingly, all three of us enlisted in the army in our late teens.

"Well, war was nothing like the way Dad described it. On my first tour in Vietnam, I watched four of my buddies killed. One had just bought an engagement ring for his girlfriend. He stepped on a land mine before he ever had a chance to propose. I had promised to tell his girlfriend personally if anything happened to him. I had to give her the ring. Can you imagine? Any remaining fantasies I had about the battlefield died during that painful conversation. The other guys' deaths weren't much better, but I was getting numb to it all. Every day, more loss, more reasons to kill.

"That was the thing about war for so many young men, regardless of what side they were fighting on. They started off fighting for their country and for their ideals. Then they fought for their fallen comrades. And when that was gone, they fought because they didn't know how to do anything else. Do you know how many soldiers returned from combat and ended up killing other innocent people or themselves? The number would make you sick.

"In any case, like I said, I was numb. But I was also decorated. I'd done a few things deemed heroic and the government put some fancy ribbons on my chest and shook my hand a few times. After a decade or so in active combat duty I was given a desk job at the pentagon as a military advisor. Basically this meant I was still killing people, but without pulling the trigger directly.

"You wouldn't believe the effort, time, and resources that the U.S. government invested in dreaming up new ways to kill people. We'd often have meetings with these young, beaming geniuses from the country's leading tech colleges who'd been brought in to demonstrate new weapon concepts. How about a bomb that had multiple delayed explosions? Let the medical teams come in to clean up the pieces and detonate again, and again, and then a fourth time, so that no one was left? Or a warhead that could drill into a water reserve and poison it with a neurotoxin? The government would later resolutely deny the development of any such weapons, but I can tell you emphatically that when those kids finished their little slideshows, there were applause and approving nods all around the room.

"Eventually, my military experience landed me an even higher position as a personal advisor to the President. I now had the opportunity, several days each week, to observe the man that made the most important decisions of the most powerful, militarized, nuclear country in the world at the time. And let me tell you, half of the time he had no idea what he was doing. I would later recall the meetings I had with the President when I read the words of Jeremiah 10:23 for the first time. No matter how confident he seemed as a leader, I can say with certainty that he wasn't any better off than the average person at directing his step."

Brother O'Donnell rubbed his chin and turned to a plate glass window behind him. I waited for a minute or two and asked how he finally learned the truth.

"I'll never forget that day. I had recently retired from my job in the White House. It was October 14th, 2006, a Saturday. I was sitting on my couch watching CNN when I heard a knock on my door."

"The Witnesses."

"You bet. And I wasn't exactly a fan of the Witnesses, you see. My father had always been prejudiced against them-another thing he passed down to his sons. I was about to shoo them from my property when the man handed me a small handbill. Had I not seen the bold, black letters on its cover I likely wouldn't be sitting here today. But I did see them, and they startled me. *The End of False Religion is Near*, it said."

"Kingdom News No. 37."

"That's correct. I asked the man on my doorstep where he'd gotten the tract, and he explained it was part of a worldwide campaign being done by Jehovah's Witnesses.

"'But how do you know about this?' I asked.

"The man didn't seem to get my meaning. You see, for years, the U.S. government along with a good number of reps in the U.N. had discussed how to ban–or at least strictly control–religion. It was no big secret that religion was one of the biggest instigators of unnecessary conflict, and since the 1950's governments had proposed various ways of keeping the churches in check, but with no real action taken.

"It was believed in those days, and probably rightly so, that any kind of religious restriction would be met with massive resistance. And at the time, the Catholic church had a say in decisions made in the U.N., so it seemed that there was little anyone could do. But it remained an unspoken agenda of many major world political organizations: get religion out.

"What surprised me, looking at that tract, was how accurately the chain of events were laid out. Even the depiction of false religion as a wealthy prostitute was right in line with what I'd felt for years. In private circles, we'd sometimes even refer to major religions in similar terms, though with a bit fouler language that I care to recall."

"So did you start studying then?"

"Not quite. But I did make a call to a colleague that morning, asking him if he'd seen the tract. He hadn't, so I faxed a copy to his desk. It circulated all the way to the President. When I went in on Monday, we even talked about it briefly. Although most dismissed it as an amusing coincidence, it had a big impact on me. When I retired the next year I contacted the brother who'd left me the tract and began studying.

"I wasn't an easy student, I'm sure. I'd been used to people yessir'ing me for years, and having a man young enough to be my son telling me, on occasion, that I was wrong, didn't feel good. But with time and molding from Jehovah, I progressed. I was baptized in 2012, along with my wife, Elizabeth.

"How were you affected by the Liberation Act?"

"Well, I knew it was coming. Remember, for decades this idea of eradicating religion had been talked about quietly in political circles. But the problem was the support of the people. Religion was a kind of drug that people needed to be weaned off of gradually. It had to be their choice, or at least, they had to feel that way."

"And when did that finally happen?"

"It's hard to put an exact date on it, but I know that two major events helped bring about the change. The first was that Whollyevil website. There had been other whistle-blowing websites like it in the past, where folks could anonymously submit damaging information regarding government secrets, corporate scandals, and so on. But this was the first time a website like this was targeted directly at churches, and the effect was devastating.

"That one website alone had, as I recall, published over one million church scandals and cover-ups in the first year it was online. Many involved church officials abusing children, and the vast majority of the offenders were never charged. But with all that information online publicly, it took the offenders from the protection of the church and into the public's accusing eye. Many were investigated and sentenced as a result of those files on Whollyevil. Others were attacked by civilians."

"I remember hearing about that website," I said. "I never visited it, but it seemed that for awhile everyone was talking about it. How did the government respond to its popularity?"

"Positively, and for two reasons. First, with public support of churches–and religion in general–at an all time low, it seemed that the idea of religious bans was no longer improbable; in fact, it was nearly inevitable. Second, it took a little heat off of the government, which was facing intense criticism for its handling of matters in the Middle East."

"And how did you know about all this? It seems that at the time Whollyevil was online, you were already retired."

"That's correct, but I maintained contact with many of my old colleagues. I thought, somewhat naively, that I could help some of them to see that the coming storm wasn't manmade. Unfortunately none of them responded to the following events the way I did, and paid dearly for it."

"What was the second event that helped bring about the Liberation Act?"

"The California church burnings. That's a little bit of a misnomer, actually; there were similar occurrences all around the U.S. and even many other parts of the world. But they began in California and remained concentrated there. It wasn't surprising; California had the largest percentage of atheists in the country, and many were particularly hostile towards organized religion."

"Was there a link between the church burnings and the website?"

"I'd be surprised if there wasn't, but there was no hard data to directly link the two. And although these were the two main events I can point to that paved the way for the Liberation Act, there were plenty of smaller things happening all over the place that was just another layer on a snowball racing downhill. There were a slew of church robberies around this same time, for example, and even a few contract assassinations of church employees."

"I don't remember hearing about that."

"You wouldn't have. They were usually reported as something else."

"So it sounds like the Liberation Act, while passed in 2020, was conceived long before that."

"Yes, but in my day we'd had another codename for it: Operation King Kong. The name had come from a four-star general who felt the churches were much like the giant gorilla on a rampage through civilized areas, until it somehow managed to perch itself at the top of the world. Quite an insight, if you ask me. But for the public, the name "the Liberation Act" was perfect. It conveyed the idea of finally being free from a kind of slavery, or drug, as I mentioned earlier."

"I remember being surprised at how people responded to the announcement. America had so many churches at the time that I was expecting more of a lash back. What was the government expecting?"

"It was a very delicate project, as you might imagine. It had to be worded just right to get the masses to accept it. If you were paying attention, you may have noticed that the government never used the words "ban" or "restrict". The idea was that this was a kind of 'new age' in America, where people could worship freely in their own homes and not be tied to a church or other religious organization. The PR team on that front was on eggshells the whole time, but in the end they succeeded. It was the right message at the right time. People were sick of church corruption and sex scandals. It was a *good riddance* kind of feeling."

"So at that point what were you thinking? You knew that things were soon to get tough for the Witnesses."

"It wasn't easy for me or my wife during that time. While we were excited along with everyone else at seeing the first prophecy of the Great Tribulation unfolding before our eyes, we knew what was coming next. What made it particularly tough was that we still had close ties to many of my old colleagues. But around that time, one of the elders in our hall sat me down after a meeting and said:

"'Don't be sitting in the middle of the battlefield when Armageddon comes. If you've made up your mind to serve Jehovah, serve him and don't look back. A friend of Jehovah's enemy is Jehovah's enemy.'

"It was exactly what I needed to hear. I'd been rationalizing my contact with old colleagues as an effort to help them, but I'd gotten nowhere with my efforts, and usually just ended up reminiscing over the past. It was a dangerous time to be doing that, though. I finally cut my ties and planted my feet firmly on Jehovah's side of the line.

"But as soon as I did I felt Satan trying to suck me back in. I started getting phone messages and emails from old friends from the White House telling me that I needed to sever my ties with the Witnesses soon. They weren't specific, but I could tell, from looking at those messages, that the final battle was on the horizon. They were as desperate to help me and my wife as I'd been to help them. Both of us thought we were on the side with the advantage.

"One day, I got an email from a long-time associate, Thomas Hayes, practically begging me to leave the Organization. We'd fought side by side in Vietnam and had stayed friends for decades after. He said he couldn't protect me from the wrong decision, and that I had to act right away if I wanted to be safe. I deleted the email before I finished it.

"A few weeks later, the attack against the Witnesses came. A few were arrested in our local congregation and many others were harassed. Belongings were confiscated, literature destroyed. A couple of Kingdom Halls in the D.C. area that had already been cordoned off were even demolished.

"And then, amidst all of that chaos, came the knock on our door. We knew it was our turn to face the final trial. We were ready.

"The expressionless man at the door was in his mid-thirties. He stood rigidly and wore the uniform of an army sergeant. He asked me and my wife to accompany him to his black, tinted sedan. I asked why, and he explained that I was being escorted to meet with a military interrogation officer. I asked why again, and he said:

"'Given your current religious affiliation, your previous military experience and government background poses a threat to homeland security. My orders are to bring you in. They just want to talk, sir.'

"I complied, and my wife and I rode in their car to the compound I'd visited many times before. But this time no one saluted me. No one was proud to know me. Elizabeth said she was scared, and I put my hands together and glanced upward, reminding her to pray.

"When our car finally stopped next to a concrete bunker, Elizabeth and I were separated and led to different buildings. Now I was scared, too.

"I was led through a maze of tunnels, stairwells, and elevators and finally emerged into an office hallway where I was escorted by two soldiers into a concrete interrogation room. I'd seen these rooms many times before, but always from the other side of the two-way mirrors. I took some comfort in the fact that my captors had decided not to handcuff me to the table.

"When my interrogator entered the room, my heart shot into my mouth: it was Thomas Hayes, my old war buddy. I could see the anguish in his face as he sat down and set his papers on the table between us. His first words were:

"'Long time no see, old friend.'

"'Yes, it has been,' I said.

"'You never replied to my email.'

"'There was nothing to say.'

"Tom covered his face in his palms and rubbed the wrinkles in this forehead.

"'I just don't get it, Jim,' he sighed. 'You knew this was coming. It was on our agenda when you were still here, for god's sake. Why would you pick a time like this to get religious?'

"'I wasn't 'getting religious', Thomas,' I said. 'I put the pieces together and did the right thing for me and my family, just like we were trained to do in the army.'

"'Army never trained us to climb on board a sinking ship.'

"'And yet, that's exactly what you're aboard now.'

"'Careful, Jim, you know these rooms are recording every word we say. If you so much as hint at treason, things could turn out much worse for you.'

"'That wasn't what I meant, Tom. You know what I believe.'

"'Yeah, I've heard your end-of-days spiel. And I don't think a soul in this country hasn't seen your little pamphlets.' Thomas pulled a copy of *The End of Mankind's Government is Near* from his manila folder and slid it to me.

"'You really believe this?' He asked.

"'We've been over this, Tom. Everything up to this point has happened right according to Bible prophecy. Right up to the ban all these world governments are placing on religion. And there's only one way it ends. We're not making this up, it's all there on the pages, see for yourself.'

"'Fine. Your beliefs are your business. Maybe I can't stop you or change your mind. Anyway, that's not why you're here.'

"'Why am I here?'

"'Frankly speaking, the government is worried. *I'm* worried. According to our numbers, there are over one million Jehovah's Witnesses living in this country. I get that you are different from other religions, Jim. You're honest, you live by what you believe, you pay your taxes and respect cops. But your people are also talking about overthrowing governments, and with an Organization as tightly knit as yours is, it's a very real threat. More incredible things have happened with much smaller groups in the past. I know I don't need to list examples.'

"'You've got it wrong,' I said. 'We're not overthrowing anything. Our God is.'

"'Yeah, that's what the pamphlet says, but you know what that also sounds a lot like? Kamikaze pilots preparing for takeoff. Militant Muslims strapped with explosives. Irish Catholics chucking Molotov cocktails. All in the name of God.'

"'Witnesses are not violent people. We don't fight in any battles.'

"'Up till now. But what happens when your Organization changes its mind, huh? What happens when one million people get tired of waiting for an act of god and decide to create their own? Its happening all over the world, Jim. These people–your people–are a time bomb.'

"'So you've brought me here to tell me this?' I asked.

"'There's more,' Thomas Hayes said, opening his folders and adjusting his glasses.

"'You see, in your fifty-plus years serving our country, you had access to untold amounts of sensitive information. If the Witnesses are planning anything, you'd be a key part of that. We also noticed, on doing some digging, that you've recently travelled to the Witnesses' headquarters in upstate New York...'

Thomas splayed a few photographs on the table of my car driving into the Warwick headquarters, me shaking hands with a few brothers in the parking lot, me entering the main lobby.

"I explained that I was merely there to tour Bethel. Thomas looked doubtful.

"'In that email I sent you, I said I couldn't protect you. I said that as a friend. But now, I'm saying it again as an officer. None of this looks good. You do realize the government has effectively stamped out all organized religion up till now, right? The Witnesses will be the same. You need to know that.'

"Thomas reached over his papers and grabbed my arms. The sternness in his voice was replaced by a soft, kind tone.

"'I'll never forget what you did for me in 'Nam, Jim. If you hadn't patched that hole in my leg, I probably wouldn't be here today. This is me trying to return that favor. I had a hard fight just to be sure I was the one doing this interview with you. Please. Make the right choice. Leave this crazy cult while there's still a chance. I'm telling you, bad things are on the horizon if you keep it up.'

"I looked Tom in the eyes and remembered the old days one last time. Then I said:

"'I appreciate all you've done for me over the years, Tom. But I'm not changing my mind on this one.'

"Thomas Hayes' head dropped into his hands and a light above the door began to blink. He bolted from his chair, cursed me, and before exiting said, 'What happens next is on your own head.'

"Moments later the door flung open again and soldiers with guns ordered me to stand against the wall.

"I now realized what Thomas had meant about this being my last chance. I hadn't seen it coming really, an execution like that. But then it did make sense, from a military point of view. They thought the Witnesses were dangerous, and I appeared to be helping them plan something.

"The soldiers ordered me to put my hands behind my head and face the far wall. As I did, I noticed big chunks missing from the cinderblocks that had been painted over in that cold, military ash-grey. Apparently the room wasn't just used for interrogations.

"There was no fear at this point, but I did worry for Elizabeth. I knew they wouldn't execute her—she didn't know any of the secrets I did—but I knew she would get more afraid the longer we were kept apart. I said a prayer to Jehovah and He helped keep me calm.

"I stood there waiting, forehead against the cool wall, for what seemed like an eternity. Were they waiting for their final orders? Had they forgotten to load their guns?

"'Is everything OK?' I finally asked softly.

"No response.

"'Hello?'

"Still only silence.

"Finally I turned my head to the side, peeking behind me. The soldiers were still there aiming at me. I flung my head back to the wall and winced. *Here it comes!* I thought.

"But still nothing. No tat-tat-tat from their rifles. No razor sharp pains in my back. What *were* they waiting for?

"I decided to take another peek. They were still standing there. I watched carefully for a few more moments and realized they were quite literally frozen. Not even breathing!

"I finally put my hands down and turned, slowly, to face them. They stood still. No reaction. That's when I noticed the man with the white beard.

"He stood in the far corner away from the door with an outstretched arm towards the soldiers. I didn't recognize him, but he looked important. When I asked him who he was, he handed me a car key and said,

"'Follow me.'

"We left the room and retraced the route I'd taken from the garage. Down the stairs, into the elevators, and back through the tunnels. When we had returned to the point where I was first unloaded from the black sedan, Elizabeth was waiting for me next to an idling Lincoln Navigator.

"'Get in and drive yourselves home. Do not come back here,' said the mysterious man. Then he left us, disappearing moments later behind a giant sliding metal door.

"We did as we were told. I said nothing to Elizabeth about my near execution and she didn't ask. The forty minute drive back to our apartment felt like five, and when we got in we sat on our rickety old couch in silence wondering *Exactly what just happened? Will the black sedans be back?*

"At eleven o'clock that same night, we got our answer when we heard the trumpet blasts. We were safe."

"No one else came knocking from the government after that, I suppose."

"Nope. I imagine they had slightly more urgent matters to attend to than disposing of an old geezer with military secrets."

"I remember the destruction at the capitol was especially severe. What was it like to live through that?"

"You know, I had thought for awhile that Armageddon would catch me with conflicting feelings. After all, I'd spent over half of my life supporting a political power. It had been a kind of family to me and to Elizabeth. In retrospect, I think that's why Jehovah let me go through that interrogation. I think it was his way of showing me the old master's true colors. It didn't care about me. Like the rest of Satan's world, it just wanted what I had to offer, and when I was used up, I was kicked to the curb.

"That night, as the angelic message gave way to hail and lightning and angelic armies, I felt no conflict. Just peace. We'd made the right choice."

The Soldier's Last Words

It should come as no surprise that the cities hit hardest during the events of Jehovah's Great Day were those with the largest militaries: Washington D.C., Beijing, Moscow, New Delhi, London, Paris, Berlin, Brasília, Tokyo, and Ankara.

When the angelic armies in these areas had vanquished their enemies to Jehovah's satisfaction, little remained apart from smoky ruins and ash. Somewhat miraculously, however, a few sheets of paper covered in hurried scribbles were found in a steel pipe in a demolished underground armory in Paris. Several brothers in a French Regional Salvaging Crew found the papers months into the New World and submitted them to the Organization's Historical department, which would later add the pages to their museum in Normandy.

After my interview with Brother O'Donnell, he handed me a small brown folder. Inside the folder was a transcription of the original French document, which is now well-known as *The Soldier's Last Words*.

I have included the full text of the document here.

***

My name is Sebastien Maxwell Laurent. I am a soldier of the French Troupes de marine. I am writing this letter because I do not believe I will survive to tell my story any other way. I do not know how much time I have and am having to write this quickly in failing light. Please God, may someone find this and give it to my parents.

Dear Mama and Papa,

We were wrong. About this war, about the Jehovah's Witnesses, about everything. Will you please forgive us? When my orders first came through, I remember what you said, Mama:

"Don't do it. Those are good people. You don't want their blood on your hands."

But it seemed like such a clear mission at the time. They called them seditionists, extremists, and I know so many in our family hated them for other reasons. We were to end it, once and for all. How were we so wrong?

Do you remember how mad I was when I got that pamphlet about the end of government from the Witness man in the street? I never told you what I actually did. Yes, I came home and tore it and burned it, but there was more. I hurt that poor man. But I was so angry, don't you see? He seemed like the reason our country was having so many problems. I hurt him badly.

Maybe that's why this is happening to me... Our commanding officer told us to wait here for the 'insurgents'. But we all know they aren't insurgents. Insurgents don't glow or carry swords or fly. And how can anyone explain those echoing voices shouting over and over and over again? How could anyone really think this was some kind of terrorism?

My mind is still haunted by those words.

Everything is gone. Everyone is gone. I saw it: thirty thousand troops ignite into red dust. And then the tanks. Before they could even fire a single shot, their shells began exploding behind their barrels. Those awful noises, like fireworks, of soldiers' bodies turning to ash as giant ghosts cursed them to the grave.

We were never trained for this. Everyone is terrified.

Papa, tell uncle Hugo I'm not angry at him. He always said bad things about the Witnesses and I know it affected me, but you can't force someone to hate someone else. There is always choice. And I chose to accept my orders. I was happy about them, even.

I ended up fighting God Himself.

On the street up above us I can hear tank treads scraping against the asphalt. No more shells being fired. This is the sound of retreat. More noise. It is so awful. My body is shaking from fear. My hands are numb and it is difficult to write. My ears are ringing. Screaming. Explosions.

My mind is spinning with regret and confusion. And yet, I can think of one way to make this right, to side for once with God and hopefully gain his favor.

What I have left: a few rounds in my service rifle and a grenade in my vest. I will put this letter in one of the lockers and pray for you.

Forgive me. For all.

-Seb

Jimmy Fukuda

We slipped into Waikiki Bay on a breezy Spring afternoon. Even before *Jepthah* made port, the strong scent of plumeria washed over us, enticing us onto the island. As the large ship rounded the harbor, we spotted groups of brothers and sisters sitting on surfboards waving in our direction as they waited for the next gushing swell. I'd tried surfing years ago when I visited these islands for a three-day conference before the Tribulation but couldn't get the hang of it. Too old to learn, probably. Maybe now it would be different.

As we eased closer to the floating dock, a couple of outriggers paddled our way. One of the men, dressed in a tank top and colorful surf shorts, clambered up a rope ladder and slipped into an open doorway a couple floors below deck. He apparently was here to give us new docking instructions, because the *Jepthah* soon altered its course and docked somewhere else.

A group of twenty or so brothers and sisters were waiting for us on the pier. They handed many of us small gift bags and leis and led us to our accommodations. As in La Unión, the captain and crew had brought with them cargo especially intended for the Hawaiian islands, although much of this cargo was stowed in unwieldy wooden crates and steel containers in the lower sections of the ship; it would require the assistance of a propane-powered forklift the next day to haul it into a storage area on the docks.

It was a good hour before all the passengers had unloaded from the ship. It probably could've gone faster, but no one seemed to be in a rush, and the slow and sleepy ukulele music lolling from a large pair of speakers only reinforced our lethargy.

"Hungry?" Asked my driver after I'd piled into the front seat of what appeared to be the limousine of golf carts.

I was. I'd unwisely skipped lunch to finish packing the last of my suitcases. Somehow my belongings had multiplied during the two months at sea. I finally had to borrow some crates from the kitchen to accommodate all of my junk. I nodded. Yes, I was very hungry. It was almost three o'clock.

"Right on. We have a luau planned for everyone tonight at

I'olani. Ever been to a luau before?"

"No, actually not. I was here before the Tribulation, but that was for business. Never really had a chance to do much other than try to catch a few waves in Waikiki."

My driver laughed, "Forget Waikiki. Even post-trib, it's just a tourist trap. If you want good surfing, I can hook you up. There's a spot not far from here that only the locals go to. Less people, no boats or hotels. You go out there on a quiet morning as the sun is coming up over the horizon–I'm telling you, there's nothing like it."

Smiling, I absolutely believed him. Hawaii had been beautiful before and I couldn't imagine how it could've gotten any better.

My room was on the fourth floor of a newly-renovated hotel. The lazy Hawaiian music had found its way to my room along with the ever-present fragrance of tropical fauna. A salted breeze tumbled off the waves and into my room. Below my window lay the harbor where we'd docked. Neat rows of yachts, sailboats, and catamarans bobbed up and down like plastic toys in a bathtub. The *Jepthah*, in comparison, looked more like a skyscraper that had fallen sideways into a puddle of water.

After the luau–a delectable though sometimes challengingly exotic collection of vegetable and noodle dishes, seaweed, mashed roots, locally grown fruits, and rice puddings–we enjoyed some entertainment put together by the local friends. The performing troupe from the *Jepthah* made a surprise appearance at the end as well, much to the delight of our gracious hosts.

As the sun set behind a cotton candy sky, I struck up a conversation with a brother at my table. His name was Jimmy Fukuda. He had lived in Hawaii all his life, the descendant of Japanese immigrants who'd moved to the islands in the late 1800's looking for work on the plantations. In the course of the four generations leading up to his birth, his ancestry had become mixed with all sorts of races: Samoan, Portuguese, Italian, and Spanish, to name a few.

"So are there any specific memories that leave an especially deep impression on you, looking back?" I asked, wondering how things had been in the end in Hawaii.

Brother Fukuda sat back in his white rattan chair, lacing his fingers together over his stomach and smiling.

"For so many tourists, Hawaii was this little gem in the middle of the Pacific where they could come and spend their money and get a massage and sit on the beach and watch the sunset. It was their way to get out of the city life, I guess. A lot of people thought of it as Paradise."

"You didn't."

"Oh, no. Hawaii was a mess! No matter how you looked at it, it was broken. Tourists could come and go without seeing what was happening, you know, in the shadows, but this was a scary place to live. In the Last Days, my wife and I were raising a small daughter. I was so scared that someone would offer her drugs at school, or something like that. It was a bad time to be anyone here, but especially a parent."

"Drugs were a big problem?"

"You have no idea. For awhile, Hawaii was the largest producer of crystal meth in the world. Did you ever come across that stuff in the mainland? It was a highly addictive synthetic drug. Made the user hallucinate and do crazy things.

"So many people were hooked on it, it was bad. And these kids, they would start using small doses that their classmates gave them. Some would try to make it at home after seeing some video on the internet, but would end up poisoning themselves and the neighbors too.

"And the drug problem was just one of many. You had the economy, the cost of living, political corruption, infrastructure problems, the crime rate was going up, unemployment was skyrocketing. A lot of people wanted to leave, but where could you go? The whole country was falling apart!"

"How was it for your family during all of this?"

"It was very unstable. We thought about moving—we had friends that had moved to California—but it was just too much for us. We'd been here our whole lives, and felt like we needed that kind of support system to make it through the end. We felt very trapped as times, but Jehovah helped us all the way."

"How was it here when the Liberation Act went into effect? How did the local brothers react?"

"At first, excitement. I mean, it was so obvious that things were right along with Bible prophecy, we could see it right before our faces. The news reports, the banners, the notices, everything. But then, after that, there was this sense of 'what now?' where we all sort of wondered how the Organization would handle it.

"Of course, Jehovah never forgets his people. Through our circuit overseer, our branch told us to be patient and to meet in our service groups in the friends' houses, and that more instruction would come later, and it did.

"There was a short time where we continued to meet together in groups for our meetings, which really fortified the friends' faith. There was this brother form the East side of the island that owned a tour bus company–you remember, the big chrome ones that tourists could get on and get shuttled to all the main attractions on the island. Well, when the Liberation Act went into effect, he had over twelve of these buses. Tourism had been slow, so his buses were just sitting in a hot parking lot starting to rust–the ocean air does that to everything here.

"Anyhow, the branch contacted the brother and plans were made to hold meetings in these buses as they toured around the coast. The friends wore casual clothes and used the on-board mic system to make comments. It felt more or less like a meeting in a Kingdom Hall, except we had a constantly changing view.

"Of course, this arrangement wasn't available for everyone. There were almost a hundred congregations in Hawaii at the time, and even with a rotating schedule, only a fraction of those were able to have these mobile meetings. Still, the arrangement worked well while it lasted. It was safer than having the meetings in private homes since the police were starting to do house calls, confiscating literature and making sure we weren't preaching and what not. If a bus was ever stopped by a police officer, there was nothing unusual about it. It simply looked like a bunch of tourists in big hats cruising the island."

"How long did these mobile meetings go on?"

"Over a year, I believe. Later, when many of the friends had their possessions taken, that tour bus company shut down and we lost our halls."

"How did these developments affect the attitude and faith of the friends?"

"When the liberation act first passed in congress, we started seeing a lot of inactive ones returning and attending the home meetings. I guess they could see that time was running out."

"Did they stay?"

"Some did. But a lot of them, well, after awhile, the urgency wore off I guess, and they would miss a meeting here or there, and then you wouldn't see them anymore. And when the final pressures came, where the government was taking private possessions, that's when we lost the most. Even some of the ones who'd been attending regularly fell away."

It was the same story across the world. So many of the retellings I'd heard of the Tribulation went the same way. In the beginning, a flurry of activity: the dirt hill had been disrupted and the ants stirred crazily. But over time they returned to their hole in the ground. When the rain finally came, they were too deep to come up for air, and drowned.

"What about for you and your family?"

"Rebecca and I were pioneering at the time. We had considered going off the list when Abby was born, but decided it would be good for her to grow up in an environment where full time service was the norm. I worked as a substitute teacher at a local intermediate school part time and did some electrical work with another brother when things were slow. Rebecca was a seamstress. We lived simply because we didn't have any other option if we wanted to pioneer.

"When the government came with the notices about confiscating the Witnesses' belongings, we just shrugged 'OK'. We had an old Honda Civic, some household appliances, a laptop, a couple of cellphones, and clothes. There wasn't a whole lot to lose. I'm so thankful we lived that way, too.

"There was a brother in our hall–Mike was his name–that owned a construction company. He'd been doing it for almost four decades and had been really successful with it. That was the business to be in at the time–all these rich families from the mainland were moving in and buying up these million-dollar beachfront properties, houses up in the mountains and in the greenest parts of the valley, that kind of stuff. And the first thing they did was remodel their home, maybe add a second floor and a swimming pool.

"Well, Mike had been busy in those days, one job after another. Sometimes he'd make his meetings, but other times he'd be out there on some rooftop in Manoa, taking down shingles for some young couple that had gotten rich doing whatever it was that kids were getting rich from.

"I remember a shepherding call we did on him and his wife once. We did our best to gently remind him not to get sucked into a materialistic way of life. But his thinking was that he was doing this to support the brothers in our hall, several of whom worked for him and were pioneering.

"'I'm doing it for the Kingdom,' he said!

"Anyway, our call didn't do the trick. We didn't see him much after that, at meetings anyway. Sometimes I'd spot him driving around town in his new Camaro, though. He'd gone ahead and remodeled his house too, and put in a swimming pool after he bought a neighbor's property. He seemed to have it all, and a lot of our younger brothers wanted to be him when they grew up.

"But then the confiscations came, and Mike panicked. I remember him calling me one night after he'd heard some of our friends were being ransacked by the police.

"'Jimmy, I don't know what I'm gonna do,' he said on the

phone. I'd never heard his voice shake like that before.

"'What do you mean?' I asked.

"'I can't let them take it. I just paid off the Camaro and Kayla loves this house.'

"'I'm not sure you have much of a choice,' I told him. 'All the Witnesses are going through the same thing.'

"'Isn't there a way I can fight it? I know a lawyer. Maybe he can help me–help all of us, I mean. Nothing wrong with trying, right?'

"'Mike,' I said. 'This isn't us versus the government of Hawaii. This is Jehovah versus Satan's system. Our deliverance isn't going to come from some lawyer, and it isn't going to come because we got to keep our luxuries.'

"Mike sort of scoffed into the phone. 'Yeah, well that's easy for you to say. You've got nothing to lose.'

"'Yeah, that's exactly the point,' I said. He hung up.

"In the end, there was never enough time to hire a lawyer. That night the police came knocking on Mike's door. He resisted, stating his rights as an American citizen. Apparently the police had prepared for this scenario: they immediately cited him for a whole list of offenses and hauled him away in a HPD squad car. His family ended up losing everything anyway."

"What happened to them, in the end?"

"His wife looked for a lawyer to help get her husband out of jail, but from what I understand no one was interested in taking it. Cases involving any kind of religious freedom were dead-ends at the time; no lawyers wanted to get involved with them. The court appointed a defense attorney to represent Mike, but the trial was over before it began. He was sentenced to four years in jail. His wife moved in with her non-Witness family, and things just went downhill from there.

"Sadly, Hawaii had a lot of stories like this. Some had just gotten complacent with the old system of things. Some had gotten sidetracked. Some were trying to build their own Paradise a little early. For a lot of these folks, the end was the same. They lost their hold on the real life. And for what? A beachfront condo with insane property taxes and termite problems. It was so shortsighted."

Jimmy finished off his maitai as a perimeter of bamboo torches were lit around the tables. Several sisters were dancing hula on the stage behind us. One was Caucasian, but the ethnicity of the others was as ambiguous as Brother Fukuda's. In a few generations, I mused, everyone's children would look like this, and ethnicity wouldn't matter.

One family. One God.

Alika Cardosa

I spent the first week in Oahu touring around with Alika Cardosa, the brother who'd driven me to my inn in the golf cart on the first day. As promised, he took me to a remote beach early one morning to re-teach me the basics of surfing. When I saw the first swell I panicked: it was well over my head, and certainly beyond my skill level. I tapped Alika on the shoulder and sheepishly asked if we couldn't possibly start over there, pointing to the far end of the beach where the waves seemed much tamer.

It seemed hopeless all over again as my first attempts to mount the board failed.

"You're paddling too late," my instructor said. "Keep your eyes on that point and paddle when I tell you."

"OK," I said, rustling up another bout of confidence and propping myself upright on the board.

I watched the approaching wave ripple and peak, slowly galloping towards the shoreline. If there was a rhythm to be seen, I wasn't seeing it.

"Now!" Alika shouted.

I anxiously flopped against the surfboard, pulling my legs from the water and digging into the sea with frantic arms.

"Paddle hard!" he ordered.

I tried, hacking at the water and wondering where my wave had gone.

"What's happening?" I yelled back, just about ready to give up. "Did the wave die?"

As if in reply to my question, I suddenly felt a surge of water pushing me up into the air. I let out a strange noise that wasn't nearly as much excitement as it was fear.

"Don't stop, keep paddling!" said a voice from somewhere below. Against my better judgment I listened, pawing at the crest of the wave without knowing exactly why. More terror went through my veins as I saw the pointed tip of the board dipping downward into the rushing water. I imagined tumbling helplessly in the wave and smashing against sharp coral or sea urchins or whatever dangerous things may have been beneath me. Instinctively, I pushed my elbows beneath me and leaned upward. Apparently, this was the correct maneuver, as my board leveled out and seemed to teeter on the edge of the wave as we surged forward together.

It was a unique feeling, as if I were riding in the saddle of some unseen beast below the sea. The wave carried me neatly to shore before it dissipated humbly back into the seabed, ready for its rebirth.

"Did you see that? I did it!" I shouted back to Alika, who was riding another wave in my direction. I felt like a little kid who'd finally lost his first tooth without crying.

"Congrats, I think you got it," he said, easing next to me on another wave and dropping his body into the water.

"Man, that must've been a big one. How large would you say that was?" I asked.

Alika just smiled coyly, "Ah, not sure. Maybe a couple feet?"

"Oh."

"Yeah, sometimes it feels bigger from up top."

We spent the rest of the morning working my courage up to the point where I could ride a wave I would actually be proud to talk about later. In other words, I had a chance to learn just how patient Brother Cardosa was. But we both laughed a lot: a couple of kids having adventures in Dad's backyard.

That afternoon, while Alika drove me around the North point of the island, he explained conditions in Hawaii during the final part of the Last Days.

"Although we knew, as Witnesses, that the Tribulation began with the attack on false religion, for the rest of Hawaii's residents, the feeling that we were really living in the Last Days probably came with the tsunamis. When California had that big earthquake in 2020, it caused a series of waves to ripple across the Pacific. They weren't especially high by the time they hit the Hawaiian islands, but they were enough. Hawaii had about eight hours of notice before the waves made landfall. In that time, people completely freaked out.

"The media didn't help much. The news of the tsunamis was the biggest thing to come over the airwaves since something related to the Liberation Act, and every local media outlet jumped on it and rode it home. You know what that's like–paddle early and paddle hard.

"You see, people on these islands would try to forget that they were living on a rock, but when a disaster like that sparked up, the realization would sink in that there's nowhere to go and everyone would turn into animals. I'd seen it before, with hurricanes and tropical storms, but this was something else entirely.

146

"First came the looting. Store owners tried to enforce some order, but it was impossible; they were overrun. People were scrambling for batteries, water, canned goods, you name it. It was later reported that dozens of people were trampled and killed during that chaos. Our family, of course, stayed in doors for all of this. The elders told us that help would come soon enough, and not to take matters into our own hands. We're thankful we listened.

"During the night before the first wave hit, a man carrying a five-gallon jug of water across our front lawn was run over by a family in a van. They stole the water from him and left him there. He somehow made it home, but I'll never forget the screams he made as he crawled away.

"We tried to shield our kids from seeing this, even from watching the news reports that went on non-stop through the night. Ashley was seven at the time, Kekoa was thirteen. But my wife and I soon realized how close we were to the end. Those horrors were the reality, and the kids would learn about it one way or another. We explained carefully to our children that everything happening was part of the end of a wicked system, and that they were going to see more and more terrible things, just as the Bible had foretold. As we talked to them, I began to suspect that we were more fearful than they were.

"I remember my little girl pressing against my leg as I peeked through the curtain covering the picture window in our living room.

"'Don't worry, Daddy,' she said like a doctor giving a clean bill of health. 'Jehovah knows how to save us.'

"Fortunately, at the time we were living in the hills, so we didn't have to flee to higher ground like many of the friends had to do. Some of them even came to stay with us, and that brought us strength. Unfortunately, there were also those who didn't listen to the instructions from the brothers, opting instead to grab what they could from groceries stores during the looting. Some of these friends were never seen again, others barely made it to safety.

"At about five AM on a Tuesday morning, the first wave of the tsunami washed onto the sands of Kailua beach, on the East side of Oahu. We later learned that before landfall, it was moving at about 500 miles per hour, which is only a hair slower than a commercial airliner.

"The thing about tsunamis, we would all soon learn, is that they aren't like normal waves which crash, wash onto the shore, and then recede. Tsunami waves can be hundreds of miles long, meaning that an entire city is flooded in a few minutes and stays underwater for hours or days. The other thing about tsunamis is that usually they aren't just a single wave, and the first wave to hit isn't always the biggest.

"What hit Oahu was a series of three waves spaced four hours apart, with the last being the largest. Hundreds that hadn't fled were killed. Thousands of homes were damaged or destroyed, including those of many of the friends. The resulting flooding also caused sewers to back up, which turned the water completely toxic and lethal. On top of that, many of the houses were built on raised platforms; the force of all that water caused them to shift, breaking gas lines and causing a series of fires that burned for days.

"That entire area of the island turned into a wasteland. After the waters finally receded and it was safe to re-enter, contractors were able to go in and start some small rebuilding projects, but with Armageddon right around the corner, they didn't get very far."

I'd previously heard very little of what Alika was telling me about the islands. With the surge of catastrophes happening globally at the time it was difficult to keep up.

"What was Armageddon like here?" I asked.

"Perfect timing. So many of the brothers had lost possessions, either due to the tsunami, the economy, or the confiscations by the police. It was getting harder and harder just to keep going. The ministry had effectively been shut down. We were trying to keep up with our informal preaching work, but people were so anti-religion that it wasn't effective. Some of the brothers, including our CO, were even imprisoned at the time. It felt like Satan had almost won."

"How did you feel when you first heard the trumpet blasts and the angelic announcement?"

"I felt...I felt sort of like I'd been holding my breath underwater for years, and finally I was able to come up for a breath of fresh air. I guess, more than anything, I felt relieved. Even before the angels began speaking, I knew we had made it to the end. The sound those trumpets made, that booming chorus of noise... I knew."

"In some areas, people put up quite a fight against the angelic forces. What was it like in Hawaii?"

"There was a mixed reaction. Oahu had several large military bases at the time, each located on different extremities of the island. A lot of people thought they'd somehow be safe if they went there. In many areas they were willing to climb over barbed wire fences with their children just to get in. Like the looting mobs before the tsunami, it was unthinking and desperate, like a wounded animal hiding from the hunter.

"Other people were different. Some thought they could bribe their way out of judgment. Since they knew Jehovah was fighting for his people, they came to closed Kingdom Halls and left presents at the barred doors. New cars, diamonds, bags of money, and so forth. Others who had persecuted the Witnesses directly tried their best to apologize, hoping to get pardoned, or something.

"Many others killed themselves, as in most other areas of the world.

"And, like other parts of the world, the military went first. From our house on the hill, we had a good view of what happened at the Kaneohe air force base below. The military sent maybe twenty or thirty helicopters to fight a couple of angels. We could hear the distant thuds in the air as they fired missiles and bullets into the clouds. Then, from beneath the helicopters, a line of angelic chariots and archers slowly rose from the sea. The sound of a heavenly trumpet blew and the archers' arrows sheared through the machines, leaving streaks of smoke and light in the sky.

"In probably ten seconds, the helicopters had been reduced to charred sections of metal sinking in the waves. A lot of that wreckage is still there, poking up from above the surf. The execution against the tanks was the same. When the war machines were gone, the angels flew through the towns, executing all who'd taken the wrong stand. By my count, the entire event lasted less than a half hour. I counted six angels.

"From what I hear, it was even more breathtaking in Honolulu, where several battleships had been stationed after the nuclear incidents in China. The battleships were destroyed by a single angel. Eyewitnesses say the angel was six stories tall with a long, double-edged sword. He walked on the water, and with each step his feet created these deafening hissing noises as the water vaporized beneath him.

"After Armageddon, that entire area, maybe twenty square miles or so, was just smoldering rubble. We let it burn out, and cleared as much as we could with chainsaws and bulldozers about a month later. Of course, this was almost twenty-five years ago. It's just a giant park now, not far from your hotel."

"So how many were left here, after the Great Day?" I asked as Alika's electric car climbed up a curvy road.

"I think the figure was somewhere around sixteen thousand, including the outer islands. Before the tribulation began, the population was one and a half million."

"So only one in a hundred or so made it."

"Yeah, that sounds about right."

"And what was disposal like?"

"Tricky. On an island like this, you can only dig so deep before you hit sand, and then water. So we had to truck a lot of the remains to the elevated areas of the islands and bury them there. We buried maybe two hundred thousand or so. The rest had been cremated directly by the angels or had been found by rats or birds before we could get to them. Not the most enjoyable part of life in the New World."

"What departments are most active here these days?"

"The RBC is in full swing now, with about half of the residents moved into permanent houses. There are a lot more developments planned as well. The Ecology crews are pretty busy, too. Last I heard they were looking for volunteers. How long are you here before you head out to Tokyo?"

"Haven't decided yet. I was planning on a short stay, but I may extend. Ecology work sounds interesting. Maybe I'll ask about it at the hotel."

We pulled up onto a grassy cliff overlooking a long and sandy stretch of coastline. Bits of rock and gravel crunched beneath the wheels as we eased to a stop. I got out of the car and felt a salty gush of air whip against my body, nearly toppling me. On the other side of the old and rusty knee-level guardrail, the ledge precariously disappeared into the frothy sea a hundred feet below.

"This is one of the few scenic spots that looks about the same as it did in the Old World," Alika said in a large voice. He had to fight to be heard over the whacks of wind.

"It's beautiful," I replied. The ocean in front of us bounded away infinitely, with the afternoon sun reflecting on its surface like chips of dancing gold. You could almost see the curve of the earth from up here, I thought.

I wondered idly if Jehovah saw it that way, too.

The Shark

For over seven years I worked with the ecology department in Hawaii. Most of that time was spent on the main island of Oahu, where our team was occasionally asked to help with construction or restoration projects, or perhaps train new arrivals. Incidentally, the ecological revival on Oahu was most obvious since the environmental damage there had been more severe than any of the other islands.

This was especially evident on the coast, where the coral reef and ocean wildlife were flourishing. In the days when Hawaii had been inhabited by Polynesians, long before the men from "civilization" had made their grand entrance, the coral reefs had been a kind of underwater forest, dense with plant and animal life and teeming with color.

One 18th century explorer from Europe described it this way:

"...The beach on this area of the coast was protected by a kind of natural underwater barrier, or reef, made of coral such as I had not seen before, neither on this island, nor in the seas of my home country, nor any other place. Using a clever device that the Ship's Corporal previously fashioned by fixing a circular plate of porthole glass to a round section of metal pipe, so that the wearer may see clearly beneath the surface of the water, I was able to get a close look at the coral reef.

"It was nearly blindingly colourful and fertile. The overwhelming heterogeneity of hues makes one think of a painter's palette; indeed, a more fitting comparison remains to be found. Equally beautiful were the multitude of living creatures swimming in and out of the holes within the massive sections of rock."

Sadly, within a century of the arrival of those first explorers, life in the seas was gradually strangled by increasing barge traffic, waste dumping, overfishing, and later, in our day, global warming and chemical pollutants. By the time I visited the islands in the Last Days, the coral was blanched and sickly-looking, though still vaguely beautiful, an old woman whose youthful vigor somehow still radiated beneath wrinkles and age.

The aquatic life then had been somewhat less disappointing, with fish of bizarre shapes and colors. Still, it was nothing like the undersea murals scrawled on my hotel lobby's walls, and worlds apart from the explorer's recollections.

Now, though, everything was slowly returning. Even in my few years on the job, I'd seen dramatic improvements. The lifeblood of the reef had returned. It pulsed with color and movement where frail dormancy had reigned before.

The fish had come back, too, and many other creatures with them. Crabs of dazzling sizes and colors skittered on the sea floor. Mantises rustled in and out of their sandy hiding spots. I was getting better at spotting octopi, too, though their skillful camouflage still fooled me most of the time.

Perhaps the most surprising of these creatures, as least for me personally, were the sharks. If you lived in the Old World, the next few paragraphs should resonate with you. If not, you'll probably find my trepidation a little ridiculous, since your mind probably imagines a very different image from mine when you hear the word "shark".

The first time I saw a shark (up close) in the Old World was in Sea World, in Florida, where my wife and I took our son, Jacob, when he was just two years old. Looking back, that may not have been the best choice for a toddler. He started whimpering as soon as the sharks drifted above us in the curved-glass walkway.

I couldn't blame him. Sharks were never my favorite. They just *looked* mean. Bullies of the seas. The feeding demonstration that followed didn't do much to allay that notion, either.

From somewhere just above the surface of the water, a dark human figure extended an arm and threw chunks of something into the water. Something thick and bloody. This didn't help poor little Jacob, who probably imagined those pieces belonged to something other than an animal. Emma, my wife, was also cringing. I could feel her tighten her grip on my sleeve and heard her sharp breaths through clenched teeth.

As soon as the meat touched the surface of the water, the sharks swatted their tails in a frenzy and tore their way towards the meal, angry and crazed. The chunks hadn't descended five feet before they'd been completely gobbled up by those razor-toothed monsters, leaving only a faint haze of blood and entrails. I shuddered. Jacob was crying. Emma suggested we go buy him a dolphin balloon, and we left.

This is why, while doing a routine reef inspection in my scuba gear one evening, I was nearly frightened to death. I felt it before I saw anything: a cold rush of water at my left side. It didn't have the force of a normal wave, which I would've ignored. Craning my head in synch with my underwater flashlight, I saw it: the streaked and speckled body of a tiger shark, nearly twice the length of my body.

Should I have been scared? Of course not. Yes, I knew animals and man were finally at peace. And yes, this had been the case for nearly twenty-five years. Nevertheless, the mere sight of its slow and calculating pace, those dead black eyes and sharp, menacing angles only inspired visions of terror: more chunks of meat–*my* meat–gobbled up as they sunk to the reef.

I panicked. My arms went first, like noodles, flapping and flailing in a cloud of bubbles. Then my legs, slowed by diving fins, but somehow trying to make it to shore on their own. I was breathing heavily, too, which isn't healthy underwater, even with scuba gear.

All this commotion seemed to excite the tiger shark, which slowly rose to my side, studying me with its cold, coal eye. I wondered, in that moment of horror, if I'd somehow gotten it all wrong: perhaps sharks *weren't* at peace with man, perhaps they never would be? My mind flipped through every related scripture and article I could think of, nearly convinced that I was about to become its dinner. *Would I be resurrected? How would that work? Would it be immediate? And where? Would I have to make my way all the way back from Atlanta to here? Would there be punishment for not knowing about the sharks?*

Sharp terror had sprung a leak in my head and lots of everything was spilling out. And then it got a little worse.

The shark edged toward me with a flick of its tail. Another gush of cool water pushed against my legs. Then, with a rolling motion, it grabbed my oxygen tank in its jaws. If there is a word to express a greater intensity of fear than 'morbid dread,' I would insert it here to describe my feelings. Surely, I knew, I was a dead man. *How come no one had told me about the sharks!*

But instead of devouring me, the shark just sort of idled there, like someone had flipped a switch and turned it off. I swiveled my head back, catching a glimpse of its sinister face and jagged rows of teeth and my scraped and dented tank hanging out of its mouth. Still no movement.

Slowly, I unlatched the buckle at my chest and slid out of the straps. I took one last gulp of air and pulled the regulator from my mouth. I moved my legs, ever so slightly at first, drifting away from the horrible beast. A minute or so later I picked up the pace, aiming straight for the shore, heart pounding in my ears.

When I finally got back to shore I found my crew sitting around a bonfire. I collapsed into the sand, chest heaving, barely believing that I'd made it out alive.

"What's with you, Mitch?" Benny said as he rotated a veggie skewer in the flames.

"And where's all your gear?" Asked Ichirou.

It was another few minutes before I had the composure to tell the story. I didn't miss a detail, all the way until my impossible escape.

The two looked at me with wide eyes, then at each other, and exploded into laughter. Benny let out great big hoops and haws, smacking his leg and pressing his stomach. Ichirou was making little choking noises as he rocked back and forth, big tears rolling down his face.

"What?" I said. It was the first time I'd felt irritated in a long, long time.

"WHAT?" I said again.

"Sorry," Benny finally said, wiping his face and nose, "we should've told you!"

"Yeah, it wasn't on purpose, really." Said Ichirou.

"Told me what? That sharks are dangerous?"

"No, of course they're not dangerous."

"Just the opposite. They're extremely playful," Ichirou explained.

I just stared at them blankly, still laying sideways in the sand.

"Playful?"

"Yeah, like dogs. And they love to chew on things."

"You're serious."

"Yes. This area is full of them. They never bite people, of course, but they often nudge us and watch what we're doing. Very curious animals."

I suddenly felt very small and stupid.

"And what about my tank?" I asked. My voice sounded exactly like a little boy's.

"Don't worry about it," Benny said, still giggling a little. "We'll get it after dinner. Hopefully the shark dropped it where you left it. Usually they do. They don't find it all that interesting if its not moving."

Ichirou handed me a cold beer and a roasted skewer. "When we go look for it we'll take a stick for the shark. They love 'em."

Twenty-five years in and still learning new things every day.

Jayna & Tim Avindelle

What d'ya think about this one?" It was man's voice from several aisles over.

"Eh, too Old World. I reckon you'd better stick to something a bit more subdued."

"C'mon, Jayna, this is *Hawaii*," he pleaded.

Jayna didn't say anything.

"Ok, ok, I'll stick with earth tones." There was a metallic *clank* as the man replaced the hangar on the rack and sauntered over to the next aisle.

I had to smile as I thought back to my younger days, shortly after Emma and I were married. We didn't argue often, but when we did it was usually between racks of clothes at a thrift outlet. Those were our golden years, before I took the insurance job and we were busy with a house and baby.

This place was almost identical to those thrift stores we used to go to, in fact. Every brand you could imagine from the Old World, in most of the styles that had been popular before and during the Tribulation, but rarely in a size that fit.

Clothing outlets like these were established in many towns several years into the New World. Salvaging crews had initially stored any usable garments in sealed plastic crates placed in shipping containers. Distribution wasn't a priority at the time since most people still had a closet full of their own clothes.

As the years wore on, however, so did the threads, and eventually new crews had to be organized to sort through what had been salvaged years ago. Unsurprisingly, our tastes had changed during the time away from Satan's system, and many of the items pulled from the crates seemed so outlandish or immodest that they were either shipped off to museums or turned into costumes for plays and films.

The rest ended up in places like *Kimo's Threads*. Browsing through Old World emporiums like this was a kind of pastime for some, a way to spend an afternoon of exploration and storytelling with post-Trib children or pick up a few trinkets for decoration. Over time, other recovered items had made it onto the shelves: antique picture frames, mirrors, bathroom fixtures, furniture, rollerblades, and so on. *Kimo's* even had a whole area dedicated to second hand kayaks.

There were always things in a place like this that gave pause for thought. The sizes of the garments, for example, said a lot about our lifestyles in the old days. In the New World, everyone was outside working in the soil or doing construction. Our diet consisted of fruits, vegetables, grains, a little dairy, and lots of legumes. There was simply no way to get fat, even if you tried. It was unlikely that many of these oversized garments would ever make their way to the front counter.

I eventually settled on jeans, grey corduroys, and a new orange beach towel. I traded a bottle of chardonnay I'd aged myself and brought back from La Unión and slipped on my sunglasses before stepping out the door.

I ran into the couple again outside.

"Where you folks from?" I asked.

"Australia," said the man. "Just got in this morning. You local?"

I shook my head. "I'm originally from Atlanta. Been here a few years though. What brings you two?"

"RBC. We're here for the new housing development in North Honolulu," said the wife.

I introduced myself and we shook hands. Their names were Tim and Jayna Avindelle, from Melbourne. A sprawling banyan tree near Kimo's entrance made a swath of cool shade across the lawn. We plopped down on a couple of benches and opened our juices: Kimo and his family made and bottled them personally. They came in a variety of local fruit flavors; mine was 'strawberry guava'. It went down my gullet sweet and cool. Paradise indeed.

"I haven't heard about that development you mentioned. How far along is it?" I asked.

"Just a blueprint. That's why we're here, actually: we specialize in irrigation and natural cooling systems. They wanted us here to go over the plans and make sure everything is done according to current building standards."

"What's a 'natural cooling system'"? I wondered aloud.

"Basically any cooling system that's not a fan or an AC, which suck the generators dry. Typically, natural cooling means reflective roofing tiles, proper attic ventilation, and so on. But recently in Australia we've been able to incorporate some really creative ideas into home construction. For example, we can run the fresh water through a system of pipes in the walls, roof, and floor of a house. This warms the water up naturally, so that less gas can be used when cooking or warming water for a hot shower. Additionally, it brings the temperature down considerably in the home. Some of the move-ins for the test houses we built using this system actually thought we'd installed hidden air conditioners!"

"Sounds interesting. When does construction begin?"

"We don't know exactly. Some modifications may need to be made to the design before it can proceed. The brothers here really want to be up to code with everything," Tim explained.

"What about you?" Jayna asked as she sipped from her lilikoi lemonade. "What brings you here from Atlanta?"

"I signed up with rotational. I've done a little bit of everything since we crossed over. Right now I'm assigned to ecological studies on the local plant and animal life."

"Huh," Tim said. "What's that like?"

"Pretty fascinating. Our work is actually related to what you guys are doing. We make sure a building site isn't home to any sensitive habitats or species. We're also called in to oversee waste management. A lot of the building materials are leftovers from the Old World, as you're no doubt aware. Some still have trace amounts of toxins, so we have to be careful with how we dispose of it."

"Returning species. You mean, like, species that return to an area, or extinct species coming back?"

"Both, actually. Sometimes they're just coming out of hiding, but in a few cases we've managed to prove that an extinct species is making a comeback. We've had a few birds do that here in Oahu. We had to pull up their records in the historical archives to be sure, but we finally confirmed that they hadn't been seen since the 1800's, when sailors from the Americas came to the islands with rats and diseases that did away with many of the native species."

"How does that work? I mean, a species coming back?" Jayna asked. Her eyebrows creased at an odd angle and a curly straw jutted from the corner of her pursed lips. She looked a little bit like Emma, I thought.

"We're still not sure. It makes sense that a species should be able to reemerge naturally. After all, the genetic potential should be there in the DNA. But what's really odd is that we've found eggshells of different species of birds in the same nest. The latest of these findings was on a cliff in Maui last year. We were able to identify the nest as that of an albatross, but the egg was far too small to be that species of bird. We're not sure how it got there. Either the albatross carried it there, or–"

"Or it gave birth to an extinct species! That's fascinating, right,

Tim?" Jayna said as she banged her bottle of juice against her husband's arm.

"Huh," Tim said. "If the bird did give birth to a different species, that might have some implications," he said.

"Like what?" His wife asked.

"Well I know people are still split on the issue, but... if Jehovah can bring back an extinct species of bird through a modern variety... Well, all I'm saying is, why couldn't he do the same for a human baby? That is, bring back the embryo of an aborted baby into the womb of an adoptive mother?"

I took another sip of lillikoi strawberry and mulled over Tim's suggestion. It wasn't the first time I'd heard that line of reasoning, but there were too many unknowns for me to form an opinion. Maybe the egg was deposited–or created?–in the nest? Maybe it had nothing to do with human babies. Did it really matter?

I didn't really think so. I'd learned, over the last thirty years, to deal with whatever came. Sometimes our hopes and assumptions were on point, sometimes they were way off. But in the end, it always worked out.

"Whatever the case," Jayna said, "I'd love to have an assignment that involves animals."

"You didn't have many animals back in Australia?"

"Nah, it's not that. A lot of Australian species are really thriving now. We just really love animals. Can't get enough of 'em," Tim said.

"Then you should definitely go for a dive as soon as you can. The ocean wildlife here is incredible. Especially the dolphins and whales."

The couple shot each other a glance and smiled. I could smell a story, and so I dug:

"I suppose Australia has its share of dolphins and whales too, right?"

"Indeed it does," Jayna said, smirking. After some more prodding, Tim began to explain...

"We used to work at the Sydney Sea Life Aquarium, back in the Old World. We were both marine biology students in college, but there weren't many jobs available after we graduated, so we ended up working there. But if you really loved the animals, like Jayna and I did, it wasn't a great environment to be in. It didn't take long to see and feel how stressed the animals were, being kept in their tanks for so many years. Many of them had to be fed special medicines and tranquilizers to keep them from getting ulcers and other stress-induced illnesses. So eventually we quit our jobs there and moved to Brisbane, on Australia's Gold Coast."

"Were you both in the Truth?" I asked.

"Eh, sort of. We were both raised in the Truth, but didn't do anything with it until after college. It was a bit of an embarrassing coincidence when we met there at the aquarium and realized we had both been raised as Witnesses and weren't doing anything with it. But eventually we were able to help each other get stronger spiritually, and just in time, too. Shortly after we moved to Brisbane, the Great Tribulation started, and that was it," Jayna said as her hand sliced through the air.

"Australia went into a panic," Tim explained. "You remember that right during the time the U.N. went after religion, there was a slew of major natural disasters."

"Sure, I remember," I said.

"Well, a fair number of those were earthquakes in or near the Pacific. Since so many Australians lived in the big cities on the coast, everyone was worried they'd be wiped out by tsunamis. There was a mass exodus to the continental interior. People just freaked out. They took as many things as they could and fled. They had no idea how to handle it."

"How were our friends taken care of?"

"The branch told us to stay put until we knew more. It was direction from Jehovah. As it turned out, the looting and rioting during the migration proved to be greater dangers than the water, which did minimal damage."

"What was the backlash against the Witnesses in Australia like?"

"I don't think it was the same in Australia as it was in the rest of the world. I don't think the Australian government was as successful as other governments in inciting the general public against the Witnesses. There were some brutal incidents, but I think that was more a result of people being scared about everything else and not knowing how to vent their anger and frustration. I don't think it was a response to the government propaganda.

"The public was very distrusting of the Australian government at the end. They'd been let down too many times, especially during the Tribulation. When the government finally sent police to round up and imprison us, some non-Witnesses even tried to fight them off. In a few instances, they even saved our brothers' lives, although the friends always insisted on being submissive to the authorities."

"And what was the end finally like?"

"Just awesome," Jayna said. "The trumpet blasts, the angelic soldiers beaming down from the sky. It was like some incredibly well-done Hollywood sci-fi movie–" Tim rolled his eyes at his wife and she abandoned the comparison, "–I mean, it was just *awesome!*"

"What was the first thing you did after Armageddon?"

"I think we were in a sort of shock afterwards. It had all happened so abruptly, and then it was over. Brisbane was in ruins. Many of the landmark buildings had been destroyed or severely damaged. A lot of the homes were in flames. It was like a warzone. In some areas, where there had been road construction crews working, the machines were still running with no one to operate them. It was a little creepy. We rode around on bicycles with some of the friends from the congregation trying to figure out what was left, and what we were supposed to do next."

"And that's when we thought about Sea World," Jayna said.

"Sea World? As in, jumping dolphins and whales? That Sea World?"

"Yeah. There was a park not far from us right on the coast. We immediately thought about the animals that might be trapped there," Tim said.

"We asked our elders about it, but they weren't sure what could be done. They discussed it as a body and finally told us that we could go and check it out, but they couldn't deal with it officially–their concern was to contact all the friends and make sure everyone was safe, which of course made sense.

"It took most of the day to ride there on our bikes, and when we finally got to the park it was starting to get dark. We stopped at a half-demolished gas station to grab some flashlights to inspect the tanks with, and then we let ourselves into the park. The gates had been left open, so we just walked right in.

"We heard them long before we saw them. The orca was especially loud. He was just a calf, and we could tell from his wailing that he was terrified. When we finally found him, we could see why. The two adult orcas with him were both dead and the water was clouded with their blood.

"The dolphins were noisy too. They were squealing and chirping from their little bay at the far end of the park. It was an agitated sound. We sensed they were just as scared as the calf, and probably hungry as well. We managed to find the freezer that kept the food, and divided the portions among them as evenly as possible. But we had this sickening feeling we were just prolonging the inevitable."

"Yeah," Jayna said. "We felt terrible seeing them like that. And the awful thing was that the park was right on the waterfront, only about thirty meters from the ocean. But it was impossible for just the two of us to move even a single dolphin. They were simply too heavy."

"So what finally happened to the animals?" I asked.

"Well, we prayed about it together and decided to spend the night in the park. We slept on the benches of one of the stadiums, looking up at the stars and wondering what Jehovah thought about it all. Our thought was that since we were now in Paradise, it was our duty to take care of these creatures. After all, no one else was there to do it, and without us they'd die. And that just didn't feel right, especially not in the New World.

"The next morning, when it was light, we explored all the storage areas in the park. There were some useful things, like chains and harnesses that dolphins could fit into, but nothing to lift them with.

"And that's when we remembered the road construction equipment we'd seen on the way to the park. One of the heavy machines that had been sitting there was a truck-mounted crane. We knew that was our answer, if we could operate it.

"We made our way back up the road and found the crane still sitting there. I got inside and started fiddling with the controls, trying to figure out how it all worked. Thankfully everything was labeled, though I still had to spend half a day getting familiar with it all. It was a good environment to learn in, though; there were all sorts of construction materials to experiment with, and I was able to figure out how to move things around quickly.

"When we drove the crane into the park, we were able to find a perfect spot on a walkway between the dolphin tank and the waterfront. Jayna helped me set the extension legs down on the side of the truck to stabilize it, and then we got right to work. I'd dip the harness into the water, Jayna would guide one of the dolphins in, and we'd lift it from the enclosure and deposit it in the ocean."

"It's funny, they were all very cooperative with us, as if they knew what we were trying to do," said Jayna. "They didn't exactly line up, but they all would wait patiently to get in the harness, and they made a different kind of noise. It kind of sounded playful and curious, not so much fearful, as it had before."

"How many dolphins did you move?"

"We were able to get all seven of them out, although it took nearly six hours. The first few were especially slow, but we got faster at it as the time went on."

"And the baby orca?"

"That was the tricky one, so we saved it for the next day, after we had gotten some rest and knew how to go about it. But it was more or less the same process: we found a suitable harness in storage, parked the crane in a central location, lowered the harness into the tank, and transported the calf into the ocean. All in all, it was an incredibly smooth operation," Tim said.

"I really feel like Jehovah was blessing our efforts out there. It was just the two of us, moving thousands of pounds of sea animals... When I think back on it, it just seems so impossible."

I couldn't disagree with that. A slurp erupted from my empty bottle as I finished off the last sip of juice.

"It's quite a story," I said, stretching as I stood and placing my bottle in a recycling carton next to the table. "Did you ever see any of those animals again?"

"Oh, sure," Tim said. "We saw them all the time. They'd hang around the ports we'd be working at. Often times at night, when we'd go for a swim, they'd be right there with us."

"That's one of the reasons I'm finding it a little hard to adjust to leaving our old home," Jayna said. "I really miss them. Their family has grown quite a bit in the last few decades, too. But they all stick together, and they always wait for us."

"Well," I said. "I'm no expert, but who knows? Maybe they'll come to Hawaii looking for you."

They smiled and gave me a hug.

"Thanks, Brother Hanson. Hope to see you around," Tim waved as I walked back to my electric scooter. The wind had picked up a little and I wondered what the surf was like. I turned the key and whizzed back down the road to my cottage.

Haru Saito

"Have you been to Japan before?" Asked the quiet man sitting in the deck chair next to me. His name was Haru Saitou. His eyes studied me from beneath the shade of his floppy-brimmed hat.

"No, never have."

The boat let out a couple of pressurized roars as we chugged away from the Honolulu pier. My crew had thrown me a going-away luau the night before and I was still wearing the aromatic pink plumeria lei around my neck. I'd miss the islands, but hoped to be back soon. I knew Emma and Jacob would love it.

"Are you from there?" I asked Haru.

"I am from Osaka, about four hundred kilometers west of Tokyo."

I knew little about the land I was destined for. Really, about all of Asia. A lot of Asian brothers, mostly from Japan and Korea, had passed through Honolulu while I'd been there, but I hadn't learned much about their homelands. They tended to speak more often of their assignments in the New World, emphasizing how much still needed to be done.

"What was it like in your area during the Great Day?" I asked.

"It was a great relief."

"Why?"

"During the Great Tribulation, our brothers and sisters there were treated very cruelly. The government used many tactics to put pressure on the friends."

"What kind of tactics?"

Haru shifted in his chair and I wondered if I'd made him uncomfortable. I explained my book project, and that seemed to assure him a little.

"To understand the methods the Japanese government used, one first must understand the Japanese. In Japan, one's honor–or reputation–was always the foremost concern. The more eyes watching you, the more important that honor was. To break from the ordinary was to bring criticism. A government guided by this kind of thinking, you can imagine, is always looking for subtle ways to achieve its less-

163

admirable goals."

"Like the goal of eradicating a religious group."

"Yes. You see, while in other countries religion was becoming acknowledged as a kind of plague to society, the Japanese people generally didn't feel this way. Some viewed religion with a kind of unconcerned apathy, but most others saw it as something to be respected, and at the very least, tolerated quietly. At the time, there were still a large number of Christendom's churches and Shinto shrines in virtually all areas of the country. It was a kind of tradition, and tradition was not to be disturbed.

"So, when the U.N. passed the laws limiting or banning the public practice of religion, the Japanese government faced a serious dilemma. Their solution was equally brilliant and sinister: They enlisted the help of Japan's crime organizations.

"In those days, criminal organizations were always just out of the public eye, but we knew they were close by. There were many indications, too, that they were cooperating with local police to continue operating. The Japanese loved to boast that their percentage of solved crimes and successful arrests were in the ninety percentile. But this was a misleading figure–if the police knew they couldn't solve a crime or didn't have enough evidence to carry on a successful investigation that would lead to a certain conviction, they wouldn't even attempt it. The idea was, keep the numbers high and maintain the public's support and admiration–again, reputation was everything."

"How did the government use crime organizations to ban religion?"

"First, the police would pressure criminal organizations to loot and damage religious sites. Shrines, temples, churches, and so forth. If calls were made to the police reporting these attacks, the police were always too "preoccupied" fighting crime in some other area. The organizations, in return, got to keep anything they looted to resell later on black markets in Japan and abroad. Additionally, they were allowed further freedoms in operating their own illegal ventures."

"So there was never a ban passed on religion?"

"There was, in a way, but it was never called a ban. After a year or so of these criminal incidents, which the media consistently blamed on bōryokudan, or "violence groups", the Japanese government stepped in. They expressed empathy towards religious Japanese and explained that similar atrocities were happening around the world. To protect their citizens, the government said it had decided to temporarily close such places of worship."

"How did the Japanese react?"

"There were some protests, but they died out after a few weeks. Many seemed genuinely afraid of those criminal organizations. They seemed to accept the government's decision as being in the interests of the people."

"You mentioned earlier that the Witnesses were treated cruelly. When did this begin?"

"Once the Kingdom Halls had been closed down, the Japanese Witnesses began meeting in homes, as many others were doing around the world at the time. We avoided discussing anything spiritual on the phone or in emails, just in case we were being watched. In time, we became quite comfortable with this way of doing things. Many of the friends even commented that they enjoyed the smaller groups, which allowed us to get to know one another better.

"One of the interesting things that happened during this time was an increase in Bible studies. In our congregation, we had many unbelieving mates who began showing an interest in the truth. They were impressed that we hadn't given up worshipping our God, whereas so many other religionists had become completely inactive.

"One of these unbelieving mates was a man named Tsune Yamamoto. In the past, Tsune had not been a kind husband to his wife Motomi, our dear sister. She had to endure his persecution for almost twenty years. But during the Tribulation, Tsune began to change. Then, one night, after a midweek meeting in our small apartment, Motomi told me that Tsune wanted to see me.

"I had met Tsune only twice before. The first time, he was drunk. The second time, he didn't speak a word to me. He was a broad-shouldered, muscular man with tattoos on his arms. He always seemed angry. I was afraid of him, really. And I did not know what he could possibly want to talk with me about. But I could see that Motomi thought it was urgent, and I agreed to call him.

"I will never forget the conversation Tsune and I had the next afternoon in a small park near the building where I worked. What initially surprised me was Tsune's changed disposition. I couldn't believe my ears when he actually asked: 'How are you?' as we sat down with our coffees.

"'I'm fine, thank you. How are you, Tsune?' I said.

"'I need to tell you something,' he said. 'It is about your people— the Witnesses. You are in danger.'

"I didn't know what to feel when I heard those words. Could I trust this man? Why was he telling me this?

"'I know you are good people. I've been observing you for a

long time now. My wife trusts you. This is why I am telling you all of this. I hope you will listen.'

"'Of course, Tsune. Whatever you have to say, I am willing to hear you.'

"Tsune first explained that he was connected to a dangerous Japanese organization. He didn't give me the name, and I could tell he was nervous just mentioning it. He kept looking around us as we spoke. He explained that the organization was working with police precincts to target religious sites. Up to this point, many of our brothers had suspected this, but now I knew for sure.

"'What's coming next is worse,' Tsune said gravely.

"'Actually, we know what is coming next,' I told him.

"He shook his head uncertainly, so I continued:

"'This is all a part of Bible prophecy. The attack first on false religion, and then an all-out attack on God's people. We have been waiting for this for many years.'

"Tsune seemed confused. Then he said: 'They are going to kill you all.'

"The words were like ice on my body. Of course, we all knew something was coming, as I had just told him. But this. It seemed...impossible.

"'The government is planning on letting the Witnesses organize a large meeting this year or next. They want to get all of you into a single place. And then, when you've gathered, they will attack.'

"'Attack?'

"'I don't know how, or what, but it will likely be called a terrorist attack later. Maybe a bomb.'

"'Can you be sure about this?'

"'Mr. Saitou, I have done many wicked things in my life. I know you people don't believe in hellfire, but I amnot sure. I want to do at least one good thing before I die.'

"And that was that. Tsune stood up, bowed politely, and walked quickly away, leaving his half-empty cup of coffee on the bench next to me.

"I didn't know what to do. I believed what he said. He had no reason to lie and he didn't look like a man who was telling one. I sat there for another thirty minutes, thinking and praying to Jehovah. The next week, when our Circuit Overseer came to meet with the elders, I explained the strange conversation I had and asked what we should do. He said he would contact the branch on our behalf.

"That Autumn, the branch offices in Japan received a formal letter from the Japanese government. It expressed the government's

166

condolences that our work had been interrupted, and seemed to acknowledge the contributions towards the community that the Witnesses had made in the past. Then the letter stated:

"'To express our appreciation for your efforts and as a sign of goodwill, the Constitutional Monarchy of Japan proposes a national convention for Jehovah's Witnesses to be held in the urban districts of Kyoto, Hokkaido, Osaka, Tokyo...

"There was one stipulation, however: the conventions had to take place on the same weekend, at the same time."

"So what was the branch's response? Were the conventions held?" I asked.

"It was an important and difficult decision. The branch committee met with me personally to ask me more about what Tsune had said and done during our meeting. I tried to contact him again, but his wife explained that he was away on business, and wouldn't be back for weeks.

"In the end, the brothers decided to accept the government's offer and hold the conventions. The reasoning was that the friends needed the spiritual encouragement and Jehovah would see to it that his people were protected. Also, Tsune's story couldn't be confirmed, and he'd since disappeared.

"I agreed with the decision, but I was hesitant and scared. When my wife and I walked into the stadium for the first day of the convention program, my stomach was in knots and my hands were sweating. I kept praying to Jehovah. I felt like Mordecai, and kept wondering where our Esther would come from."

"Did you tell your wife any of this?"

"No. The brothers decided to keep strictly quiet about all of what we'd heard. It would only cause a panic.

In any case, the first day ended without incident. Then, on the second day, during the morning session, an alarm went off. The brother on the stage continued to give his part, but a minute or so later the chairman walked on stage and handed the speaker a note. The speaker told the audience to calmly exit the building, and that the police and fire department had been notified. We were evacuated.

"About fifteen minutes later, several police cars and a fire engine pulled into the parking lot. The officers and the firemen shuffled into the arena. One of the brothers asked a policeman if there was anything we could do, and he told us to leave them alone and move away from their vehicles. The brother complied, immediately helping to direct the friends farther away from the building. It was a hot, cloudless day and the parking lot seemed to intensify the sun's heat, but everyone–nearly 8,000 people–were cooperative and calm.

"I don't know exactly how to describe the noise that came next. It was a terrible, deathly sound. The sound of absolute obliteration. I was facing away from the arena when it struck, but its force pushed us to the ground. When I turned back, the walls of the building were caving inwards, tearing the metal in the window frames and roof like newspaper. Glass shook loose from its frames in jagged sheets, splintering onto the pavement in great crashes. Plumes of fire and smoke erupted from the doorways and windows.

"We just stared at the dying building in shock. I'm sure no one said a word for at least two minutes. There may have been some children crying, I'm not sure. Because as the flames rose to consume what the explosion hadn't devoured, a new sound came, an unearthly sound: The sound of a thousand trumpets in the clouds."

There is a kind of wondrous light in Haru's eyes, as if he's seeing the angels appear right now over the hull of our ship.

"All I could think of in that moment was Isaiah 54:17: *No weapon formed against you will have success.* This intricately crafted scheme to annihilate us had failed miserably, and had even claimed the lives of some of its own. It was a victory that only Jehovah could have been behind. And so we sung, right there in the parking lot, as the angelic forces began descending from the darkening clouds."

"What ever happened to Tsune?"

"Motomi never heard from him again. It is possible that his employers found out about our conversation, but we cannot be sure. I do hope, however, to see him again soon."

168

Into Tokyo

Tokyo wasn't what I had been expecting. It didn't, in fact, feel like any place I had been to before in my life, Old World or New. Long before we even reached the shore, dark blotches in the sky above us caught my eye. They drifted in and out of the cloud cover and it wasn't until I peeked through the eyepiece of the observation deck's telescope that I managed to identify the specks as a series of hot air balloons.

In another thirty minutes, the sky above us was full of them, in every imaginable color and design. They looked like jellyfish suspended in a pool of light blue water.

"What're they doing up there?" I asked a Japanese sister who held a pair of pocket binoculars up to her face. Her name was Ayame.

"Some are probably working, seeing if the coastline is changing, maybe looking for ships sunk during Armageddon. Others just do it for recreation."

One of the balloons, decorated in purple and blue stripes, had dipped close to the sea level. Two women were attaching a giant grooved wheel to a metal arm that extended from the edge of the large basket and over the water. A rope was laid over the wheel. The remaining length of rope was dropped into the water below. I noticed that the end of the rope was blinking red.

A few minutes later, a gloved hand erupted from the surface of the water and coiled itself around the rope. A bell began to chime in the basket, and there was a flurry of activity as the two sisters, using a mechanical winch, hauled the diver out of the water and into the basket. The flame from the burners was adjusted, flickering a bit brighter and hotter to compensate for the extra weight.

The suited diver flopped into the basket and the three lifted back into the air.

"Where do all these balloons come from?" I asked.

"A sister makes them here in Tokyo. Sumi Ishikawa. She has a workshop at the Uruyasu Complex. It isn't far from the port we're heading to. You should try to arrange a tour."

I nodded gratefully, "Yes, that'd be wonderful."

Tokyo seemed to be decades ahead of the rest of the world in terms of restoration and rebuilding. Neatly organized villages (somewhat dense, but never cramped) covered the coast as far as I could see. Farther inland, the same attention to detail and design shone through in the agricultural regions. The perimeter of each lot was ruler-straight, the rows of plants tidily groomed and perfectly parallel.

The architecture here, too, was unique from anything I'd seen before. At first glance, it was easy to assume that the buildings had been leftovers from the Old World. They seemed far too large and too advanced to have been constructed post-Tribulation.

The welcome center, a half kilometer from the shoreline, was a prime example. It was a wide, sprawling complex with angled walls and tall windows that swung sideways on tracks, allowing residents onto the balconies. I realized, after some observation, that the crooked angles at which the rooms jutted from the building exterior had a purpose: each guest had an unobstructed view of the sea and yet was kept private from the other balconies.

Arching lazily over the complex's impressive four stories was a clamshell half-dome. It wasn't clear how or with what materials it had been built, but I noticed that it was covered in grass, vines, and other fauna. On the dome's underside, a network of water pipes ran from the outer edge back along the spines of the clam structure and down into the residential area of the building below.

"Welcome to the Tokyo Harbor Inn," the grinning brother behind the counter said with a bow. "How was your trip?"

"Nothing to complain about," I said.

I followed the brother as he came from around the counter and led me through the lobby. The lobby was immaculate. Every inch of the interior had been carefully designed and manufactured. From the ceiling hung white paper lanterns that glowed on and off as we walked past. The air was sweet and quiet.

In the area farthest from the entrance, a large pond was sprouting flowered water lilies. It was fed by a solitary finger-thick beam of water as solid as glass and made only the slightest gurgling noise. Plush, velour recliners had been placed beneath the hanging lanterns in this area. A low, wooden bookshelf next to these chairs followed the curve of the pond. A few guests were seated with books in their laps.

"This hotel was built in the New World?" I asked.

The concierge gave a slight smile and tilted his head. I realized I had asked a dumb question.

"Yes, brother. Everything you see here is post-Tribulation

construction. We tore everything down after Armageddon."

"Everything?"

"Yes, all of it. The area here was mostly filled with skyscrapers and shopping malls anyway. We had no use for it. Also, during the Tribulation we had a few bad earthquakes. Many of the buildings were damaged. We didn't want to risk anyone's safety."

I followed the brother into a dimly lit corridor. A moment later, I realized in astonishment that this place had elevators. In another moment, I was ever so slightly disappointed to find that they were only used for luggage. We'd still have to take the stairs up to my room.

"So where did everyone live, after the Tribulation?"

"Tents, mostly. Some were able to find boats here in the Tokyo harbor to live in, but they were a minority."

"And how long did that last?"

"In Tokyo? About ten years."

"Ten years in tents?"

"Yes. Why do you ask? Didn't brothers and sisters in America do the same thing?"

"We lived in houses."

"Houses built by the RBC?"

"No," I said with the slightest scoff that immediately triggered a ripple of guilt. "We lived in houses from before the Tribulation."

"Oh, you mean your houses."

"Well, some of us were able to return to our houses, but many of them, you know, moved into other houses."

The brother seemed to struggle with that idea for a moment. "I see," he finally said.

"So, this hotel, it was built after the Tribulation? That's pretty amazing. It looks so... modern." I said.

"It's adequate. We're still working out many of its issues. The awning pipes still don't absorb as much water as we'd like. You may have noticed the hanging garden on the dome roof. The soil there catches and filters rainwater that is then piped to the residences. Only fifty percent of the inn's water comes from soil precipitation, but it was designed for eighty percent."

I let the attendant's words quietly boggle my mind. I suddenly felt very foreign, and very backwards, a country boy riding his horse into the big city for the first time.

"I love the design."

"Ah, yes, that's coming along. It's all done by a local brother, Kiro Ushihara, and his design team. He was the lead architect of this building. He uses a lot of natural materials in his designs. The result is always very organic and very at harmony with its surroundings. His motto is, 'build it like it was meant to be there.' Ah, here's your room."

The brother slid open the wooden door and placed my luggage squarely in the center of the room.

"Supper is prepared at six o'clock. Until then, I suggest you get some rest. Travel by sea is exhausting."

Another bow. And then he left.

The room was simple and elegant. The floor was a polished, smoky stone that kept the room comfortably cool. The walls were covered in a kind of tan felt, designed with those same crazy angles that pronounced the exterior of the building. I assumed this was for acoustic considerations; I could barely hear the sound of my own footsteps as I walked across the floor.

The only thing missing, strangely enough, was a window. I mentally retraced the turns we'd taken to get to the room, trying to work out what side of the building I was on. Perhaps I was in the middle? I ran my hand against the fabric of the far wall and noticed that it gave a little against my palm. Then I discovered a handle at the far edge of the wall and pulled on it. The wall creased and bulged as it folded against itself like an accordion. I pulled it all the way back to the other wall, revealing a seamless floor-to-ceiling window that spanned the entire room.

I sat down on my mattress and took in the sight, as I had many times before. Baltimore, Los Angeles, San Diego, La Unión, Honolulu, and now Tokyo. Each area a little different, with its own fingerprint of beauty. I sat, and my eyelids sagged, and I laid down, and I slept.

Todd Renner

"Quite a hotel, isn't it?" Said a voice to my left. I realized that I probably looked a little funny standing there, mouth open, gazing at the ceiling in the lobby. I hadn't noticed the sculpture hanging there before. It had to be about fifty feet across, and spanned the height of several floors.

"Do you know what it is?" I asked, looking at the stranger and pointing up.

"It's a kind of tree, actually. It's formed that way by an artist as it grows, which I imagine it's probably been doing for a couple decades now. Gets a good amount of afternoon light once the sun dips past the cover of the canopy."

"It sounds like you've been here for awhile," I said.

"Yeah, longer than it feels I guess. Name's Todd. Todd Renner. Originally from Canada."

I introduced myself and we shook hands. We sat in the recliners I'd seen earlier, next to the pond.

"What brought you to Tokyo?" I asked.

"Architecture."

"Oh?"

"Yep. As with so many other things, Japan's way ahead of us Westerners when it comes to post-Tribulation architecture."

"Yeah, I guess I've noticed. I have a hard time believing all this was constructed in the last two decades."

"No kidding. From what I understand, almost all the survivors after the Great Day were given shovels and pickaxes and told to get to work clearing away the rubble."

"No wonder. I was in California a decade after Armageddon and it was maybe fifty percent cleared."

"Yeah, Canada was about the same. I think a lot of the friends were hoping to get right to the Paradise part, and sort of forgot about all the cleanup that was required. Did you have that too?"

"We did. There are still a lot of Old World neighborhoods where our friends live near the big cities. The roads are falling apart and they're still trying to run off of generators, from what I hear."

173

"What about you? Did you leave a lot behind to come here?"

"No, I've never felt that way. I was happy to say goodbye to that old house. My wife and I put so much work into that thing in the Old World, it practically consumed us. In the end, a storm knocked one of our neighbor's trees down and it landed right in our kitchen. The house was never the same after that. Roof leaked, doors wouldn't close right, just a nightmare."

From Todd's smile, I could tell he'd had a similar taste of suburban life. Then he asked:

"Were you in your house through the Great Tribulation?"

"We were. A lot of the friends were giving away possessions or having things taken by force by the police, but we managed to somehow avoid that. What was Canada like?"

"More or less the same, it sounds like. The police first confiscated only Bible literature, but eventually they came back for more," Todd explained.

"So what was the first thing you did, after the Great Day?"

"We had a huge congregation picnic. It was our coordinator's idea. He wanted to make sure everyone was safe, and sort of help everyone to recoup after all the things we'd been through. It took about a week to contact everyone, driving from one place to another through blocked or partially destroyed roads.

I'll never forget the day of the picnic. It was so... surreal. We'd had many gatherings at that same spot in the past, a little park right outside downtown Vancouver that overlooked a few apartment complexes and business buildings. On that day, about half of the buildings had disappeared in a pile of rubble, and the others were missing windows, or still smoking from the fires that had burned themselves out of tinder.

And amid all that ruin and destruction, there we were, this throng of celebrating people, eating and singing together with a carefreeness that none of us had felt before."

"A lot of people talk about feeling like the Israelites after crossing the Red Sea."

"I certainly can't think of a better way to describe it. It's exactly how we felt. And just like those Israelites, our joy was coupled with a slight uncertainty about the future. I think a lot of people thought it would be a completely clean slate after Armageddon, that we'd go back to wearing fig leaves and everything modern would evaporate somehow. I remember one brother looking over the ruins of the city who kept saying, 'I'm sure it'll all burn up eventually. It has to, right?

How are we supposed to clean this up?'

"Of course, all those questions were answered a few months later at the Super Convention, but at the time, it wa daunting. Overwhelming, even."

"What about the non-Witness survivors?"

"That was a surprise too. I don't think any of us were expecting so many of them; we thought we were working our territory pretty well! I never learned the exact numbers, but there were a lot of them. Many of them, perhaps even most, were foreigners, especially Chinese exchange students who'd never heard of the truth before. One of them that I ended up studying with hadn't even seen a Bible before."

"How did they take to the truth?"

"If anyone rejected it, I didn't hear about it. How could you? You'd just seen angels completely wipe out the world's military along with billions of wicked people after mankind had nearly destroyed itself. Could there still be any doubt as to what the right decision was?"

"How did Canadian friends respond to the Organization's directions for the New World?"

"Again, I think a lot of people were hoping to step right into Paradise, and some were a little disappointed to know that the resurrection was still a ways off. But most had the right attitude. One thing that helped was a talk from the Super Convention called *Adam's Descendants, not Adam's Imitators*. It reminded us that we, like Adam, had been given a task to carry out. That, just as in Adam's day, we had to work towards a global Paradise one step at a time. I especially liked the point that one of Adam's shortcomings was his desire for instant gratification, and that this took priority over the assignment he'd been given. The talk encouraged us to temporarily put aside our personal desires and work towards global restoration as a brotherhood."

"What other talks stand out to you from that assembly?"

"Oh, there were so, so many. That program was entirely different than anything we'd attended in the Old World. Back then, it was constant reminders about Satan's traps, worldly influences, materialism, and so on. But that first post-Armageddon program never mentioned any of that stuff. It was specifically tailored to our new lives.

"I remember one part that my wife and I especially enjoyed entitled *What is Macedonia?* It explained that our preaching work was a thing of the past, but that now we had new tasks to conquer, and new "Macedonias" to step into. The part encouraged us to join one of the new RCs that had been established, Salv'ing, Demo, or Transportation. It carefully outlined the kinds of work that these crews would be doing, and we even got to see some short clips from the work that was being done around the world. We were also reminded that teaching those who had come through the Tribulation without knowing Jehovah was of upmost urgency. They had to be taught, trained, and tasked.

"I remember scribbling notes madly into a large yellow legal pad. I think I filled the whole thing after just the first session; fortunately during the lunch break the brothers passed out more notebooks!

"Widen Out was another outstanding talk. Now that countries, national borders, and travel visas were a thing of the past, we were free to go wherever we wanted and this talk encouraged us to do so. We were told to get to know our brothers and sisters in other areas, to experience other cultures and cuisines, and to *keep widening out.* I really loved that talk. I had always been a little hesitant to travel, but now I had no excuses! It was shortly after that convention that my wife and I signed up for Salvaging work and were sent to New York, and then, five years later, across the Atlantic to Lisbon."

"Do you remember the talk *Can You Make Room for It?* on the second day of the convention? How did the friends in Canada respond?" I asked.

"Ah yes, that talk. Again, I think some were a little disappointed, but most responded well. The fact is, the Organization wasn't *forbidding us* from having children, they were merely encouraging us to consider it. The reasoning made sense: if we were going to apply any of the other suggestions–to move abroad, join one of the traveling work teams, or even get involved with local restoration work–it'd be easiest to do it without young children."

"Did you have children at the time?"

"No. We wanted to, but it never happened. My wife had really hoped to start a family right away in the New World, but we both really wanted to travel, especially to Europe, and to help with the restoration work there, so we agreed to follow the direction of the Organization and put off the plans for a family. Here it is, almost thirty years into the New World, and we've just been too busy with everything to think about it. Maybe after the Resurrection. We'll see."

"So how did you go from Salvaging to architecture?"

"I haven't been doing architecture long, actually just started a few years ago. Maria and I were with Salvaging for over twenty years. After Lisbon we were in Rome, then Athens, and then spent a few years in Cairo, learning basic agriculture. After that we sailed from a port in the Red Sea all the way to the Arabian Sea and through to

Manila. The brothers there explained that salv'ing and demo crews were just about finished with their work, and that architecture would be a much-needed skill in the decades to come. We were instructed to come here, to Tokyo, to learn what we could."

"Is there an architectural school here?"

"It's just a six-month class, but it's held at the Uruyasu complex not far from here. Have you heard of it?"

"Yes, I'm actually supposed to be touring it with friends sometime. Something about hot air balloons."

Todd's eyes lit up, just as mine had when I'd seen the air speckled with balloons two days before as we pulled into port.

"You're gonna love it."

And something told me I most certainly would.

The Uruyasu Complex

The area surrounding the Port of Tokyo was filled with things I'd never seen or imagined. Glass buildings that jutted from the water, sleek electric stations powered by the sun and wind, gliders that drifted over the bay like motionless birds.

It was as if I'd stepped into a world of dreams. It was hard to wrap my mind around it all. That so much could've been accomplished here in such a short time seemed impossible. Still, the Japanese of the Old World had been famous for their self-discipline, precision, and innovation, and there was reason to believe that ethic had lived on, even if the flag hadn't.

Our means of transportation was an electric-powered, beige monorail that threaded its way along the contour of the Tokyo Bay. A pleasant voice announced each stop, where passengers piled on and off in small groups.

My travel companions for the day, Gabe and Ayame Tucker, pointed out sights as we whizzed by.

"A lot of this used to be military," Gabe said, waving his arm at a park on our left. "After Armageddon, it was just a big, black smudge on the ground."

I leaned slightly out of the open window to my right, trying to get a look at where we were headed. Oddly, we seemed to be heading for the edge of the pier, and it was approaching quickly. Maybe one hundred meters. And beyond that, all I could see was ocean.

Seventy-five meters. Fifty. Twenty-five.

The monorail shot off of the pier and down towards the water. For a moment, I wondered crazily if the track had been broken in some kind of accident. The decent was sharp, and some braced themselves against the handrails, but everyone was composed and quiet.

In another moment we were gliding along the surface of the water, creating slight ripples in our wake.

"How...?"

"There's a rail under us, right above the surface of the water. It's only a foot wide or so, but it's there. Wild, huh?"

I nodded.

The monorail continued forward, banking slightly at each turn. It eventually lifted back onto a pier and eased to a halt.

"This is it," Gabe said as we slipped backpacks onto our shoulders and stepped onto the platform. The air was bright and clear and smelled like the sea. We walked for a few more minutes inland, passing knots of people here and there on the dock.

The Uruyasu Complex was unmistakable. Had it been an art museum in some bohemian district in the Old World, it would've fir right in. Here, though, standing solitarily in a field of grass, surrounded by a flatness interrupted only by the occasional sapling, it was an oddity.

The complex was a series of boxy brown buildings linked by arched wooden bridges. The bridges looked very Japanese, with their sloped terra cotta roofs and intricate carvings. Were it not for the broad glass windows, the buildings themselves resembled some kind of fort, impenetrable and daunting. At their bases, the buildings faded into a blur of green where local fauna had begun its slow takeover.

The complex grew as we neared; what looked like two stories suddenly became three, and finally five. As we passed under one of the bridges between two of the buildings, a walkway became visible. It led downwards, below ground level, to a circular garden, like the footprint of some long-extinct beast. Several artists were scattered about in stools painting each other.

"They have art classes here too?" I asked.

Gabe and his wife nodded as we stepped into a doorway next to the garden.

"First I want to show you the gallery," Gabe said. We walked down a narrow corridor that slanted slightly uphill.

When we passed through the next door, I found myself in a stark white room. Walls that didn't quite reach the ceiling cut through the room in a dozen different directions. Paintings and sketches hung on every section of every wall, each lit by a different spotlight from somewhere high above in the blackness in the ceiling.

The drawings were all architectural. A few were accompanied by photographs of the completed structures, but most were by themselves. One of them, I noticed with some surprise, was captioned "Gabe Tucker, Windmill, Concept 45"

Gabe was smiling proudly when I turned back to him.

"My first in the gallery," he said with a slight bow that looked very Japanese.

"What happens to all these ideas?" I asked.

"Most of them just come here to be displayed, but a few go

into development. RBCs come through here regularly to pick designs that they feel are both suitable for a project site and practical to construct. The first part of our curriculum here was learning about building materials and design styles, learning what kinds of structures are in demand right now, and then learning all the math behind the art."

"Sounds difficult."

"It was at first, but I'm really starting to enjoy it now."

"What happens after the course is finished?"

"Most of the architect graduates will be assigned to different countries where there's a need. The stuff you see here is more creative and conceptual than they'll likely be building when they get to their destinations, but hopefully, when other regions catch up to Tokyo, they'll be able to start making some really cool stuff."

"So how did Tokyo get so far ahead of everywhere else?" I asked, glancing at Ayame.

"The Japanese are a disciplined people. After the Super Convention just about everyone went full-time into the demolition and clean up effort. I think it was done in maybe, ah, four years?"

"That's incredible," I whistled. "Wasn't Tokyo a huge city in the Last Days?"

"One of the biggest," said Gabe.

"Once the coastal cities were cleaned up, half of the task force moved inland while the other half stayed behind to work in the fields and build farmhouses and storage buildings. They were very crude structures, made from pipes and tarps and sheets of metal and wood that had been stripped from the wreckage of the Old World. The idea was to get on with the work as quickly as possible." Ayame folded her arms.

"I think you had the right idea."

"I think so, too," Gabe said. "Here in Japan, everything's been cleaned up, most of the residences are done, and education centers like this complex have been up and running for awhile."

"I wonder what's next," I thought aloud.

"Well, in Osaka they've started clearing land for Welcoming housing projects."

"Welcoming?"

"Yeah, for the resurrected. They're supposed to be coming back there."

My heart jumped into my throat for a moment and the room spun. I suddenly felt very cold and hot at the same time and needed a drink of water.

"Are you ok?" Ayame asked, taking a step toward me.

"I...I'm fine...I just..."

A spark ignited in my mind's eye. I glimpsed my son's bright face, still missing those two front teeth, imagined him tugging at his mother's hand as they ran through these corridors towards me. They moved in slow motion, their feet not quite touching the ground.

The resurrection.

"I need some fresh air," I finally said while Gabe and Ayame looked on in worried silence.

When we finally surfaced, we were in a totally new part of the complex. It was similar to the area we'd entered with the rust-colored buildings and ancient-looking bridges, but in this area a waterfall poured from a horizontal slit in one of the building's walls and fed into a long, rectangular pond. Smooth black stones surrounded the pond, and on top of these, chair-sized concrete cubes that looked a little like giant dice. We sat and took a moment.

"I'm sorry for that, back there," I said after taking a swig from my water bottle.

"Not a problem," said Gabe.

"I apologize if I said anything in the gallery to–"

"No, no, it wasn't anything either of you said, Ayame," I said. "I just had this sudden urge to see my family. They passed during the Tribulation–a car accident. I've been so busy with everything these last few years, I sort of hadn't thought a lot about the resurrection. Just hearing that word, though. It really hit home."

"I understand, Mitch. If you want to head back to the inn, that's fine," Gabe put a hand on my shoulder.

"No, really, I'm ok. I'd really like to see more of this place."

Ayame looked at Gabe and then smiled at me. "Let's go see Sumi's workshop–you know, the one who makes the balloons you asked about. I think you'll enjoy meeting her."

I nodded, and the three of us slipped into another doorway.

Sumi Ishikawa

"No, no, that's not quite the right color. We need something more reddish. Check storage. Avery, can you please come down here and help Miki?" The woman spun around, her silk dress tossing in splashes of color. Her hair was tied in a tight bun and she held a clipboard in the crook of her arm.

A tall, blonde boy wound his way down a spiral iron staircase, his feet thomping loudly on each step.

"Thank you. See this color? This is too orange. We need something a bit more red, almost fuchsia, do you see?" She held two swatches of shiny fabric in the air for him to compare. He squinted studiously and nodded, running out a door in the back of the warehouse.

"Sister Ishikawa?" Ayame said in a voice just above a whisper.

The woman raised her head with a serious look that quickly melted into a smile.

"Well hello! Ayame, Gabe, good to see you. And you are–?"

"Mitch Hanson," I said, shaking her outstretched hand. Her wrist was covered in bangles that clanked as she moved.

"Brother Hanson, good to meet you. My name is Sumi Ishikawa."

"Hello. Seems like you've got quite an operation going here."

"Yes, it's amazing how busy things always are around here. You'd think life in the New World would be a little more relaxing, eh? Soda, anyone?"

Sumi lifted the lid of a plastic cooler on the floor with her foot. As it yawned opened I saw it was full of ice and canned drinks.

"A friend of mine in Colombia makes them. All natural flavoring, plus a little carbonation for old time's sake."

The cooler scraped against the concrete floor as she pushed it with her foot towards us. We each fished through and grabbed one. They were almost too cold to handle. They hissed open and tasted wonderful. I hadn't felt that cold burn in my throat in years; it was so strong that I had to wipe away tears in my eyes.

"I feel like we're seeing more and more balloons around Tokyo

183

every day. Are they all yours?" Gabe asked.

"I think so. At least, I don't know of anyone else who's making them. But Tokyo's been growing a lot lately, it's hard to keep track of all the new faces. Who knows?"

"So, I just have to ask, why balloons? And how?" I asked, almost woozy from all the fizz and sugar.

"Why? I've always liked them, I guess. Or, to be more specific, I always liked the idea of flight. I thought I'd be a pilot when I grew up."

"Where did you grow up, by the way?"

"New Zealand," Sumi said, smiling. "My parents were originally from here, but moved our family there when I was a little girl."

"Oh," I said. I tilted the can back again and was slightly embarrassed to find it empty.

"So how did you get into making balloons?"

"After Armageddon, when I was with Salvaging, we went through a lot of military bases. Sydney, Port Moresby, Manila, Jakarta, et cetera. There wasn't much left over after the angelic forces trampled through, but we did find a lot of parachutes. No one really had any ideas on how to use them, but I remembered, back in the Old World, reading about hot air balloons on the internet, and how they could be made with the same nylon found in parachutes.

"I convinced the overseer to let me have the 'chutes and I drew some diagrams and patterns. It took a couple weeks, but finally I was able to cut up all the fabric and stitch it–by hand–into the basic teardrop shape of a balloon."

"That's incredible. And did it work?"

"Technically, yes. I attached a gas burner to the underside and it flew just fine, but it was far too small to lift a person. The way parachutes are designed, cut into short, narrow strips, makes it very difficult to turn them into large balloons, so I sort of gave up at the time."

"Then what?"

"Then I came to Japan. I did some work in textiles, since the brothers and sisters here were already starting to make their own clothes at that time. They had these huge warehouses in Nagoya where the Salvaging teams had found all kinds of amazing fabrics. Including, believe it or not, exactly the kind of nylon needed to build balloons. And better yet, in all sorts of colors, as opposed to the ugly greys and greens of military parachutes."

"The desire of every living thing."

184

"OK, so I thought that, of course, that this was a little blessing for the work I'd been doing, but I'd also matured a bit since those days with the Salvaging crews, and I worried if perhaps some might be a little unwelcoming to the idea of balloons."

"Because they're dangerous?"

"The Japanese tend to be a bit more conservative," Ayame said almost apologetically.

"Both of those reasons. So I decided to talk with some elders about it first. My uncle, at the time, was working at the branch in Tokyo, and I figured that if anyone could tell me a straight yes or no, it would probably be him. I would've asked my Dad, but he and my Mom were doing ecology studies in Lima at the time and we didn't talk too often."

"What did your uncle say?"

"Nothing at first. He tilted his head and pursed his lips a little, looking this way and that. I thought for sure he was going to say it was a terrible idea. And then, out of the blue, he said, 'I think this may be the answer to our prayers.' I couldn't believe it! He explained that the brothers had been trying to figure out a way to travel quickly between different areas, especially the outlying islands, and from inland areas to other places like Seoul and Shanghai. He asked if a balloon could make that kind of distance and what the travel time would be like.

"He took my proposal to the brothers in the Transportation Committee and the overseers all gave it the go ahead. They did ask about safety, but after I explained that in the Old World, balloons were statistically much safer than commercial airlines, they seemed satisfied. They gave me a small team of assistants and this warehouse as my workshop. And I've been a busy little bee ever since."

"How long ago was that?"

"A little over eight years. In that time, We've built over two hundred balloons. The first few were just for ourselves, small ones to experiment with. We wanted to test everything out completely and make sure it was safe and effective. Around that same time the branch sent us some balloon assembly instructions that the information committee had recovered from Germany. It explained how to put together the envelope–that's the big teardrop balloon section–how to correctly build the throat–the part where the burner feeds into, the correct kind of fuel needed, and so forth. It took about a year to get everything right for the first manned trial, and we had a huge crowd show up just t watch."

"I'll bet that was nerve-wracking."

"You have no idea."

"And how was it?"

"Incredibly, it was fine. It was tethered to the ground, just in case, but all the instruments worked and we knew we were ready to move forward."

"So how long did it take to catch on here with the public?"

"Well, at first we were building them exclusively for the branch. They asked for ten in a year, and we weren't sure if we could make that goal. But Jehovah must've been blessing the effort, because it came together way ahead of schedule and we were able to do twice that. And before that year was even over, friends were already asking about when and if they could trade for a balloon for themselves. In the end, the extras that we made never even went into storage–they went right to private owners."

"And what about operating them? Who does that?"

"That, we had to learn ourselves first. We spent a lot of time–me and my assistants–learning how to pilot them correctly, how to descend smoothly, how to read wind currents, and so forth. Now we have a pilot training program headed up by my lead assistant, Avery."

"Wow, really? He seems so–"

"Young, I know. Only twenty-three. But he's a smart kid, I trust him completely. He's in charge of teaching the private owners how to safely manage the balloons. He also taught the pilots to fly balloons for the branch."

As if on cue, Avery jogged back through the doorway with a patch of nylon in one hand.

"Take a look at this one, Sister Ishikawa. I think it's the color you're looking for."

Sumi compared the samples, ran her long fingers across the smooth material, and nodded.

"Yes, this'll do. Do we have enough?"

"Yes. I'd say enough for four or five mid-sizers."

"Perfect. Tag it and we'll pull it in tomorrow."

The boy nodded and walked through the doorway again.

"What happens when the nylon runs out?" I asked.

"That's a good question, and I don't know the answer. The Tokyo branch has put out a request around the world for more nylon to be sent here, but to my knowledge we haven't heard anything back yet. If we do run out, I guess I'll do something else."

"You don't seem worried."

"I'm not. Whatever happens, happens. I know I won't be disappointed. In the meantime... anyone up for a flight?"

Into Jeju

Japan was a world in itself. Time moved quicker, things happened faster. On their days off, people were still working, still moving forward. This spirit was contagious. After only a few months in Japan, I found myself pushing my own barriers, seeing if I couldn't possibly outdo my past accomplishments and refine my skills.

This intensified pace of individual lives and the greater societal whole therefore allowed for a endless stream of exciting new projects: the intercity solar monorail, the Tokyo telescope, and the construction of blimps (A project overseen by Sumi, who did eventually get more Nylon from a storehouse in Moscow).

Months turned into years, and the years added up. You can imagine my surprise, one day, when I realized I was almost sixty-five years old. I thought back to what that age looked like in the Old World: the wrinkles, the slowly hunching figure, the daily pills for aches and pains.

When I was ten years old, my family had gone to a nursing home to visit a great-uncle on my Dad's side of the family. His faltering memory put him in a state of constant emotional turmoil: confusion, frustration, paranoia, anger. In time, he lost control of his body just as he had his mind. His knobby hands jittered sporadically, as if operating a marionette only he could see and feel.

I never wanted to get old. Dad said I wouldn't have to, so long as I obeyed Jehovah. I asked what would happen to Uncle Fred. Dad said he didn't really know. Uncle Fred didn't know much about Jehovah, but who knows? Only Jehovah sees the heart.

Sixty-five years old. That was hard to believe. I didn't feel sixty-five. I didn't look it. Not like Uncle Fred. And yet, on the inside, there was age. Growth. Some of that, no doubt, could be attributed to experience, the stuff that brings the wisdom of old age. But the rest, the greater part, was and is perfection.

Perfection, as a human quality gradually being restored, is more subtle than I used to think. Of course, it still needs to be coupled with accurate knowledge and obedience to be worth anything. These latter two elements require time and effort to build. This is especially so in the case of an imperfect human coming out of the Old World and moving towards perfection. His inclination has changed for the better, but the previous habits of the mind and body, like dirt paths beaten into the brush, need time to fade.

Perfection has not brought super-human abilities or pre-programmed skills. We can't breathe underwater, we still need to eat food and drink water. A perfect child still needs to be taught to read, to swim, to know Jehovah. Obedience, however, comes naturally.

It is as hard to sin in the New World as it was to avoid sin in the Old.

Thoughts like these drifted through my consciousness as my balloon bobbed between the clouds and the sea. I tugged at the vent catch a few times, letting out a bit of hot air from the top of the envelope. A slight mist was creeping in from the East. It was a sight that would've worried me when I was new to ballooning, but after hundreds of hours in the air with Avery and Miki, I shrugged it off and focused on my instrument readings. I'd already been in the air for nearly six hours, meaning that land would be appearing in the next few minutes far beneath by basket.

Another yank on the vent cord and the balloon dipped slightly towards the sea. I took another glance through my telescope eyepiece and finally spotted it, a hazy grey-blue outline sitting placidly in distant waves. Old Korea.

A flicker of static came through over the HF radio in the balloon basket. I turned up the volume a few notches and hailed the tower:

"This is Black-Seven-Nine to Jeju ground. Do you copy?"

I waited a few moments for a response. The mist was still moving in, and nearly under me. It worried me a little, but I tried to shake the thought as I hailed the tower a second time.

Then, finally: "Jeju East Tower to Black-Seven-Nine. You are clear for landing on lot thirty-two. Follow the lights. Over."

I peered over the edge at the incoming island. I still couldn't see the tower I was communicating with, but two parallel lines of blinking lights began to flicker in slow succession, guiding me to my landing lot.

Tightly organized landing fields for balloons and the occasional (though very rare) prop plane were a necessity these days. Although it never felt like heavy traffic in the skies, there were more and more people using balloons for travel, and even one collision would be unacceptable.

The landing was smooth and uneventful. I set the basket down in lot thirty-two and locked the vent open. As I waited for the envelope to deflate, two brothers stepped forward to greet me.

"Brother Hanson?"

"That's right, that's me."

We shook hands and one of them marked something on his clipboard and radioed the tower to confirm.

"It looks like you just beat the fog. Twenty more minutes and we would've all been worried for you."

"Sorry. I hit a strange weather pattern after leaving Osaka. It took me longer to get here than I was expecting."

"It's no problem. We're glad you're here safe. Welcome to Jeju island. This is Taosun. He'll be escorting you to your dormitory. We've got radios in each of the rooms there, so if you need anything, feel free to call the base. Someone is listening twenty-four hours a day."

I nodded, thanked him, and followed Taosun down the grass slope to a dirt road. Waiting for us there was an electric dune buggy. The long radio antenna on its back was still bobbing up and down from the vehicle's previous motion. It resembled a friendly mechanical dog wagging its tail.

Taosun asked the usual questions as we jounced down the dusty road. Yes, this was my first time to Old Korea, and Yes, I did think it was beautiful, quite like Hawaii, in fact. No, it was just me. Yes, I was originally from the East Coast of Old America, oh really, you had some friends there too? And so on.

It was a five-minute drive from the landing field to the dormitory, which resembled a seaside villa I'd once seen pictures of in a travel magazine. Somewhere in the Mediterranean. The walls were porous and white, the roofs were plated in curved sections of dried, blue terra cotta. Twisted and curled iron bars formed the railings for the balconies and stairwells.

The whole place was set, somewhat precariously, on the ledge of a cliff, a few stories up from the ocean. I peeked over the edge and watched the waves, relentless and powerful, smashing against the cliff below. I noticed that several man-made ledges jutted from the face of the rock, where water would momentarily catch, go inert, and then dissipate.

"What's that?" I asked.

"Those vents drive the water into hollow columns in the rock," explained Taosun. "The water then moves a series of turbines as it flows down, which gives this place electricity."

"Which explains why we're perched on a cliff like this."

"It's the only reason, really. Although the area you see here, above ground, is just the lounge and observatory. If this mist clears up by tonight, you should come back and take a look through the telescope. It's a brand new Newtonian reflector we acquired from Old Germany. Anyway, most of the complex, including your dorm, is below ground."

I was a little skeptical about this as we entered the scissor-door elevator and lunged down into the abyssal building.

Moments later the door clanked open, beckoning us into a long hallway. The smell of polished cedar flooring was rich and warm, and the natural fluorescent lamps that hung from the walls added to the aura. The far wall of the hallway was an enormous glass window. I jumped back a little when a wall of foamy water lashed up against it from the outside, leaving a web of bubbles as it smeared back down.

A low bass hum could be felt more than heard from the floor beneath us: the ocean-powered generators, no doubt.

And there was another sound too, floating around in the hallway. The sound not of machines or of nature, but of humans. The sound of music. Someone, somewhere nearby, was playing a saxophone.

Taosun led me to my room and waved goodbye. As always, I fell asleep almost immediately.

Yuhan, Eunmi, and Payu

Before I continue with the events in Korea, and specifically the research I did while there, it's important to backtrack just a bit and explain what had been happening up to this point with the animals.

The animals of the Old World, with the exception of a few domesticated species, had been at odds with the human race. Part of this, we knew, was divine intervention on their behalf, a kind of mental and instinctive reprogramming that sent them into hiding at the first scent, sound, or sight of man. This was for good reason. From at least as early as the time of Nimrod down till the Last Days, wild animals had been hunted and harvested mercilessly, and not always out of need.

Sharks in Asia were captured and mauled by fishermen for their dorsal fins. When returned to the ocean, they were unable to swim, hunt, or survive. Elephants hunted for their ivory tusks experienced similar fates in India and Africa. Tigers, even when on the brink of extinction, were poached for their claws, heads, and hides. The list of atrocities went on and on. The animals that suffered the most intensely were the ones harvested like produce for their meat and organs, often fed chemical supplements to speed up their growth and increase their meat output. Their lives were short and miserable.

With the arrival of the New World and the subsequent sharp decrease in human population, animals finally had a chance at peaceful, natural lives. Their fear of man, however, didn't subside overnight. No one is sure exactly why, but some have hypothesized that this fear of man was somehow linked to their diet. After all, once Armageddon passed, rodents, birds, and even domesticated animals did their part in cleansing the earth of human remains.

It was several years after this cleanup process that previously wild animals began showing signs of docility. Like Ferra's bear in Baltimore, they slowly crept their way back into our lives. The more dramatic change, though, came with the second and third generation of animals. They were born domesticated, friendly, trusting of humans. They also subsisted primarily on vegetation. Thus, it was at this time that the Organization began establishing animal research centers. The

191

animals were no longer hunting for their own food, so we had to help feed them.

At the time I flew to Korea in my Black-Seven-Nine hot air balloon, there were a dozen major animal research centers (organized by Regional Wildlife Committees, or RWCs) around the world. Each center was located in a different habitat, and organized into smaller research outposts that specialized in understanding and caring for specific species.

Our complex was the South Jeju outpost of the Seoul RWC. We were there to focus on studying marine life of the nearby seas: fish, whales, octopi, dolphins, and, of course, sharks.

To facilitate our research, an underwater lab had been built. It had been constructed, unsurprisingly, in Japan, then ferried over to Korea and lowered into the sea. It connected to the rest of the complex by a metal corridor that jutted from below the sea bed, about fifty feet underwater. It took ten minutes from entering the complex from the cliff to ride the elevator to the lowest floor–B5–and walk through the corridor to the lab.

The lab made me uneasy. There wasn't anything to be legitimately concerned about, of course; the most vigorous of safety precautions had been taken to ensure our safety, and the animals were by now passive and friendly. Still, there was nothing natural about being in a pressurized glass bubble far beneath the waves, hearing the muffled churning of water at our sides and the supple scrape of silt and sand below.

For the first few months of my work there, my companions were Eunmi and Yuhan Li. They were a couple originally from Incheon, Old Korea, and, after Armageddon, had ended up migrating as I had. Their travels had taken them to many corners of Asia, but had finally brought them back here, where they were taking the lead in marine research at the South Jeju complex.

Eunmi was small, with long, delicate fingers that tapped precisely on the controls. Her job was piloting the drone submarine. It had been found by a Salvaging team years prior on an Australian research vessel and was put in storage. It took another five years to find its operating manual, which was finally located on another ship in Indonesia. Eunmi and Yuhan taught themselves how to operate it, and were eventually shipped back to Jeju island together with the submarine and an assignment.

The sub was roughly two feet in length, width, and height. At its center, a plastic hub bulging with numerous convex glass windows housed the sensitive components: five high definition cameras, a sonar device, an infrared scanner, two batteries and the radio receiver and transmitter. Outside of the housing, the sub's rotating directional propellers and LED headlamps, and protecting all of that, a reinforced metal frame that gave the sub its cube shape.

On my first day in the lab, Yuhan patiently walked me through the sub systems and displays.

"The screens here are the camera feeds coming from the sub," he said, pointing to the top row of monitors. "The colorful display is the infrared feedback. The circular display is for the sonar."

"And what are we looking for out there?" I asked.

"Well, most of the fish and aquatic life has been documented; we know they're living off of the remains of other dead fish and algae. But there are a few reclusive animals out here we're still trying to understand. And then there's the wrecks."

"Wrecks?"

"Ships that went down during the Great Day. We know that military vessels of at least four different countries were in these waters when Armageddon hit: China, Korea, Japan, and the United States. Most of them sunk off the East coast of Japan, but we've found a few here, too."

"What do we do if we find them?"

"Fortunately, we don't have to worry about the weapons on board. Just about everything went inert with the angelic attacks; a lot of the guns and bombs simply disintegrated. Still, we're required to report the coordinates and information of all the vessels we find. This is used to make accurate charts of the waters, just in case we need to come back for something."

"We also find on-board recorders once in awhile," Eunmi said quietly as her fingers danced on the controls.

"On-board recorders from sunken ships?" I asked.

"Yes. Most military ships had them. They usually aren't recoverable, but we have found a few."

"What kind of information is recorded?"

"Video feeds from different parts of the ship before it sunk, instructions coming in from Navy bases, captain's orders to the crews, all kinds of information."

"And what do you do with a recorder once you find it?"

"We download the information and send it to the branch. Then they either discard it or send it to one of the Armageddon Archives."

The Armageddon Archives, I'd learned some years back, wasn't just one location confined to La Unión. Archives were popping up all over the place. Unlike the one I'd been to, which had been bits and pieces from around the world, these newer ones were assembled solely with local footage. The Tokyo Archives documented the angelic destruction in Japan, the Seoul Archives told the tales of the South Korean Navy standoff (and the foiled North Korean nuclear attack), and so on.

"Hey, Yuhan, look who's back for a visit," Eunmi said suddenly. Yuhan's chair squeaked as he swiveled in her direction, peering out through the 4-inch-thick glass wall.

"Payu?" He said, tapping against the glass with a knuckle.

I walked over to get a closer look and didn't see the animal at first. Just a small school of tuna and a lot of sand and rocks.

But then one of the rocks rolled over, exploding in a radiant flash of color. It startled me and I almost fell backwards.

"Don't worry, Mitch, he's harmless," Yuhan laughed.

I leaned back toward the glass, and realized that the 'rock' was actually a giant octopus changing colors. Apparently, he had some rapport with my two colleagues, who were now huddled around him, cooing and scratching at the glass.

"Payu belongs to a species of giant Pacific octopi," Eunmi explained. "Octopi are the most intelligent invertebrates man has discovered so far—watch this." Eunmi trotted over to a desk drawer and produced a crumpled piece of tin foil. When she returned to the glass wall, she held it up next to the octopus.

Payu slowly twisted his head to get a better look at the strange object. His right eye seemed to study it for awhile, and then, with a ripple of hues, he began to change: a greyish, speckled color that was undoubtedly an imitation of the foil now dominated his skin. But there was something else, too.

Payu's skin, which had been smooth and even, now took on a new shape and surface. Parts of his tentacles were extended while others were indented. Certain bits seemed to stick out straight like spines. And the edges of his body seemed more ragged than before. The octopus's skin had changed textures.

"I've never seen anything like it," I whispered.

"Try showing him your hand," Eunmi suggested.

I inched closer and raised my palm, pressing it against the cool glass. Again, the octopus seemed to study it for a moment with its dark, marbled eye. Then it carefully laid two tentacles against the outside of the glass, closely matching the shape, color, and texture of my hand. It was simply awesome.

"He's able to imitate all kinds of things: backpacks, hats, books, bottles, oxygen tanks, you name it. Once we had a musician in here doing sound experiments with the sea life, and when she took a break, Payu contorted himself into the shape of her saxophone," Yuhan explained with another laugh.

"A lot of the animals down here seem to be really curious about what we're doing, and sometimes we get the feeling that they want to communicate with us. Especially the dolphins and whales. A lot of scientists in the Old World had speculated about the complexity of those mammals' ability to communicate, but no major breakthroughs were ever made. It didn't help that a lot of whale and dolphin species were hard to study due to their rarity. Now, however, we hope to be able to break some new ground in that field."

"And in the meantime, you have Payu," I said, still looking at the octopus that was now imitating my brown leather work boot.

Valeriya and Darya Popov

It was around this time that we experienced what was later called the Great Breakdown. Up to this point, we'd still been using computers, printers, digital cameras, and numerous other digital devices. Minor problems could be fixed by maintenance centers, and major problems meant merely switching the device out for a new one.

But after roughly forty years in the New World, those devices finally began to wear out. You can imagine how much of a challenge this was for us. It wasn't that we necessarily needed the devices, it was that they made life a little less primitive than we were willing to accept. When they were all gone however, acceptance was all that was left.

The problem was production. All of us knew how to use the devices and many of us knew how to fix them. But no one knew how to make them. And even if we did possess the knowledge, we didn't possess the means. The factories to build the devices had either been destroyed in Armageddon, demolished during the cleanup, or experienced the slow fate of decay in the New World. There was simply no way to make more.

At least, not now.

And so we regressed, somewhat reluctantly, to the ways of antiquity. Typewriters were dusted off, the last computers and digital cameras were abandoned, and we said our final farewells to our beloved tablets. Even Eunmi and Yuhan had to retire their RC submersible.

Fortunately, radios were still in operation. The Organization had put their manufacture near the top of the priority list, so we were still able to communicate globally long into the New World. We could fix them and we could build them.

It was remarkable, though, how much we realized we didn't need. After just a year of parting with my computer (which I was really only using for writing anyway), I barely missed it. My typewriter, while bulky and less convenient (no more copy & paste), was perfectly suited for my needs. And taking a bicycle from the complex into town was no worse than the buggy. I got to see a lot more wildlife that way, too, since there was no snarling motor to scare off the animals.

And if it hadn't been for my bicycle, I would never have heard the enchanting tones pouring from Valeriya Popov's cabin in the woods.

The cabin stood at the end of an old road lined in foliage. I leaned my bicycle against a rickety wooden fence and knocked on the front door.

The music halted. There were impending footsteps, and the door creaked open. Behind it stood a tall, thin woman with pale skin, red hair, and freckles.

"I'm sorry to disturb you," I said. "I just heard your music from the road and came to investigate."

There was an almost imperceptible smile on the woman's lips. "It's no disturbance. I have visitors often. Please, come in."

The house was decorated plainly. A long, gnarled bookshelf made a spacious perch for a few lonely books. Three pale lanterns hung on thin wires from the vaulted ceiling. Several pairs of shoes were neatly lined against the wall. In the dormant fireplace sat a single piece of wood, waiting. And there, on the far side of the main room, against the tall, paneled window frames, sat the piano.

"This is my sister, Darya," my host said, motioning to a woman I hadn't noticed in the other corner of the room. She was sitting in a rocking chair, cradling a cup of something warm in her hands.

When I introduced myself, she nodded slightly and smiled.

"My name is Valeriya. It's nice to meet you," my host said.

"I apologize for just barging in like this."

"As I said, it's no problem," Valeriya stowed my shoes next to the others in the line and offered me tea. I thanked her, and soon the three of us were enjoying the warm afternoon sun flittering in through the glass.

"The music I heard, before I entered, was that a recording, or were you...?" I glanced at the piano.

"Yes, that was me."

"It was beautiful. I'm sure I haven't heard anything like it before."

Valeriya silently took a sip from her mug.

"Where did you learn to play?"

"My mother."

There was a pause as the two sisters exchanged glances.

"We grew up in Russia in the 2000's," said Darya. "Those were relatively good times for the Witnesses. The government tried to restrict some of our freedoms, but things were still much easier for us than they had been for past generations."

"The two things I remember distinctly about my childhood was field service with my father and piano lessons with mother," Valeriya said. It seemed that she was speaking more to her sister than to me, but I didn't mind.

"So how long have you two been in Korea?" I sipped from my mug. There was a touch of sweetness to the red liquid.

"Over twenty years," Darya said. "We came to study botany."

"Here in Jeju?"

"No, farther north, what used to be North Korea."

I thought back to the North Korea of the Old World. When I was a child, it had been a land of secrets. During the Tribulation, it emerged as a daunting nuclear power that tried to impose its authority over South Korea. Nuclear war had been evaded narrowly, but not without several disasters, all of which occurred in it's own regions, or in neighboring Chinese territory.

"We built this cabin a few years ago after moving to Jeju island. There are some unique plants here. And it's a perfect setting for the music."

"Do you write your own music?"

Valeriya gave a slight nod.

"Ah, well that explains its...uniqueness."

"Thank you."

"Your mother must've been an incredible musician."

Again, the sisters exchanged a surreptitious glance.

"Go ahead, Val, you should tell him," Darya said.

Valeriya sighed. "You're right, my Mother was, by reputation, an incredible musician. She was a pianist in a Russian orchestra before learning the truth. But me, well, I never actually heard her play."

"How's that?"

"I was born deaf. It was a surprise to everyone. In all other respects, I was completely normal."

"What was deafness like as a child?"

"Lonely. I was always very aware of my condition. Normal children could simply look at each other and move their mouths and understand everything, but I couldn't. I felt like a large, invisible wall was around me my whole life. Sign language helped, but I was still so angry at not being like everyone else. I'd often throw tantrums out of sheer frustration."

Darya nodded with wide eyes. "You wouldn't believe the magnitude of sound that little girl's lungs could produce."

"Well that was another thing: I knew what sound was, even if I couldn't understand it. I knew I could cry and shout and get others' attention, and I used that a lot to manipulate others. I didn't have many friends, but I did have a lot of people doing my bidding."

"And how did you discover music?"

"My father and mother knew I needed something to focus my energy on. I was often yelling and being disruptive, even at meetings, and they were exasperated with me. One day, while my Mom was playing the piano, Dad noticed me staring, and asked, in sign, if I'd like to try. I said yes, and he sat me next to Mom on the bench.

"At first, I did what all little kids do: I mashed on as many keys as I could. Mom just waited patiently for me to finish. Then, she showed me how to play a simple song, an old Russian children's lullaby. I played it back to her, missing only a few notes. When I looked up at her face, I saw an expression that was new to me. Her mouth was open and her eyes beamed. I realized, for probably the first time ever, that I had done something to make her proud.

"Even though I couldn't hear what I was playing, I had a good memory for the progression of notes, and more than ever, I wanted to see Mom and Dad's smiles. So I kept practicing and practicing. Soon we were learning Mussorgsky and Balakirev, Abramsky and Beethoven and Bach."

"Sounds like you were a bit of a prodigy."

"I'm not sure about that, I just knew it made my parents happy, and I lived for that, as any child does, I guess."

"Around that time," Darya said, "Our father starting making business trips into North Korea. He was a mechanic by trade, and apparently they were having problems with their Russian-built trains, and somehow through our Father's company he was offered the job. It seemed a little odd at the time, since it meant he'd be away for days at a time, often missing meetings. He was a spiritual man and raised us as a spiritual family, but this job was apparently very important to him. It was only long after, when we went to North Korea ourselves after Armageddon, that we found out what he was really doing there."

"And what was that?"

"He was smuggling literature in for the brothers there."

I'd heard about the smugglers in North Korea before, but thought they had all come from South Korea or China.

"How long did he do that?" I asked.

"About five years. It was an incredibly dangerous assignment. We didn't even know about it, which was probably his way of protecting us if something happened."

"And eventually," said Valeriya, "something did happen.

Something terrible."

Valeriya was interrupted by a knock on the door. Darya hurried over to answer it.

A young man stood in the doorway, probably in his late teens. He wore the signature cap and uniform of couriers from the RTC. "Is this the residence of Valeriya and Darya Popov?" He asked.

"Yes," Darya said, taking his envelope. Moments later, he'd retreated back up the drive to his bicycle.

"Another one from the branch. Probably just another recording request?" Darya slipped the brown envelope under her arm and returned to her rocking chair.

"What was the terrible thing that happened, Valeriya?" I asked.

"Actually, we never found out exactly what it was that happened, but on one of his trips into North Korea, our father simply disappeared. There was no letter, no phone call, no notice, he was just...gone."

"How old were you two at the time?"

"I had just turned fifteen. Darya was eighteen."

"What was that like, losing your father?"

"The not knowing was the hard part. Even up until the few years after Armageddon, we hoped that one day he'd just show up again. We thought maybe he had been imprisoned there. It wasn't until years later that we were finally able to accept his death."

"And what about your mother?"

"She raised us as best she could after our father disappeared. We eventually moved to a city about five hundred kilometers to the West. It was good timing, because just two years later, North Korea had that awful nuclear incident."

"Although, it didn't help that we thought our father might still be alive at the time. We worried that he was locked away in some dirty prison cell as the radiation descended upon him," Darya added from across the room. "Well, who knows... maybe it did."

"And where is your mother now?"

"She died a year before Armageddon. She had been battling cancer for a few years by then."

We sat in silence for a few minutes, slowly draining our mugs. I could almost see the division between the shade and the afternoon sun move across the uneven floor as the grandfather clock in the hall ticked the moments away. A few egrets were poking around in the hedge on the other side of the picture window. Their comical shadows bobbed and wobbled on the floor next to the piano.

"What was it like," I finally asked Valeriya, "when your hearing was restored?"

"It was a gradual process that lasted a few days, actually. And it didn't start right away, either. I think that's because there was a lot of explosions from building charges in our city after the Great Day, and Jehovah didn't want to startle me. It wasn't until after those crews left that I began hearing very slight shuffling noises. Everything sounded like this."

Valeriya held her palm against her ear and, reaching across with her other hand, scratched against a knuckle with a fingernail. I tried it. The sound was as she described, a sort of dense and nondescript scraping noise.

"The sensation of suddenly being able to hear when you've been born deaf is something almost impossible to explain to a person that has heard all their life. When your ears sense the vibrations in the air and the information is transmitted to your brain, you give it no conscious thought. But for me, even that initial indistinct *sound*... it made me shiver with excitement.

"As the days went by, the sounds became clearer and distinguishable. I could tell between different voices, and I could hear, for the first time, *laughter*. When I first heard it, I could only smile. I tried it myself, forcing a giggle up from my diaphragm, and just hearing that little bouncing sound was so amazing that I made myself *really* laugh, and that sounded even funnier, and soon I was rolling on the floor, crying because everything was so new and bizarrely wonderful."

"She isn't exaggerating," Darya said. "I thought she'd hurt herself because she was crying on the floor, curled up in a ball."

"And what about the sound of music? What was it like hearing that for the first time"

"Well, I waited to hear that sound. I didn't want to ruin my first impression by hearing it with damaged ears. I gave myself three days. And then, when I was sure I was hearing everything clearly, I sat down to that very piano and played the first song my mother had taught me, the Russian lullaby, *Sleep*."

Valeriya slowly moved to the piano bench, sat, and unfolded her fingers against the white keys. There was just a moment of silence, and then the notes came, one at a time, filling the air inside the cabin and spilling out into the dusty road and tall pines and rolling hills outside. Her fingers lilted with an unhurried, natural kind of movement, a feather caught in a gush of summery breeze.

"It's a simple song," Valeriya said, again, as if to apologize.

"You could've fooled me. It seemed that there was a lot behind it."

"That's exactly what I felt when I first heard it. So few notes, and yet each one aches with longing. Don't you agree?"

I did. And again, feelings of my own aching surged through my body, memories of my little Jacob and his mother. I saw her wearing the dress I'd bought her on one of my trips to New York; a colorful floral print with a wide, white belt and matching white hat. She'd worn it once when her and Jacob had waited to pick me up at the airport in Atlanta. I missed them so much on that trip. Just like I missed them now. A stray tear trailed down my cheek.

Yes, I knew longing.

Darya, still in her rocking chair, had set her mug down and taken to opening the envelope in her lap. She had some trouble with it; the material was thick and pliable. She went to the kitchen for a knife and sat back down, sawing at the flap once she'd squeezed the serrated blade into the slit she'd torn.

Reaching in, she produced several sheets of paper and two small blue stubs. Frowning, she held the paper up and began reading. Her lips moved slightly as her eyes slid across the page.

"Oh my..." she whispered.

Valeriya and I looked at her curiously.

"Oh, oh my..."

"Darya, what is it?" Her sister asked a little impatiently.

"Val... You won't believe this."

"Well, tell us, what is it?"

"This is an official notice from the Welcoming Committee."

"Welcoming Committee? We haven't travelled anywhere in years... What does it say?"

"No, no, this is something new. This is a resurrection notice."

"WHAT?" Valeriya was up from her bench and running across the room-- "What did you say?!"

Valeriya leaned into her sister's lap and grabbed the paper, going over the same words.

Dear Darya and Valeriya Popov,

We are happy to inform you that your Father, Alexei Iosef Popov, and Mother, Polina Taisia Popov, are to be resurrected on N.E. 53, Nisan 20th, at approximately 3:00 PM. Enclosed are lodging reservations and two attendance tickets. The branch will provide all necessary food, clothing, and shelter arrangements for the first week, but kindly ask your cooperation in helping to relocate your family after that. For recommended settlement information, please see the included information on pages 2 through 5...

The two sisters leapt into the air, sending the papers flying as they jumped and hugged ecstatically.

"It's finally happening! It's finally happening!" Valeriya was nearly screaming hysterically.

"Thank Jehovah!" Darya said, tears in her eyes and sobs in her chest.

"N.E. 53, that's just eight years from now," Valeriya said, with wide, focused eyes darting around the room.

"Eight years should be enough to expand the cabin here, at least for a place to live in the beginning."

"We can radio Mike and Leah tonight about building supplies and possibly getting some friends over to help."

"Do you still have his frequency? I can try him now."

"Wait, did the letter say where they're coming back. Is it Korea?"

The two women scrambled for the papers on the ground, suddenly asking a million questions needing, then and there, a million answers.

And that's how I left them, slipping quietly out the door I came, out the door the courier had knocked on just minutes ago with a message that would forever change Darya and Valeriya's life. Well, maybe not *change*. *Enhance*, perhaps, was the right word.

I was happy for them, and I smiled as I picked my bike up from the fence, pushed the kickstand up with the heel of my boot, and pushed at the pedals back up the hill. Yes, I was happy. And I'd be happier still when my own courier arrived. Maybe tonight?

I pumped the pedals a little harder.

Sy Deeker

There weren't many of them–the genas, that is–in the first few decades after Armageddon. A few, like Aria whom I'd met on my way to Honolulu, had been conceived during the Tribulation and born around the start of the New World. Others would be born later. The desire to procreate, however, seemed to naturally recede from the conscious desires of many. In the wild, plants and animals with exceptionally long life spans had few offspring. As humans, we were now at the tip of this pyramid, and our offspring, who would live as long as ourselves, were in no hurry to exist.

Still, the genas gradually emerged onto the world scene, and brought with them the birth of the New Culture.

That's what we called it, anyway. Of course, this wasn't anything like the divisive, destructive *cultures* that had marred the Old World, the culture of flags and emblems and petty conflicts and racial prejudice. It was the culture of progress towards a unified goal, and a culture of looking at things in a new way.

It was most evident when the bulk of the reconstruction work had been completed. The land was cleared and tilled, the houses for the soon to be resurrected were nearly completed, and we were raising a scattered first generation of perfect children. This new generation drew a lot of nicknames: some called them newgens or New Worldies, Post-tribbers, or simply "the kids". The term used most, though, was 'genas', a derivative of "Gen-A's".

We, the Great Crowd, had battled with imperfection and Satan's system and every other imaginable (and unimaginable) evil. Genas hadn't. They saw the universe for what it was–the product of an awesome and intelligent Being that wanted nothing more than peace and happiness for His subjects.

Objective, mentally uncluttered thinking was the beauty of the genas. When genas looked at a problem, they saw it with minds that pondered the Divine. *How would God solve this? Is this a physical problem? What applicable scientific laws had Jehovah established?*

This thought pattern was their foremost guiding principle in life. Once they had been taught by their parents who Jehovah was and what he wanted, they understood and complied. More than that, they yearned to be His friend. They talked to Him with an intimate congeniality free of even the memory or hint of sin.

We, on the other hand, still struggled with seeing any issue through chipped and smudged Old World lenses. *How did we solve this back then? What machines did we build to get around this? Could we build them again?*

Our thinking remained, for some time, fundamentally flawed.

And this is why it was sometimes difficult for the two generations to understand each other. I don't mean to imply dissension here, the problem was never so severe. But sometimes, there was a division, however slight, between the two kinds of minds. Almost as if a different language was being heard and spoken on each end.

This was most evident to me when I met Sy Dreeker. Sy was the son of a brother from Old Iceland and a local sister from Korea. The couple had met on a restoration project in Shanghai and had been married sometime later. Another thirty-three years passed before she became pregnant with a son.

Sy was tall like his dad but with his mom's vaguely exotic features. The color of his wavy hair had averaged out to a dark brown that glowed blonde in the sunlight. He was a fine-looking young man, and had been accorded such a reputation by many of the single sisters with whom he'd crossed paths.

Sy was also brilliant. My job was to train him in wine agriculture. A plot of land that had once been occupied by a botanical research outpost had been recently repurposed, and once the building had been emptied and the equipment shipped to other parts of the world, I was asked if I could move in for the two-year vineyard project. Although I dutifully pointed out that it had been thirty years since last bottling my now-exhausted cabernet, I was apparently the only one on the island with such experience, and so I finally accepted.

Sy was waiting for me among a shipment of crates near the empty lot. A tent had been erected on site and he was beneath it, fanning himself with a sheet of paper he'd cleverly folded for the purpose. He wore a long-sleeved button down that was tucked into his light blue corduroys and he wore an old baseball cap. Probably his father's.

"Hello, Brother Hanson," he said when my bike had pulled up next to him. He stepped behind a crate to shield himself as a small wave of dust climbed from my back tread.

"That's me. You must be Sy Dreeker?"

"Yes. Were you expecting someone else?"

"Uh. Nope. Just you and me for this project, for now."

I pushed my bike around to the back of the tent and grabbed the equipment manifest to make sure everything had arrived. I noticed that one of the crates, marked P79-003, wasn't on the list. "P" usually stood for personal effects, but I hadn't made any personal requests, and wondered if it might be an error. Then I noticed a note etched on the crate in pencil:

"Mitch,

"Thanks for your help with this vineyard. May Jehovah bless your crops to the full! Miss you. Love you.

"-Your Friends,
Hansu & Dina,
Seoul Branch

I smiled, wondering what the box might contain.

"Ty, can you throw me the crowbar?" I said, pointing to the corner of the tent. Ty walked over, picked up the metal rod, and brought it to me. I wedged it beneath one of the wooden struts and pulled back, pushing the sole of my shoe against the top of the crate for leverage. The wood groaned and gave.

When I removed the packing straw, I was astounded to see a familiar orange and black cardboard box laying inside. I yanked it out and opened it up, holding the contents to my face in disbelief.

"What is it?" Sy asked.

"A new pair of Nikes!" I said, pulling the box apart and turning the sneakers in my hands. "I thought these things were all long gone. I haven't seen a new pair in decades. I used to love this style!"

"That white is going to stain quickly with all this dirt," Sy pointed out.

I thought about that for a moment. "Well, sure. But I can still wear them when I go into town, perhaps. The condition is just incredible. I wonder how they found these?"

"I'm not sure how those shoes are better than just standard work boots," Sy said, clearly puzzled.

I felt just a tinge of irritation with Sy's questions. They were honest, and I had no legitimate reason for being upset, but still. I didn't like feeling impugned.

"Look, Sy, I know it's hard to understand, but objects like these hold a sentimental value for some of us from the Old World. They may not be entirely necessary or practical now, but we enjoy them, and in any case, it's just a pair of shoes. We have to be reasonable."

Sy seemed to realize that it was time to abandon his line of questioning, and went to opening the other crates.

It took the rest of the day just to itemize and organize all our supplies: there was a palette dedicated just to construction materials for the gardening shed, a simple but effective structure which we'd assemble together on the following day to store bags of fertilizer and gardening tools. For the remainder of the month, we tilled and prepared the soil, just as I had in La Unión decades ago.

One night, while I sat at my typewriter organizing notes from an old interview in Tokyo, I heard a strange noise coming from the shed. It was close to midnight, and a strong eastern wind was battering against the back of the residence building. The barometer that was nailed to the wall above my desk had dropped swiftly since the afternoon, and the air smelled like a storm. I didn't really want to go outside, but the noise from the shed was curious. I grabbed the electric lantern from off the hook in my room and slipped out the front door to investigate.

The wind was stronger than it had seemed from inside. I almost lost my balance as a sudden gust pushed from behind. I could now see that a light was on in the shed, a single bulb hanging from a wire that was linked to a solar panel on the roof. The bulb was spinning helplessly in the wind let in by the shed's open door, causing rays of light to dash wildly back and forth on the ground outside.

More noises, metal banging against something.

"Hello?" I called out warily. The noise stopped. I slowly rounded the doorway and peeked inside.

Sy was sitting on the ground in a tangle of multi-colored wires. "Hi," he said.

"Sy, you scared me half to death. I thought you were in your room. What on earth are you doing out here?"

"Working. I'm running out of time. I needed to finish this tonight."

"Finish what? What are you working on?"

"An idea I had."

"Why now? You do realize a storm is coming, don't you?"

"Tell me, brother Hanson, when you read 1 Corinthians 3:7, what do *you* think of?"

"What?"

"The scripture about Paul planting, and Apollo's watering–"

"Yes, I know the verse. God makes it grow."

"Yes, precisely. *Jehovah makes it grow*. I was thinking about it earlier this morning, while you were sleeping, and I think we may have been relying on ourselves too much lately with this project."

"Sy, that scripture is a reference to the ministry of the good news, not planting a vineyard."

"Of course, but the Apostle Paul was reasoning logically with a natural process as his illustration. Ultimately, Jehovah makes everything grow."

"OK, and?"

"Then why are we still using fertilizer? Have you read the labels on these bags? They're full of chemicals we don't see anywhere else, and I'm not entirely sure how safe they are."

"Sy, agricultural teams, including the ones your mother and father worked on for many years, all used this stuff. When it runs out, we probably will never make more, but in the meantime, it's here, so let's just use it and worry about other problems, OK?"

"Brother Hanson, most of the air in our atmosphere is nitrogen, about seventy-eight percent. The other twenty or so percent is oxygen, with a bit of hydrogen as well. These elements are combined in molecules floating around in our air.

"When storms like these occur, they often cause lightning. When lightning strikes, it generates immense amounts of energy, breaking the bonds of air molecules. When that happens, the individual atoms are released and free to bond with new atoms. These new bonds result in compounds like ammonium, nitrate, and nitrite. Those compounds then mix with water vapor, which, in a storm like the one about to land, usually becomes rain. When that rain falls on the soil, it fertilizes it. *Naturally.*"

I generally understood the process already, though I hadn't known the specifics as Sy had explained them. A frigid breeze blew in through the door and sent a shiver through my body. "Ok, I get that, but what does that have to do with all this?"

"Well, metal attracts lightning. If we can get the lightning to focus on the soil in the vineyard... Well, I don't know exactly what will happen, but it just seems more natural than spreading chemicals all over the ground. We're going to be drinking those grapes one day, after all..."

I had to admire the young man, sitting there in his giant knot of wire. He was just trying to do the right thing, after all. And here I was, a grumpy old curmudgeon, still stuck in my Old World ruts.

"You're right," I finally said. "Let's give this a shot."

Sy's face beamed as I sat down and helped him fasten the wire structure together. We squeezed it out of the shed door and stuck its pronged legs in the ground. Since it was only a rough framework, there wasn't much for the wind to blow against, and it managed to stand up without any problems.

"Let's get inside," I said. "It's probably not too safe to be standing next to this thing."

The first heavy droplets of rain rapped against the glass windows just as we were filing back into the building. I made us some ginger tea and we sat there in silence, watching the incoming storm.

"Did you really think of the lightning rod idea from First Corinthians?" I finally asked.

"You don't believe me?" There was a look of slight injury on Sy's face.

"No, it's not that. I know you were telling the truth, it's just... I wouldn't have put that together from just reading that verse. Not in a thousand years."

"Maybe it's because I recently read through Ezekiel's vision, you know, about the lighting going forth between the living creatures?"

"Yeah, still wouldn't have thought of it," I said with a laugh. "Sometimes I really wish I could get in your head, see the world the way you do."

There was a new look in Sy's eyes. A flash of distant lightning cast bright blue light over his face.

"That's quite ironic. I always feel the same about members of the Great Crowd."

"Oh? Why's that?" I refilled my cup of tea and wrapped a blanket around my legs.

"You were there on the other side. You faced all those trials. You were attacked my the most evil creature in the history of the universe, and you stood firm. You're here because you fought for it. But us genas... we were born into it."

"Are you saying you feel...unworthy?"

"Yes, I do. I've never been attacked. I've never been hated. I can't even imagine the horror of death or sickness. I've never felt that kind of pain in my life. I'm not sure I could handle it."

"You're worried about the end of the Thousand Years."

"I'm terrified."

Sy's sentence was punctuated by a stray bolt of lighting that dove from the stormy mass right behind the tree line not fifty meters from the wire tower. We waited for a second hit, but only rain fell.

"Well, Sy, your feeling is similar to the way a lot of our brothers and sisters felt before the Tribulation."

"How so? Those were the Last Days, life was difficult for

everyone, wasn't it?"

"That's true, but we knew the Tribulation would be the real trial. We knew it would be like nothing before it. A lot of us were scared then, too. We wondered, just like you, if we were going to make it through to the New World–this world."

"And?"

"And most did make it. The key was consistency. Luke 16:10. Those faithful in least..."

"...Are faithful also in much," Sy said, nodding.

"The ones who were doing the right thing before the Tribulation, making their meetings regularly, keeping a simple life, staying free of bad associations, going in field service often, they did just fine. It was the ones on the fringe that had it the toughest. Faith, endurance, and obedience don't sprout overnight. They're like the grapevines out there in that field. They take time to grow, to get strong, to be of value."

"But that's just it–I'm not going through any trials now. How do I know I'll be able to make it through the final test?"

"By looking at how you spend your life now."

"What do you mean?"

"Think about the direction we've been given in the New World. Just like the Garden of Eden, we don't have a lot of commands forbidding us from doing this or that. But we do have a series of tasks to complete. You and I both know that there are different levels of enthusiasm being displayed when it comes to completing these tasks. It takes hard work. Some are less willing than others to put forth that effort."

"Do you think they'll be the ones who follow Gog?"

"It's not my place to speculate. We'll have to wait and see. However, there has always been a link with working diligently in carrying out Jehovah's will and being saved. Noah and his family built the ark and lived to tell about the Flood. Jeremiah prophesied an unpopular message for over six decades and survived Jerusalem's destruction. First century Christians preached in spite of torture and death and are now ruling over all of mankind. You know these examples as well as I do. Industriousness and salvation are inseparable. Laziness, on the other hand..."

"The wicked and sluggish slave..." Sy said in a whisper.

"Exactly. The point is: *Don't bury your talent.*"

Another crack of a lightning, like the extended branch of an upside down tree, materialized from the storm and landed directly on the wire tower. A shower of sparks erupted from the structure, scattering and fading on the wet soil. Somehow, the tower managed to stay upright. In the next half hour, it would draw another four bolts.

"Thanks, Brother Hanson," Sy said. "I needed that."

I nodded, suppressing a yawn and pulling the blanket closer to my chest. It felt good, helping a gena like that.

Sy and I would continue to become close friends as the two years progressed. Unsurprisingly, he was adept at producing healthy, tasty crops of grapes, and when I finally left two and a half years later, he was ready to teach a team of novice vinedressers from Guangzhou, Old China.

Zhougan & Qiaomei

The man stands facing us on the road. He is an old man, from the Old World, with long wrinkles etched into his old face. His outstretched arm raises to the height of his shoulder, where we catch a glimpse of something small and black in his unclenched fist. We realize it is a seed.

The man drops the seed to the ground, where it falls into a neat hole in the soil next to the asphalt road. The background flutters with activity, winds come and go, clouds breeze in and out of the picture. But the man remains.

We see that the man is changing, ever so slightly, from one frame to the next. The grooves in his face and neck are fading. He appears to be growing, upward and outward. He stands straight now, and his hair is darkening and thickening.

The hole in the ground has become a mound, and the mound is producing a small green cord. The cords writhes upward, snaking toward the sun. The cord has a leaf, and now two, and now too many to count. The stem is thicker, then darker, and then it is a twig.

The road is changing, too. It is a more subtle change at first, detected only with careful observation, and then it spasms, as if alive, rippling and bending against the ground. Then it cracks. Green tongues lick at its wounds and shoot into the air. Some become flowers.

The man is still facing us. He is young, a boyish shadow of his former self. And then he stops changing.

The sprout is as high as the man's knee, and then his hip, and on it moves. Thicker, taller, stronger. It sprouts a branch, and another, and continues to expand. The man is now standing in its shade.

The road is almost invisible now, consumed in a sea of vegetation.

The sprout is a tree now. Several dozen bulbs erupt from its branches and grow, quickly, turning a vibrant green yellow.

The jittery picture becomes smooth. The man reaches for the fruit above him and takes a bite, smiling.

***

The lights glowed on in the room, revealing a half dozen faces staring at a blank wall. Then someone started clapping and we all joined in.

"Simply beautiful," said Myra. She had red hair and was dabbing her eyes with a handkerchief.

"How many years did that take?" Myra's husband asked. His name was Aiden. His arms were crossed and he wore a look of intent analysis.

"This is one of the older ones in the collection. We started photographing in N.E. 1 and filmed that final shot eleven years later."

"How did you do the clothes?" I asked.

"That was one of the trickier parts, actually. We wanted my outfit to stay the same throughout the time-lapse, so we had them specially made by a sister from here in Shanghai. She stored the material away and later made more garments to fit my growing proportions. The result is pretty convincing, eh?"

"Yeah," I said. "It really looks like the same outfit the whole time."

"Where did you get the idea?" Saveedra asked. Her head was tilted and her finger and thumb made the shape of an L against her jaw. She seemed mesmerized.

"My wife," Zhougan said.

Qiaomei shrugged with a sheepish smile. "I wanted to document the process of age reversal. At the time, no one really knew how long it would take. Some thought it was more or less the reversal of the biological clock, so if you were seventy-five, it would take fifty years or so to return to normal, peak bodily condition. But with our background in biology, Zhougan and I suspected it would be much faster. After all, it was simply a matter of generating new cell structures, and, in the case of wrinkles, getting the body to produce more collagen. It wouldn't likely take many years to see that kind of an effect."

"Or so we thought," Zhougan added. "Like Qiaomei said, we didn't really know, we were just making an educated guess."

Qiaomei was nodding. "Anyway, we thought that, just in case it took longer, we'd do the pictures of Zhougan standing next to a pear tree. Pear trees tend to be some of the slowest to produce fruit, so we were safe."

"But it didn't. Zhougan looked like a young man long before the tree had fully grown," Aiden said. He still had that look on his face.

"Right. Zhougan looked like a young man after just a few

months. However, if you watch carefully, you'll notice his posture continues to straighten as time passes. That's because bone cells don't restore themselves as quickly as skin cells."

Saveedra opened her mouth as if to say something, and then changed her mind. "What was the idea behind the road in the pictures?"

"We wanted to show the difference man and manmade. Perhaps, one day, we will be able to create as Jehovah does, with eternity in mind. At present, though, our creations are disposable, eventually overtaken by nature and outlived by us," Zhougan explained.

"So the road is a symbol for the Old World?" I asked.

"It's more than that," said Qiaomei. "It's a symbol for all we can achieve materially. Fleeting, temporary, ultimately meaningless."

"And the tree symbolizes Jehovah's creations?" Asked Aiden.

"Creation subordinate to mankind," Qiaomei corrected. "Unlike man, it dies as an individual, although it reproduces."

"Whew," said Myra, visibly overwhelmed. "I thought we were just looking at a tree and a road and a man!"

Then Aiden spoke, his voice triumphant. "It's brilliant. The time lapse begins right after the Old World, and captures its essence: The road is new and formidable, which is what we used to think of the things we accomplished. The man is old and frail–our weakened, imperfect condition coming into the New World. And the seedling, I guess that's like a new beginning. Not yet visible, but soon to bear fruit. And as time passes, the balance returns. Man is made perfect and strong, man's creation fades, and Jehovah's creation once again fills the Earth."

Zhougan and Qiaomei were nodding, pleased.

"Aiden has always been interested in art," Myra explained, as if to excuse her husband's excitement.

"We were the same, in the Old World. Never had time to study it, though. Not that our parents would allow it, of course. Chinese parents demanded that their children enter a profession that could guarantee wealth. That's why we studied medicine."

"What year was that?" I asked.

"I graduated from college in 2012, Qiaomei in 2013."

"Is that how you met?"

"Yes. We attended the same university here in Shanghai. The school was actually very close to where we are now. You could probably see it from these windows if it was still there."

"So your parents weren't Witnesses?" Myra asked.

"No, I'm afraid not. In fact, my father was a communist party member. It was considered disloyal to the party to have any religious affiliations. At the time, China wasn't really a communist country, though. It was pure capitalism, and many were getting rich off of the system."

Zhougan led us from the room around a corner, where a similar space had been sectioned off with white walls. He dimmed the lights and pressed a button. Colorful lights danced on the far wall and fused into a clear image. An Old World cityscape.

"This photograph was taken less than one kilometer from where we now stand, facing East. You can see here the waterfront, the famous Pearl Tower, and a few other landmarks from Old Shanghai. This isn't my picture, but it's a fortunate find, because it's one of the few pictures that remains from the city right before Armageddon. I found it in an old travel brochure in the wreckage of a hotel. This is the first slide in this time lapse." John pressed another button, and the images began flickering by.

The sky was clogged with smoke that glowed orange from the fires of the buildings below. The fires disappeared after the first few slides, leaving the city scape charred and deformed.

"Each frame you see here was taken at the same time each morning. I would climb up to the rooftop of an old warehouse and snap a picture on a camera attached to a tripod that never moved. I built a little canopy above it and covered the camera when I wasn't there, just to protect it from the elements. Everything you're seeing now is part of the first year. But you'll notice, in a minute, how things start to change..."

Everyone took a slight step forward, peering at the images flicker by. The sky began to change colors, from a lifeless, featureless charcoal to a greyish green color, and, eventually, to a deep, clear blue. The water was changing, too. And then there were new colors, flashes of orange, blue, and green at the base of the buildings.

I realized that these were tents, similar to the ones we'd used in Baltimore.

Then the buildings began to disappear. I almost thought I'd imagined it when it first occurred, it was so abrupt and absolute. But then it occurred again, and then again.

"Demolition crews..." I said.

"That's right. They brought down the big buildings first, the ones that posed the biggest safety risk," Zhougan said.

"We had a lot of foreign crews coming in from Japan and Korea for that initial phase of the clean up. Chinese building materials were so poor that the Organization gave top priority to demolitions in the major cities here. It was estimated that they'd pose three times more of a safety risk than the abandoned skyscrapers of other countries."

The buildings in the time lapse had all but completely vanished now. Myra let out little gasps of glee with each disappearance, as if watching a delightful little trick.

Finally, the ground was flat, but for a few solitary buildings on the waterfront, no doubt for lodging and storage. Sailboats and barges now filled the frame, zipping here and there as the days wound on. The ground was now slowly turning green. In some of the images, large flocks of birds would materialize for the slightest moment, only to disappear again in the next frame.

Now came the houses, which I knew, from experience, would be for the agricultural learners. It was certainly too early for anything else. I glanced at the timestamp and noticed that it was now twenty-six years into the New World. A line of houses zigzagged across the plains, followed by neat patches of tilled earth. The earth burst with vegetation. Dots of workers were scattered among the fields, and then vanished. The vegetation retreated slightly, and the cycle renewed.

With time, a larger building here and there scrambled to its feet. No doubt assembly halls, museums, archives, and schools. Possibly some were hotels. I wondered if any of what I was seeing was designed by Kiro Ushihara.

The time lapse froze on the last frame, and, as in the previous room, merged into a few seconds of video. Windsurfers swept by in the foreground as a flock of seagulls drifted out of sight. The sea was clean and restful. Workers milled around in the fields. A hot air balloon descended in the background.

"You can barely tell it's the same place," Saveedra said. "I wouldn't have believed it if I hadn't seen the process here."

"Again, how did you even think to do this?" Myra said. Her hands were on her hips and she was shaking her head. Her curly hair was bouncing gently against her shoulders.

"This one was all Zhougan's idea," Qiaomei said, beaming at her husband. "I thought he was crazy, hiking out to that dirty old building each morning, but I'm glad he did. It's a reminder of how far we've come."

"Every time I watch this video, I'm shocked and repulsed by how dirty the Old World was. And then I remember that on some days, the air was so unbreathable that the news told us to *stay indoors*! To not to go work! It was dangerous just to *breathe*." Zhougan was shaking his head. "In the end, some Chinese companies were actually selling compressed oxygen tanks for personal use. It was becoming a big industry."

"That's just incredible," said Aiden. "It never got quite that bad in Australia, but then of course we had UV radiation and sweltering temperatures to worry about."

"Don't forget the hurricanes," Myra whispered.

"I haven't," Aiden retorted.

"How did you two learn the truth?" I asked the Chinese couple.

"There were a lot of Witnesses in Shanghai at the time. They came from all over: Japan, Korea, America, Russia, all over Western Europe, and so on. I was first contacted by a brother from Sydney. His Chinese wasn't so good, but I was also majoring in English, so we studied in that language," Zhougan said.

"I remember hearing a news report way back about most Chinese being atheists. Was that true?" Asked Saveedra.

"It was true, although some would argue that the Chinese viewed money as their deity. That's how I was when I first met Donald. I thought: *Another superstitious Westerner trying to make us Chinese believe in a mythological God.*"

"What changed your mind?"

"I remember a conversation Donald and I had in a McDonald's. I proudly stated that I would 'never believe in God'.

"Donald asked, 'Why?'

"'Because I believe in science, of course.'

"'That's good,' Donald said. 'Science helps us to know the truth about our environment and the universe we live in.'

"I was surprised that we agreed on that point.

"'I, for one, am thankful for all the progress science has brought us in the fields of medicine, biology, and astronomy, to name a few.'

"I didn't know what to say, so I just shook my head. Donald continued:

"'I especially like the way scientists think: make a hypothesis, test it, and then make a decision based on the results.'

"'It's the only scientific method,' I stated.

"'Right, and it's the way the Bible teaches us to think.'

"'Really?' I said, unable to hold back my curiosity.

"Donald showed me a verse on his iPad: Romans 12:2. *Quit being fashioned after this system of things, but be transformed by making your mind over, that you may prove to yourselves the good and acceptable and perfect will of God.*

"'You see, the Bible teaches that believing in things blindly is not only foolish, but harmful. To protect ourselves, we must train our thinking ability. Like a scientist, we must compare what we believe with established fact. Do you agree?'

"'But how can you say that? You believe in an invisible God. That is not an established fact.'

"'If I agreed to only use established scientific facts to discuss my belief in a Creator, would you agree to discuss the possibility?'

"It sounded reasonable, although I wanted to laugh at the idea of someone using *science* to prove *God*.

"But Donald kept his word. In the next hour or so, I came to realize that Donald's knowledge of biology was equivalent to that of some of my professors. He was able to explain, in detail, the structure of a cell and the production of proteins and DNA. He used the *Origin of Life* brochure as a basis for our discussion, and I'd never seen such complex topics explained with such clarity. I realized that I needed to refine my viewpoint of him. He was not uneducated or superstitious in the least. In all honesty, I began to feel a little insecure about my knowledge of the subject I was supposed to be majoring in, especially when he asked if I remembered studying the things we were discussing.

"'More or less' was my answer.

"It was the first discussion of many I would have with Donald. I began to see that my science textbooks had left out important details regarding the origin of life and the ability of a species to change over time. The more I learned about established science, the more angry I became with my university. After all, my lessons with Donald were free, whereas my school was charging me tens of thousands of yuan in tuition and dormitory fees."

"When did you finally start believing in a Creator?" I asked.

"Although the scriptures and prophecies and scientific evidence Donald showed me were all very persuasive, I felt my life was already on the right track, and I didn't want to disrupt my future or upset my parents. It wasn't until I left school and began working that I realized the world had nothing to offer me worth wanting. That's when I started taking my study more seriously, started praying, and really starting believing in Jehovah."

"And what about you, Qiaomei?"

"I first learned about the Witnesses from Zhougan. We were dating at the time. I thought he was a little crazy for studying religion when his parents were party members and had done a lot to secure his education. But I didn't try to stop him. I figured it was a phase that he'd eventually get tired of. But the opposite happened. I remember that he started talking more and more about what he was learning, and he kept saying how much it made sense, and that I should start studying too.

"Eventually I met Donald's wife, Carrie, and we went through the same discussions Zhougan and Donald had. But I was probably a little easier to convince that Zhougan. I always had a feeling that *something* was out there, even though I was like most young Chinese and I didn't particularly like religion or the idea of a God. Also, I was most concerned with my future, being a successful doctor and one day a wife and mother.

"Carrie was able to show me so much from the Bible that made sense, and when I tried the principles, they worked. Before then, I was used to the nebulous thinking of Chinese philosophy where nothing could be proven as right or wrong. When I started to read the Bible, the clarity of the teachings was just amazing. And like Zhougan said, it was all free. Anyone could read it and use it. That equality really appealed to me. Justice in Old China was scarce, and everything had a price tag. The Bible's message was refreshing."

"Did you get a lot of opposition from your parents when they found out what you were learning?" I asked Zhougan.

"Yes, but not at first. At first they supported my discussions with Donald. They thought it was good for me to learn about Western culture and practice my English for free. But after awhile, they saw that I was changing my mind on certain issues, like my view of the Chinese government, nationalism, materialism, morals, and my goals for the future. That's when they tried to stop my study."

"But they weren't successful..." Aiden surmised.

"They made a lot of threats, telling me that as a Chinese I could only get ahead in the world if I used the Chinese system, even if I didn't like certain parts of it. They insisted that Westerners like Donald couldn't possibly understand the complexities of our culture. He was, after all, from a country with less than three hundred years of history, whereas China had been around for much, much longer.

"When that tactic failed, they pressured me in other ways. They even forced me to attend extracurricular biology seminars. They wanted to occupy as much of my time as possible so I wouldn't be able to meet with Donald. Interestingly, however, their plan backfired. The more I learned about biology, the more I reaffirmed my belief in a Creator. And I used the opportunity to share my beliefs with other attendees, a handful of whom later studied with our brothers and sisters as well."

"What about you, Qiaomei? Did you face any opposition?"

"Not from my parents. They didn't care much about my personal beliefs, so long as I pursued a career in medicine and found a rich husband. My father and mother were both doctors in a prestigious hospital in Beijing and expected me to follow in their footsteps.

"After getting my Ph.D., I was able to get a job at the hospital where Zhougan worked. But it wasn't anything like I had expected all those years."

"How so?"

"First, the pay wasn't very good. At the time, so many young Chinese were graduating from medical schools that the profession was flooded with new doctors. What the hospitals really wanted wasn't kids with Ph.D.'s, but with staff with experience in medicine: medical technicians, surgeons, physical therapists, and so on. Most of these young doctors only knew general practice medicine. It was a competitive field, unlike the previous generation where doctors were paid well for their scarcity."

"And that wasn't the biggest problem," Zhougan said. "The thing that really bothered us was the corruption." Qiaomei was nodding grimly. "I remember one day an old woman carried a small child into my office. The child's eyes had rolled back into his head so that only the whites were showing and his body was shaking slightly. It looked like a seizure, and I immediately began to examine him. The old woman crouched next to the examination table, rocking back and forth. I asked her how long the boy had had these symptoms.

"'He shakes like this every few days. It started when he began taking the medicine.'

"'What medicine?'

"The woman pulled a small vial from insider her coat jacket and dropped it into my hand. I could tell that it was fake. It was a cheap imitation drug, probably purchased because she couldn't afford the real thing.

"'Where did you buy this?' I asked.

"'Downstairs.'

"'In this hospital?'

"'Yes.'

"I told her to stop taking the medicine, that it was probably doing more damage than good. She nodded mournfully and wiped her eyes. I told her that the boy needed to get the chemicals out of his system, and that he should rest for a few days. I asked what the boy had originally been taking medication for.

"'A flu,' said the woman.

"I wasn't quite sure if I could believe the woman's story or not as I took the elevator down to the pharmaceutical floor of the hospital. I showed the bottle to the receptionist and explained the woman's story. She called the senior pharmacist over and he led me into his back office.

"'Is this pharmacy really selling fake drugs?'

"'Zhougan, fake drugs are everywhere. Even in reputable hospitals.'

"'Wouldn't we be shut down, or fined, or something, for selling them?' I asked.

"'I wouldn't worry about it,' he said, lighting a cigarette.

"'I've never heard of a fake drug causing such a serious side effect in a flu patient, though. Doesn't that worry you?'

"'Not really. I don't make the drugs. Look, Zhougan, you have to look at this situation realistically. These peasants that come in here can barely afford the bus fare here. They're living in poverty. They're sick. Their kids are sick. Everyone's sick. Today it's the flu, tomorrow tuberculosis. They can't afford appropriate treatment, so we give them what we can. We have to worry about helping the ones that can help us.'

"'What does that mean?'

"'It means you have to care for the ones that matter.'

"'By giving better treatment to the rich ones.'

"'Of course. Or do you expect to live on your current salary until you retire?'

"'It's enough.'

"'Not enough to put your kid through college, or get him a house when Shanghai property prices continue to rise. How do you think I got here? I took the right patients. They buy their place in line, we get them healthy.'

"'I don't like it,' I finally said.

"'Who does? But the system is here, we have to make use of it. And–what's this?'

"I handed him a scribbled piece of paper from my white coat pocket.

"'It's a prescription for the boy.'

"'And who's paying for it?'

"'I will.'

"He just glared at me. Then he touched it to the end of his cigarette, where it singed and disintegrated. 'No,' he said. I was speechless.

"'One day you'll thank me. All you first-year doctors are the same. You think you can come in here and right the system. Save your time. Look after your own. Or do you think that old woman will be the last one? No, I'll tell you about reality. You give her free meds and she'll weep and thank you and bow at your feet. And you'll feel like a real hero. But then she'll go back to her dirty little village and bring back more sick people. They'll crowd into your office and ask for more free treatment. And maybe, in the process, bring a few diseases with them. Maybe get you sick. And then, you can explain to the hospital management how you were just trying to do a good deed.'

"'It's worth a try.'

"'No, it's not. If you plan on giving out free medication, go find another hospital to practice medicine at. Or I'll see to it that you're removed from our staff. I don't want beggars in these halls.' And with a wave of his hand, he dismissed me from his office.

""I later found it wasn't just our hospital, malpractice was everywhere. Some poor patients died from purposeful misdiagnosis or taking the wrong medications. They had no real power to complain, either, or file a lawsuit as Westerners would, and so the atrocities just kept happening."

"We were silent for a few moments. I imagined that each of us was remembering our slice of the Old World with all its darkness and iniquity.

Qiaomei pressed a button, and a new image appeared on the wall: a small boy with dark skin and no legs.

Qiaomei pressed play.

The Welcome Center

"OK, so the rooms are all located on the top floors of the Center... If you look here at the side view, you can see that the front end of the rooms, which is plate glass, is slanted slightly forward, which will give them a better view of the waterfront," the man was gesturing to the paper using the back of his drafting pencil.

"That's good. Very peaceful."

"Right, the water is an integral part of this design."

"Will they be able to see the harbor?"

"According to the way we've positioned the building, no. We were afraid it'd get too hot in the rooms if the windows were facing directly East."

"That's sensible. And they feed into the hallway, here?" The man jabbed a stocky finger into the paper.

"Actually each room has a separate hallway. We're thinking we can decorate each hallway with something familiar to the individual. Perhaps we can theme them culturally," Iva said. She was the lead interior designer and, as such, was in charge of decorations.

"I see your point, but let's not get too carried away with it. It's just a walkway. The focus should be on the receptionary. And that is—" He trailed off, eyes roving over the schematics. Todd peeled the page back, revealing a floor plan for a different part of the building.

"This is the receptionary. Anise, can you show him the color rendering?" The tall woman glided across the room, producing a cardboard tube from her carrying case and unrolling its contents on the large, oak table.

"Thanks. So," Todd continued, "here you can see how the textures and colors will come together. We want this to feel very natural, so we'd like to use lots of earthy tones and textures. You can see the ground is slate and mortar, the walls are roughly-cut red bricks."

"Is this a window?"

"No, that's an open balcony. You can see the bannister better in this shot—wrought iron."

Anise was still standing behind Todd's shoulder and leaned forward to say, "According to our current plans, this balcony will be facing southwest. It's currently occupied by a few vineyards and wheat fields."

"Huh," the man said, rubbing his chin. "And the plants here?"

Todd motioned for me to step forward and explain. "Yes, those are Chinese wisteria. It's a kind of flowering vine indigenous to the area. In the rendering here, it's suspended from a stained wood trellis."

"Again, we're trying to emphasize the natural element here," Todd said. I thought back to my Old World career selling insurance to large corporations. Todd would've been good at that job. He was very convincing.

The visiting overseer flipped back and forth over the diagrams and renderings with little grunting noises. We held our breaths.

"Well, brothers and sisters," he finally said, "I can't see any reason to change these plans. With the amount of glass you've got here, and these outdoor patio receptionaries, it looks like artificial light will be kept to a minimum, which is good. I still have to confirm the blueprints with the overseers to give it the go ahead, of course. But I'm really happy with what you've come up with."

An audible sigh of relief went around the room. We'd been working on the plans for the Shanghai Welcome Center for almost a year and had been fretting over endless details.

We wanted everything to be perfect.

The plot of land for the residences had already been cleared. These buildings would be based on a series of plans that another team had put together months earlier for the Beijing Welcome Center. They'd worked some cultural flair into the designs, but practicality had always been the reigning factor, and the houses would be built for comfort and longevity.

My time in Shanghai had been busy. While I had been originally assigned there to monitor the local wildlife, I was later switched to interior botany, working with architects and other designers to put together sturdy, attractive complexes like the one we were currently designing.

Being busy was good for me. I still hadn't received any resurrection notices from the RWC and was beginning to feel anxious.

"Don't worry," Todd told me the evening after we'd met with the project overseer to pitch our plans for the Welcome Center. "It'll come. Just be patient and rely on Jehovah."

Easier said than done. Todd's wife had made it with him through Armageddon, and his parents had been resurrected the year before. *It was the happiest moment of my life*, Todd later told me. More than anything, I wanted to have that moment, too.

***

"Todd, what would you say is the greatest personal change you've undergone since the New World began?" I asked. We were sitting on the back porch of his house, a raised wooden deck with a perfect view of the sunset.

Todd mulled over the question for a few minutes before replying. "Maturity," he finally said.

"How?"

"I've come to realize that there are many ways to get from A to B. Not just Todd's way. I've learned that I'm still not perfect, and that even when I am, I will still be able to learn from a small child. And I've learned that Jehovah truly knows what's best all of the time. What about you?"

"I've changed in many ways. I sometimes imagine that my family won't even recognize me when they come back."

"I don't think that's likely..."

"No, I don't mean physically."

"Then what?"

"Spiritually," I said.

"Well, we've all grown spiritually."

"Todd, when Armageddon started, I was terrified. I was literally shaking from fear and shame. I didn't think I was going to make it."

Todd face was blank, neither surprised nor dismissive.

"The truth is, I hadn't been that strong during the Last Days and I wasn't much better during the Tribulation. I'd been so concerned with securing my position with the company and running every which way to make the year-end bonuses... And then, after my family died in that crash, I hit an all time low. I'd never been so despondent in my life. I came very close to ending it all.

"And then, suddenly, the Great Day came and I was standing on the other side. I couldn't believe it. I still remember that first meeting I went to, in the New World. Everyone was crying and singing and celebrating and congratulating one another. But there were some that saw me and just sort of stared. As if to say, '*He* made it?'

"To be honest, that was one of my reasons for joining the traveling crews. I felt like it was time for a clean slate, a perfect way to reinvent myself. And when I look back, I barely recognize my old self."

"Well, it's the *now* that counts."

"Sure, and I understand that Jehovah isn't looking at the old me anymore. I get that. But what about my family? When they see me, they'll only know that version of me. I failed them. As a father and as a husband. Emma tried to help me. So many times, when the company would tell me to go on these business trips, she'd beg me not to go, and tell me how sad Jacob would get whenever I left, sometimes for weeks at a time. I didn't understand then, of course. *I'm doing this for you!* I'd think. Emma had always wanted to pioneer, and I figured she'd never be able to reach that goal if I didn't stretch myself a little further to provide.

"And then of course there was the accident. On their way to pick me up from the airport, of all things. It had been raining, the road was slick, and I'm sure Emma was exhausted. I had caught a red-eye flight from London. And for some reason, she brought Jacob along with her. Just wanted to see his Dad, I guess. It had been a long trip.

"When the paramedics arrived at the scene, there was nothing that could be done. The semi had completely demolished our SUV. When the fireman pried the wreckage open to remove what was left of them, they found a little gift box with my name on it. I'd missed our anniversary while in London. Emma had bought me a new watch."

Todd let out a sigh. He'd never heard my story.

"And you know the worst part of it all?" I said.

Todd shook his head.

"When my wife didn't show up at the airport, I thought she forgot about me. I called her cellphone, which was dead, and was so upset with her. She had a habit of forgetting to charge her phone, you see. So I just kept calling, not knowing what to do, and getting more and more irritated. I even left a few angry voicemails...I..."

"Mitch, you had no way of knowing–"

"But that's not the point. The point was that it was my fault. I don't mean the accident was–I know that was time and unforeseen occurrence. But me, going out of town like that constantly, neglecting my family–if any one should have been irritated with the situation, it was my family.

"Anyway, I finally had to catch a cab all the way home, about forty-five minutes. When I finally got to the house, I was furious. I stomped up the front steps and that's when I saw the note from the Atlanta Police Department. I called right away and heard the news. I can't even begin to describe how awful I felt."

Todd slipped his arm around my shoulder.

At the horizon, the sky was a bright pink that fed back into a cool indigo. Orange cirrus clouds had strung themselves from north to south. A silhouetted flock of birds took to the air and were forming into a slanted *V*. Probably Chinese bulbuls, I thought.

Finally Todd said, "I can't say I know a lot about the

resurrection. I don't think anyone does, yet. It's still so new. But I have a hard time imagining that your family will judge you as harshly as you've judged yourself. I think they'll just be happy to be alive, here, with you. And they'll be thrilled to hear all your experiences. And I think it's brilliant that you've kept a record of everything you've been through. In the future, the Great Crowd will make up such a small percentage of humanity. These memories, and all the work that's going on now–that has to be preserved. I think you've made the most of your time here, Mitch.
Don't worry about the rest."

"Yeah," I said. "I know you're right. Still..."

But before I could finish, a bike courier called up to us from Todd's backyard.

The Notice

"Sorry to bother you brothers," the young man called up from the ground twenty feet below. "But is there a *Mitch Hanson* here?"

"Yes, I'm he," I said, getting up and descending the staircase.

"Finally!" The boy said. "The RTC has had a *real* time trying to track you down. You move a lot, huh? You should see the rerouting stamps on here–Seoul, South Jeju, Pudong, and finally here in Shanghai."

"I suppose I do move a lot," I said anxiously, trying to get a look at the package in his hands.

"Well, anyway, glad we finally found you. Here you go," he said, handing me a thin envelope.

"Thanks," I said. The courier jumped back onto his bicycle and pedaled up the driveway, whistling. I watched him go, wanting to savor every moment of it. I knew, without even looking at the sender's address, what was inside. It was the same size and type that Valeriya and Darya had received years ago, the exact same envelope that so many had preserved in glass cases in their houses.

It was a resurrection notice.

Todd was gripping the bannister of the porch above me, watching in silence. He knew, too.

"Uh, Todd, I think I'm gonna open this back at my place."

"No problem, Mitch. Let me know what it says, ok?"

"Uh-huh."

I walked back to my beachfront cabin, seeing everything with new eyes. There would be so much to explain. Jacob, especially, would be full of questions. I could only smile as I heard his quizzical voice bouncing in my ears. And then there was Emma. Oh, Emma. I held the envelope tightly under my arm. My hands, I noticed, were slightly damp.

I flipped on the solar lantern and the room filled with orange light in the little wood cabin which smelled of cedar. I sat down in my red leather recliner and took a deep breath. Then, after a brief prayer, I tugged at the paper tear cord of the envelope and reached inside.

"Dear Mitch Hanson,

"The Atlanta branch would like to thank you for your tireless efforts in the restoration and rebuilding efforts. We have been in close contact with your overseers, all of whom have mentioned your name with commendation and gratitude. For decades, you have displayed the attitude of Isaiah, who when commissioned by Jehovah God replied, "Here I am! Send me." (Isa 6:8)

"Therefore, we are extremely pleased to inform you that your son, Jacob Riley Hanson, and his Mother, Emma Kate Trenton, are to be resurrected on N.E. 59.

"As you may know, the branch typically determines the location for such resurrections. However, we have decided to make an exception in your case, since you have served in many different areas and possibly would prefer to have your family resurrected in a place other than your Old World hometown.

"Therefore, we have provided available resurrection dates with locations nearby your current assignment in Jeju island. Please choose from among these locations. Once you have decided, you may either respond by post or by direct radio line. The frequencies for our transceiver stations are listed on the next page.

"Available resurrection locations and dates:

"Osaka Welcome Center

"Iyyar 1-13, 17, 19 / Tammuz 12-22, 25, 29 / Ab 3, 9, 17, 18, 20-22

"Tokyo Welcome Center

"Nisan 2-5, 18-25 / Iyyar 1-10, 14-20 / Sivan 4-22 / Tammuz 1-7, 9-24 / Ab 4-19, 22-24 / Elul 3-6, 14-19, 23-25

"Seoul Welcome Center

"Nisan 9-12, 16 / Sivan 12-14 / Iyyar 19-23 / Ab 2-10 / Tishri 8-10, 14, 19, 22, 25

"Qingdao Welcome Center

"Iyyar 15-18, 22 / Sivan 20 / Tammuz 19-23, 28 / Elul 8-11 / Tishri 2-4, 7-12, 19, 22

"Shanghai North Welcome Center

"Nisan 5 / Iyyar 19-22 / Sivan 17, 20, 23, 25 / Tammuz 16, 17 / Ab 1, 19

"Shanghai South Welcome Center

"Sivan 4-25 / Tammuz 4-9, 17 / Ab 2-4, 9-12, 15 / Elul 3-19, 21-29

There were a few more locations on the list, but when I saw the Shanghai South entry, I froze. That was the center I was *helping design!*

***

"So, what's the news?" Todd asked with a big smile the next day as we walked into the drafting office.

"They're letting me choose the date and location," I said.

"What year?"

"Fifty-nine."

Todd bit his lip. "The year we finish the South Center."

"Yeah, it's incredible. I didn't know they scheduled resurrections for places that haven't even been finished yet."

"Yeah, well now we *really* have a deadline... Although that word seems... a little ill-fitting," Todd winked.

I made the call on the office radio and picked the date: Sivan 5th, the May of our Old World calendar. The grape harvest would just be beginning and I could spend the summer teaching Jacob about vineyards, even if he was a little young to enjoy the wine. Maybe we could bottle his first batch and drink it when he was a little older?

Conditions on the sea were comfortable at that time of year too, with just enough of a breeze to make sailing in the bay the perfect way to spend a free afternoon. There would be so many people that would want to meet them, so many friends from both the Old World and New. I was grinning just thinking about it, and it was still twenty months away.

After I ended my call, a transmission came through from the local branch.

"Plans look good, Todd. Send us your materials inventory and we'll get it started for you. How many workers you need?"

"Ah, we've got a crew of about thirty finishing up residences on the north side, plus another dozen local workers. But we're gonna need more, especially without the cranes."

"You haven't heard about Kenya?"

"Heard what?"

"Some brothers there just developed a new fuel system for heavy machinery. Clean, renewable, and easy to install. Dozers, forklifts, and cranes are all back to work, so long as they haven't fallen apart. I'll call up the branch there and see if they can't send you some machines."

"Wow, that'd be great, thanks."

"Don't mention it. Oh, and tell Mitch I heard the good news. Can't wait to meet them."

233

"He'll appreciate that, Jack."

"All right, I'll let you folks get back to work. I know you'll be busy from here on out."

"Nothing we can't handle."

"I know that too. Take care."

The signal clicked off.

Plans

Over the next few months, sleep was evasive. I pushed myself to the limit each day, often working into the night after my colleagues had retired. Though I returned home exhausted, flopping onto my mattress in a pile of lifeless limbs, I found it impossible to shut my mind off. There were so many things that I needed to tell my family, and still so many tasks I needed to complete to prepare for their arrival.

I thought a lot about Jacob's room.

I'd kept some photographs from our old house–the one we'd lived in together in Atlanta half a century ago. They were faded and ragged, but they preserved important details that helped me design the room. Jacob hadn't been a materialistic kid: he preferred romping around outdoors to playing video games or preoccupying himself with other electronic devices, something for which Emma and I had always been grateful.

But if there was one *thing* Jacob loved, it was his skateboard. On any given afternoon, he'd either be riding it or tinkering with it in the garage. That had always fascinated me–at just seven years old, he seemed to possess a mechanical mind, and enjoyed working with my tools in our garage.

But skateboards weren't easy to come by in the New World. Some of the Great Crowd children had ridden them shortly after Armageddon, just as the cleaning work was beginning. They'd sometimes cruise around in the empty streets, running errands for us as we worked the Salvage crews. But with the passage of time those kids grew up and their boards were nowhere to be found. But if I was going to really make Jacob's room just right, the skateboard was a detail I couldn't miss.

Then I remembered Scottie Lorenzo. Scottie and Jacob had been best friends before the accident. Scottie and his family had lived in our neighborhood and we'd been in the same congregation. If anyone knew where a New World dad might find an Old World skateboard, it might be Scottie. After some searching, I was able to track him down. By some incredible coincidence, he was in Guangzhou, Old China, where his entire family had been working on temporary residences for the resurrected. Guangzhou was a several-day journey by sailboat, and since we were ahead of schedule with the Shanghai South Welcome Center, I decided to take a couple weeks off to visit the Lorenzos in person.

Guangzhou bore similarities to Shanghai, but for its slightly more tropical flora and warmer climate. In fact, it reminded me Hawaii, right down to its colorful array of tropical birds and towering banyans. I wondered about Hawaii. After another quarter of a century in the New World, could it have possibly improved?

I also thought back to my time with Sameer Sengupta when I first learned to cultivate grapes in La Unión. His tales right after Armageddon had depicted Guangzhou with a smoky, grey skyline and crippled, jagged buildings on the brink of collapse. It was, of course, nothing like that now. The harbor was tidy and peaceful. The land was groomed and cultivated. The sky was fresh and clear.

There were a few buildings. One of them stretched placidly across the beachfront, as if hoping for a suntan. Its white walls were interrupted by tall windows with red shutters and dark green canvas awnings. I wondered if it might be the Welcome Center. It reminded me of the buildings in La Unión, and I thought about that place, too, imagining what it looked like after several more decades. And that was the beauty of living forever. You really *could* do everything you wanted to.

Cory and Alisha Lorenzo were waiting for me on the dock when I sailed in. They'd made a sign with my name on it and were bouncing and waving on the bobbing platform. It was good to be welcomed into an area by someone I'd known from before. I realized that it was a first, and was a little surprised to find tears welling in my eyes. It wasn't that I ever felt like a stranger in any of the areas I'd been to. The brotherhood truly was one big family. Still, it was nice to see familiar faces.

"You look great, Mitch!" Cory said as he cupped his hand around my shoulder. "Young, strong, nice tan." I laughed a little. It was funny because we all looked that way at this point. 'A globe full of fashion models in their prime,' as someone had described it.

"So do you guys. Where's Scottie?"

Alisha chuckled, "Oh, he goes by Scott now. Haven't heard 'Scottie' in... it feels like forever. He's waiting for us."

My old friends led me from the pier and over to a metal stand lined with colorful bicycles. Public use bicycles had become common, and most small towns had stands on every corner.

"How long have you guys been here?" I asked as we pedaled

down a magnolia-lined road.

"Over twenty years now. We left Atlanta a decade after Armageddon and moved to Mexico, then here," Alisha explained.

"What about you?" Cory asked.

"I've been all over," I said, listing the places I'd been to and some of the assignments I'd had, up to my current task in Shanghai.

Cory let out a whistle, "You've been busy. We would've loved to have left immediately after the Great Day, but Scott was so young then. Looking back though, it was the best thing for us."

"So, when are Emma and Jacob coming back?" Alisha asked.

"Four more months," I said, barely believing it. I hadn't seen them in fifty-eight years.

"What's left to be done on the Center?"

"Almost everything is completed, actually. The floors went in last week, all the plumbing is working. We're just waiting on furniture and plants now, and some of the room decorations."

"And your house? Is everything ready?"

"Just about. We'll be living in a joint family complex. The other couple are good friends of mine. We met years ago in Tokyo, and they've got a small boy, eight years old. I thought it'd be good for Jacob to have a friend. And of course, Emma will have her own cottage on the complex, until she decides what to do."

"So you stayed single all these years?" Alisha asked.

"To be honest, remarriage never appealed to me. There have been lots of great single sisters along the way, but I was content as a bachelor. I needed time to think and mature, and all I've really wanted all these years was to see my family. Even if Emma isn't my wife anymore, she'll always be my boy's mom–that makes us family. I never really considered it any other way."

The bend in the road descended into an open plain dotted with lychee trees. Clump clusters of the aromatic red fruit clung from their branches. Alisha stopped briefly to pull a bunch from one of the lower-hanging branches. She placed the fruit in the basket above her front wheel and continued on.

At the bottom of the hill, the road forked. A white, wooden sign was painted with curvy, red letters: L-O-R-E-N-Z-O. We turned left. Moments later their house came into view. A young couple was sitting on a purple swing bench on a porch that wrapped around the colonial-style house. A white tiger and its three cubs were sprawled out on the steps next to them.

"Scottie?" I said, forgetting what his mother had told me about the name change.

"Brother Hanson!" His hair was still red and wild, but he was a man now. "It's been so long, I'd almost forgotten what you looked like! I think I was what, eight when I last saw you?"

"That sounds about right," I said, a little distracted. Looking at him, all I could think of was Jacob.

"This is my wife, Xiaoli," Scott said.

***

We feasted that night on old favorites from our past—bean chili topped in sharp cheddar cheese and sour cream, honey cornbread, coleslaw, and strawberry cheesecake. Every bite was impossibly delicious. In the corner of the dining room, a wind-up phonograph spun a jazz vinyl.

"Salvaged from the Old World?" I asked Cory as I wiped crust crumbs from my mouth.

"No, actually. A brother here in Guangzhou makes them by hand."

"Really?" I got up from the table and examined the machine. An intricate hummingbird had been carved into each side of the mahogany base. The brass horn was gleaming and spotless. The record spun evenly with the rotating handle.

"It's just gorgeous. And the music?"

"A fleshly brother and sister from Australia. We met them back in Mexico while they were writing the music. They sent us this finished record a few months ago," Scott explained. I realized it had been awhile since I'd heard recorded music, and found myself as amused by it as my ancestors had probably been at the turn of two centuries prior.

There were lots of things to marvel at in this house. A baffling three-dimensional painting hung from the wall above the couch in the living room. It came from some friends in Africa who had visited several years back. A vertical maze of cross-sections of bamboo was fixed to another wall in the dining room. Water trickled its way down the structure, turning wheels and moving levers as it climbed, on its own power, back to the top. A sister in Florida was making them, Cory said.

But the greatest marvel in all the rooms of that house was Scottie. The red-headed kid from our neighborhood back in Atlanta. The kid that once convinced my little Jacob to 'rescue' a family of toads from the lake and give them a new home in our guest bathtub. The kid that had raced Jacob down the hill on a cardboard box placed precariously on a pair of skateboards. The kid that had now turned into a calm, perfect young man.

"What is it?" He asked. I'd been staring.

"I'm just thinking about how strange it'll be when Jacob sees you."

"Yeah, I've been thinking about that too. Ever since you contacted us," Cory said from the kitchen. He was washing the dishes with Xiaoli.

"This whole resurrection thing... It's still pretty unreal, huh?" Alisha said, cleaning up the last plates from the table. "I wonder if we'll ever get used to the idea."

"I hope not," Scott said. "We need to remember how special it is. I never want to take it for granted."

"You know, Scott, I was wondering if there's something you could help me with," I began.

He wore a look of intrigue as he leaned forward in his recliner. "Sure."

"You remember when you and Jacob used to play in our neighborhood, as kids, right?"

"Sure."

"You remember how you both used to skateboard a lot?"

"I do."

"Well, I've been trying to get a hold of a board, you know, for my son's room. I'd like it to be there when he comes home."

Scott leaned back and rubbed his face. "Hmm," he finally said. "I haven't seen a skateboard in decades. You checked with storage?"

"Yeah, I've made calls all over the place. No one's seen a skateboard in ages. Most of them must think I'm crazy for even asking"

"What about carpenters?"

"I've asked the ones in Shanghai, but most are post-Tribbers. They've never seen or heard of skateboards."

"Well, I've got a friend here that might be able to help us. He was part of the Great Crowd, lived in Old Canada during the Last Days. We can go see him tomorrow."

Yuanyuan

"A what?"

"A skateboard. You remember, don't you? Flat piece of wood about this long, had wheels underneath?" Scott's hands drew the shape in the air.

"No, I know what it is, but why? Why not use a bicycle?" The girl's hands were on her hips.

"It's for my son," I explained, stepping forward. "He's going to be resurrected soon and I want to get one for his room."

"Oh," the girl said. There was a long, flat pencil behind her ear. "I'm afraid I've haven't seen one in decades."

"How hard would it be to build one?" Scott asked.

"Uh, well, it wouldn't be impossible. I'm sure we could form the wood for it. The hardware on underneath might be a little tougher to track down. I can ask the guys in the metal shop, though. They'd probably be able to put something together."

"And what about the wheels?"

"Hm. That'll probably be the biggest challenge. If I remember correctly, they were made of some kind of plastic, probably polyurethane or something similar. As you know, plastics aren't as common as they used to be. I don't think we'd be able to replicate that part exactly."

"What're you guys working on?" Asked a voice behind us. A tall dark-skinned brother emerged from the doorway and stood next to the girl. They appeared to be a couple. She explained the project and his eyes widened. He tore a sheet of drafting paper from the wall and began sketching the shape.

"This look about right?" He asked when he'd finished. "Probably seventy centimeters long, maybe ten to twelve wide?"

"Seems right to me," Scott said. He looked at me for confirmation but all I could offer was a shrug.

"Sorry guys, you'd know better than me," I said.

"I dunno, it was a long time ago," Ashley said. "What do you think about the wheels, babe?"

Her husband lifted the baseball cap off his head and began

scratching. "What about something a little heftier than traditional wheels? I mean, the kid's going to have a hard time finding a paved road to ride this thing on as it is. Give him something with treads, maybe?" The others were nodding.

Ashley took her husband's pencil and sketched wheels beneath the frame. "What about something like this?"

There were more technical terms being thrown around the room than I could handle, and I realized that the project was safely out of my hands. I wanted to remember that moment, new friends and old working together to welcome a boy back to the first day of his second life.

That afternoon, Scott and Xiaoli took me to the Welcome Center they'd helped design and build. It was the same building I'd seen from my sailboat the day before, and I was happy to get a tour. Then they took me through the residential complex to on the north side of the Center. It was a cluster of about thirty houses neatly concealed within a ring of dense woods. A river ran through the stream, and at the far end of the stream, I could make out the Education Hall's sign clearly.

Residence complexes like these housed the resurrected before they decided where they wanted to live, and subsequently, build their own house. The residences were simple but sufficient. Their goal wasn't to be permanent dwellings, but rather a way for the resurrected to get acquainted with New World Organizational arrangements. Education Halls were places where meetings and private classes were held by qualified teachers.

The only exception to this system was in the case of family members who were reunited with resurrected loved ones. The resurrected would, in most cases, return to their family's living complex, where the family would study with them personally. There were, of course, books to help with New World Education, primarily the *Welcome to Paradise* book and its historical counterpart, *The Times of the Nations*.

Both had been released at a convention the year before the resurrection began.

The three of us had lunch together on the shore next to a large pier that extended out into the lake. At the end of the pier stood an elaborate gazebo that had been painted to resemble something from ancient China. Several children were diving into the water. Their parents watched from the shade of palm trees nearby us.

"Is that your daughter?" I asked one of the men. The answer was obvious. He nodded.

"Yes. She just came back to us last week. That's my wife there–

in the canoe," he pointed.

"My son's coming back soon, too," I said. The man looked at me and smiled.

"You won't believe it," he said. "Even when you hold him in your arms again, it just won't feel real."

"Does it feel real for you now?"

"Nope. I'm not sure it ever will."

The man's daughter was splashing water at her mother. Several panda cubs were wading over to join the play.

"What's her name?" I asked.

"Yuanyuan," he said sweetly.

"Did you live here, originally?"

"No, we were from northeast China, many miles from here."

"What was it like, during the Last Days?"

"You've heard about the nuclear incidents?"

"Sure. The North Korea ones in 2020?"

"It wasn't just then, and it wasn't just from North Korea."

"What do you mean?"

"Most of them were accidents in Chinese nuclear plants that the government blamed on North Korea."

"I thought China and North Korea were allies in the Old World?"

"Sure they were, but you know how alliances between world powers were. China somehow managed to convince the world that they had nothing to do with those incidents, but we knew what had happened. The nuclear testing facilities weren't far from our village."

"What happened, then?"

"Everyone knew the government had been testing weapons there for years. Many guessed that they were somehow linked to North Korea's nuclear programs, but of course no one had proof. We were warned from talking about any of this stuff, too, under threat of political imprisonment. Every once in awhile some students from a college in another city would come through and distribute flyers telling all the locals not to drink the water or eat the local produce, that it was all contaminated with radioactive materials from the nuclear plants, but there was nothing we could do about it. And a lot of those students were arrested and never seen again, so we were afraid of doing or saying anything to get us in trouble.

"And then, one day, one of the plants had an accident. I don't know what it was, but I know that suddenly there were thousands of men in radioactive suits being trucked through our village up to the plant. That's when I decided I'd had enough, and moved out with half of the others in our small town. The government, of course, never offered warnings or help, but at least they didn't try to stop us.

"Still, it was too late for our little girl. She was just starting kindergarten at the time and was so smart, but none of it was enough to stop the cancer. And we were so poor, there was nothing we could do but watch her die."

"Did you know the Truth at the time?"

"No, we didn't. We'd heard of the Bible, but didn't have a good impression of it. In those days, there were many extremist Christian cults in rural China. We wanted nothing to do with them, especially when they told us that Yuanyuan had died because we didn't believe in Jesus.

"After Yuanyuan's death, we felt so hopeless. Our only child, gone. She was the reason for our marriage, the reason for everything. There just didn't seem to be anything left to live for. My wife and I almost divorced. We reminded each other too much of our little girl.

"But then we met a couple in a fast food restaurant who would forever change our lives. They were Witnesses, though we didn't know it at the time. They could tell we were having problems, and gently began to encourage us to talk about our situation. It's a little strange now, when I think back on how personal that discussion got in just a couple of hours talking with complete strangers, but for some reason I just felt I could trust them. I think that was Jehovah opening our hearts."

"Did you begin studying then?"

"Well, when we finally realized they were Christians, we were a little offended; all we knew of Christianity was what we'd seen in our village. But it wasn't difficult to see that they were different, and they began explaining things to us that were just so beautiful and simple, even if they were a little hard to believe.

"We agreed to meet them again, and again, and before we knew it we were studying two and three times a week, and then attending meetings and going in the ministry. In just a few months our marriage improved greatly, and we were beginning to find happiness in life again. It helped knowing that if we kept at it, one day we'd have a chance at... at *this*." He waved his hand across the lake and everything got a little blurry as we both began to tear up.

"I'm so happy for you," I said.

"And I for you. You'll never forget that day."

Zhang Xulei

The flat cardboard box arrived one late afternoon by courier. It was in pieces to keep the size down, and I briefly considered leaving it that way so Jacob could put it together. I later decided, however, that I wanted to bring it with me to the Welcome Center so he could ride it right away if he wanted.

The craftsmanship was beyond anything I'd imagined. Had the result been sitting next to a factory-made model from the Old World for comparison, I'm not sure I would've been able to judge the difference. The dimensions–as far as I could remember–were just right. Even the coarse surface on the top of the board looked right–they'd cleverly glued a long sheet of low-grit sandpaper to the pressed maple. The metal hardware looked good, too. They'd even added a small shock absorber between the trucks and the board, since Jacob would be probably using it mostly on rougher surfaces that he'd been used to. They solved the wheel problem ingeniously, too. In a paper bag, they'd included six rubber tires: four for now and two as replacements. And on the underside of the deck, they'd branded Jacob's name in a funky, weaving font.

It was flawless.

The South Shanghai Welcome Center was finished ten days ahead of schedule. The last part–my part–had been arranging the interior plants and decorations. It had come together even more beautifully than the renderings we'd prepared months ago. Each of the rooms had a unobstructed view of the sunny, windswept oceanfront. It was a scene that soaked into the eyes and healed the soul.

The floors, as we'd planned, were made of slate, warmed naturally by solar receptors that fed from the building's roof and ran beneath the floor. The wisteria in the receptionaries had grown especially well; pink and purple bunches of flowers hung from each of the trellises on the back balconies where they overlooked a vineyard waiting to be cultivated.

Everything was ready, but I still had a bit of waiting to do: my family was not the first scheduled for resurrection at our Center.

Each event took a lot of planning. First, our staff had to contact the immediate family (if there was any) to be sure they'd received the Resurrection Notice. When we'd confirmed that they had made plans for travel, the date would be 'locked in'. Although this simply meant that a checkbox marked "Confirmed" was filled in on a piece of paper in a notebook, it had *immense significance*. Once that mark had been made, the resurrection was *sure* to take place on that day, at that time, without exception. Working so directly with the Holy Spirit was a profound and unparalleled experience.

Unsurprisingly, the first to be resurrected at our Welcome Center were local Chinese brothers and sisters who'd died during the Great Tribulation. Some were from nearby areas, but most weren't. The first one came back on Sivan 1, NE 59, at 10:00 in the morning. His name was Zhang Xulei. It took him almost five minutes to emerge from the room. In my mind, I saw him sitting upright slowly on the divan, looking around the room as he pieced things together. Then he'd be at the window, taking in the ocean view at first, then noticing himself in the mirror—marveling at the changes perfection had brought.

I heard the scraping of hangers on the wooden rod in the closet— he was looking for an outfit now. Finally, he opened the door.

He didn't notice me at first: his eyes were dissecting every detail of the hallway. He was wearing the cloth slippers still, meaning he'd probably missed the shoe rack beneath the closet. I made a mental note of it for possible review later with the rest of the staff.

When he did finally see me, he looked a little startled. I wondered if I'd scared him.

"Please, don't be frightened. I am one of your brothers."

"This is it, then?" He said, his mouth forming the beginnings of a wide grin.

"This is what?" I asked. We had been trained to encourage the newly resurrected to come to as many conclusions as they could naturally. These mental exercises would help them to rebuild the neural connections in their brains, which was a process leading to perfect memory recall.

"This is...Paradise... Right?"

"That is correct," I stated with a slight bow of my head. When he was ready, I led him to a receptionary where a meal had been prepared especially for him, according to his hometown's culinary preferences. He was speechless when he saw the spread of dishes. Then he lunged forward, gripping the table as he inspected each of the delicacies. I couldn't understand all of what he said. Apparently, some of the foods' names had no New Tongue equivalent.

"Please, help yourself. This is all for you. Don't feel bashful, enjoy. It's been a long time since you've had anything to eat."

A wide, boyish smile glowed on his face and he plopped down into one of the chairs, jabbing his chopsticks into the assortment of dishes while I poured him a cup of tea.

"You aren't going to eat?" He asked me between mouthfuls.

"Thanks, but I'm not hungry. Please, enjoy." He seemed a little embarrassed for a second, but quickly overcame it. Five minutes later, he had cleared most of the spread and was leaning back in a chair with a look of utter contentment on his face.

"This place... it's so beautiful. Where are we? America?"

"Believe it or not, this is Shanghai," I said. His smile disappeared and he leaned forward in disbelief.

"Eh? No, that can't be... Unless... How long was I... You know... gone?"

"If you had to guess, what would you say?"

"It's hard to imagine Shanghai ever looking like this, but I don't think you're joking so... Well, you'd need to get rid of all those buildings, first, I suppose. Wait, how did that work? Did Jehovah wipe everything out, or did you have to?"

"Let's talk about one thing at a time. First off, the year is 59 of the New Era. We started a new calendar system after Armageddon. Do you remember your name?"

"Yes, my name is Zhang Xulei. What's your name?"

"My name is Mitch. Mitch Hanson."

"American?"

"By Old World classification, yes. Now, though, we more commonly use the term Caucasian to refer to a person of my ethnicity."

"Oh. That's right, no more nations. But you speak good Mandarin, for a, ah–Caucasian."

"Actually neither of us are speaking Mandarin. This is a new language. We call it the New Tongue. Our languages were reunified after the Great Tribulation."

"Oh... Like Hebrew?"

"Almost. It does share some aspects of ancient Hebrew, but it also borrows a lot from more modern languages that we were familiar with, like English and Mandarin."

"That's great. I used to have such a hard time communicating with foreigners. We had a few in our congregation and had the most difficult time interacting. I guess I won't have to worry about that anymore."

"That's right. And I'm glad your memory of the past is so clear. If you could, try to remember some other details for me. For example,

247

do you remember how old you were when you died?"

Brother Zhang thought carefully for a few moments. "I must've been eighty-two. I was diagnosed with lung cancer and it progressed rapidly."

I checked his biographical information in my notebook. His answer was correct.

"And do you remember how you contracted lung cancer?"

"The doctor said it was from smoking too many cigarettes. It had been one of my vices before I started studying."

"And when did you start smoking cigarettes?"

"Oh, I was just a boy in high school I believe. Maybe fifteen or sixteen years old."

That was good. It meant that Brother Zhang's childhood memories were already coming back. How incredible that just one hour ago, he didn't exist, and now, not only had he returned from the grave, but with a decades-long set of memories.

"And what is the last thing you remember before your death?" I asked.

"I remember... Being cold. And tired. And numb. I couldn't think clearly, either. The doctors had me on all this medication to keep the pain down. There were a few friends there from my congregation, too. Shanlin, Jinli, Linghan, Wangzi were there, I think. Maybe some others, but I can't remember that too well. But I know I wasn't sad, not for myself anyway. I was happy I knew Jehovah, and knew that my next experience would be...all this."

"That's good. That faith is a large part of why you are here now, in Paradise."

"May I ask a question?"

"Of course."

"My wife, Yangsong... Is she here?"

I knew this question was coming, and I'd prepared a response, but the words came with difficulty.

"I'm sorry, Xulei. Yangsong never accepted the Truth."

He looked sad, but unsurprised. "She persecuted me fiercely when I was studying. Perhaps you already have that in your notes. But I always hoped she would change after she saw all the support of my spiritual family. I guess not."

"There is good news, though," I said. Xulei's eyes raised expectantly.

"Your children made it."

"My *children*? Which ones?"

"All of them."

"But how? We were estranged for decades. They barely came to visit when I was sick! What changed?"

"*That* you can ask them yourself. They're downstairs in the courtyard waiting for you."

"When can I see them?"

"Soon. Very soon. Just one more question for you, Brother Zhang."

"Yes?"

"How do you feel, having just been resurrected?"

"I feel good. Strong. Young. And I feel ready to work."

"Good, good. Now come, let's go see your family."

Sivan 4

Sivan 4, 59 NE fell on a Wednesday. The sunrise was purple and the clouds were light streaks high in the stratosphere, just below where the expanse was reforming. I hadn't slept much the night before, but didn't mind. Today was the day.

Everything had come together. The rooms to welcome them back were finished. I traipsed into the garden to cut a few fresh flowers, and noticed that a family of deer had been sleeping next to the house. I hadn't seen them before. But then, it was becoming difficult to keep track of new wildlife. I'd been so busy with the house and the Welcome Center I'd seldom turned my focus to anything else.

I made myself a simple breakfast on the gas stove in the kitchen: a couple of fried eggs and a slice of toast and jam. A neighbor up the road–Chent Samway, from Old Ireland–was well-known in the area for his delectable selection of jams and homemade breads. I'd helped him put a new roof on his seaside cottage a couple of summers ago, and ever since then I'd had an endless supply of breakfast treats.

At eight o'clock I closed the front door behind me and set off down the road, a skateboard with big, rubbery wheels tucked under my arm. The deer, ever curious, decided to follow me to the Center. I could hear their hooves clip-clopping against the road behind me. Perhaps they could sense my excitement.

"Today's the day," Anise said with a smile as I walked into the Center. She was sitting behind the main desk in a white dress with sky blue lacing.

"It's hard to believe," I replied, taking a deep breath. It's what people usually said when they came for their welcoming appointments.

"Would you like me to give you the instructions, or do you want to just go ahead and wait outside?" Anise asked. I'd done dozens of receptions for the resurrected in the last few weeks, and I knew the procedure well. Still...

"Go ahead and tell me. I'd just like to hear it," I said.

"I understand." Anise walked from around the desk, cleared her throat, and began. Her eyes twinkled as she spoke, and the smile never faded from her lips.

"Brother Mitch Hanson, welcome to the Shanghai South Welcome Center. My name is Anise Lycroft and I'll be the receptionist for your son, Jacob Riley Hanson, and his mother, Emma Kate Trenton. At ten o'clock this morning, they will be resurrected in these rooms to my right. When they emerge from the rooms, I will have a brief discussion with the two of them. This will help them ease into their second life and reconstruct some of their Old World memories. After our discussion, they will walk out of the north end of the building, where they will meet you near the vineyard. Do you have any questions?"

I shook my head. Other parts of me were shaking, too, though involuntarily.

"Ok. In that case, please follow me."

Anise walked ahead of me down the ramp leading into the garden. I knew every detail, every unseen corner, every shadow of this entire building, and yet it was all new that day. The flowers seemed especially vivid, the bunches of grapes unusually plump and aromatic. I sat on the bench I'd built myself under a white gazebo. Looking back at the building, I noticed how everything glowed with the sunlight streaming from the opposite side. We had done a fine job with this Center.

I rested the skateboard against the bench and waited.

Despite having been on the other side of the garden so many times, nothing could have prepared me for what came next. Even as I sat there waiting, I realized anew how incredible, how utterly unbelievable what I was about to experience was.

They are dead, I kept thinking. *But in just a few minutes, that will change.*

I remembered clearly going to the morgue that night with the coroner standing there in a shroud of silence. He saw bodies everyday, and the two lying on metal slabs in front of us were no different to him. Death was his job. But to me, those two cold bodies were everything that meant anything. I stood between the two people I had loved more than anyone, holding their lifeless hands in my own and wondering if it was all a kind of punishment. I knew it was fallacious thinking, but the mind wanders into dangerous territory when confronted with tragedy. And that tragedy was like none I could ever have imagined.

I knelt there weeping, asking Jehovah over and over why he had taken them from me. If there was a way, I would have exchanged those two lives for my own. I left the morgue drained and hopeless.

The friends did their best to rally around and encourage me, but I was inconsolable. For a time, I even stopped going in service and going to meetings. Seeing the other families there, and especially the Lorenzos with their little Scottie, brought feelings of bitterness that only enhanced my misery. I had lost everything.

I poured myself into my work to avoid dwelling on the pain of loss. I worked overtime, worked nights, took more business trips. But as the economy continued to crumble and the pressure on any who claimed to be Witnesses intensified, even that refuge vanished.

I thought nothing could ever make me happy again. Yet here I was, in Paradise, sitting on a bench with a smile on my face.

And that's when I saw him.

He was just a small, grey figure at first, leaving the shadow of the walkway into the daylight and gradually taking form. He was wearing the plaid shirt and khakis that Sister Adewale–my neighbor–had especially made for him. He'd get to meet her soon enough, and I knew he'd just love her. He was running to me, but it all seemed to be happening in slow motion. His dark brown hair–the exact color of his mother's–was bouncing up and down slowly as he came my way. His teeth were just as I remembered them–the two in front still seemed too big for the rest. But to me, he was perfect.

"Daddy! Daddy!" Jacob yelled–words in an impossible dream.

My son ran into my arms and I gripped him tightly. I held him and felt his arms and back, the little bumps of his knuckles, even the dimples in his cheeks that, like all his best features, came from his mom. And I said his name over and over, so that he finally had to tell me,

"Dad, dad, it's ok, it's me, I'm fine. I promise!"

But how does a dad let go of a son he lost for six decades?

And then, looking back towards the shadows of the walkway at the far end of the garden, I saw his mother. She was as I will always remember her–beautiful, mild, and knowing. She seemed to float across the grassy path in her frilly, turquoise skirt. She was wearing the floppy, woven hat that I'd found in an emporium almost twenty years back and put in the closet. I knew she'd pick it.

We hugged, and I knew I was the happiest man to ever live on Earth.

On the way home, Emma and I talked as Jacob raced ahead on his skateboard.

"How did you choose Shanghai?" She asked.

"It's quite a long story. I've been busy. Sixty years is a long time, you know."

"Anise said you were one of the designers of that building we came from. Part of the sixty year story, I'm guessing?"

"Just one small part of it. I've done... so many, many things, Emma. I've been to so many places and met all sorts of incredible people. The New World is just... endless."

Emma stopped for a moment on the side of the road, climbing the bank and staring into the sea. A few windsurfers were bobbing along on distant waves. A cool ocean breeze caught the brim of her hat, letting her brown hair spill onto her shoulders as it blew into the road. Jacob picked it up and brought it back to her.

"What do you think of your new home, Jacob?" I asked my boy.

"It's pretty awesome. A lot better than Atlanta for sure."

Emma and I laughed.

"And what do you think, Emma?"

"It's hard to know what to think. It looks just like a picture from one of our publications. It's... beyond gorgeous."

"Wait till you see the house," I said with a wink, jumping back onto the road as Jacob scrambled to his board.

"Mitch?" Emma called.

"Yeah?"

"Thank you."

"For what?"

"For everything. For just getting us here."

"Emma, that was more you than me. I can't tell you how many nights I've spent thinking about how I should've been more of a spiritual head to you and Jacob. I'm sorry."

Emma tilted her head a little, measuring my words.

"Mitch, all that stuff that happened before–it's all behind us now. Jehovah doesn't think about it, so why should we?"

The Reunion

It took me more than four years to finish the stories I'd been compiling for the last six decades. Many made it into this final copy, others did not. Perhaps, one day, they'll find a home in another book.

After Emma and Jacob came back, I focused on helping them get acquainted with their new lives, teaching them how to care for the Welcome Center vineyard and turn it into high-quality wine.

Jacob enjoyed his skateboard for the next few years, even sharing it, on occasion, with monkeys that had wandered East from central China and had proliferated in forest areas that hadn't yet been reclaimed by humans. He was experiencing the New World in a different way than I had, and our home between the woods and the sea was a good fit for him.

Emma helped me edit much of the book you hold in your hands. She contacted many of the friends I'd interviewed over the years, combing through facts and making sure everything was accurate. She also helped me organize a book release party, inviting many of the friends I'd met along the way.

Mark and Elise Raven were the first to arrive in Shanghai. They'd been reassigned to Antarctica to survey the land there for habitability. With the waterspouts helping to reform the expanse above, Earth's climate had begun to even out drastically, and the ice at the polar caps was slowly thawing. Mark estimated that it would be livable in the next ten years, and explained that it would be an important radio relay station for the southern hemisphere once a complex was built. I had never considered voyaging out to Antarctica, but Mark made it sound exciting and fun, and Jacob was ready to jump on the next sail barge.

Otto and Tonia Weber came next. Otto had long since perfected the geothermal coil he'd been experimenting with when I met him just three years into the New World. He was now working on natural-powered engineering systems with a small team in New Zealand. Their goal was–among other things–to uncover the building secrets behind ancient construction projects so as to promote non-reliance on electrical power. By some incredible coincidence, he had crossed paths

255

with the brilliant Sy Dreeker, and they were now part of the same team. I promised that I would go visit them soon. I was convinced they would discover and develop significant things together.

Abdel Yassin and his uncle, Umar, arrived just a few hours after Otto and his wife. They'd long since finished work on the Demoliton crews and had since been building resurrection residences in different parts of South America. They looked even fitter and stronger than I remembered, now appearing similar enough to be brothers. Abdel and Umar were both currently dating sisters from Rio de Janeiro.

Yeasa Valdez and Sameer Sengupta came on the following day. The two had remained in La Unión together and had eventually married. When they arrived in Shanghai, Yeasa was two months pregnant with their first child. They were currently working on a full-scale model-slash-museum of Noah's Ark. It was being built on a massive dock just north of Miguel's Inn, where I'd stayed while in La Unión. Once assembled, it would be placed in the bay, serving as both a permanent attraction and an important teaching tool for the resurrected.

Alika Cardosa also made it to Shanghai along with his wife. They had opened a ship-making academy in Lahaina, Maui, sometime after their children had grown and moved to other parts of the world. They had actually sailed into port on one of their creations–a thirty-foot catamaran built to mimic the creations of the ancient Polynesians who'd first settled the Hawaiian islands. Alika looked forward to meeting them and teaching them about the true God of the seas and the volcanoes, the God his ancestors never had a chance to know.

When Alika's catamaran eased onto the beach, he hopped off with a giant slab of polished wood under his arm. It was a longboard hand-carved from Hawaiian koa wood which Alika had fashioned himself. I insisted that I'd forgotten everything there was to know about surfing, but he assured me it would come back when I felt the first wave rising beneath my board, and he was right.

Then came Hank Haynes. His military edge had dulled some, though his mind was sharper than ever. Hank had eventually married and settled in West Europe. He and his wife were studying cellular biology there with a team of scientists who were working on an exhaustive volume of science textbooks, books that would give the credit of creation back to the rightful hands of its Creator. Hank was also working with a team of engineers from Old Germany on a side project–a scale model of a human blood cell that was as big as a seven-story building. When finished, a series of complex machines would mimic the various cellular mechanisms.

Of course, Todd and Kay Renner were there as well, along with all the other local friends from the Welcome Center. Todd and I had become close friends after all our work together on the project, and I never forgot the first time I met him in the lobby of the Tokyo Hotel. Todd and Kay were now the official caretakers of the Shanghai South Welcome Center, where roughly a dozen souls were daily being resurrected.

Sumi Ishikawa was the last to make it. She had come all the way from India, where she was teaching the local brothers to build solar-powered dirigibles. We were able to get a first-hand glimpse at her newest creation–a red-and-purple bulk of nylon wrapped in an aluminum frame–as it drifted ungainly across the plains high above us. I'd never seen Jacob's eyes so wide with wonder.

I watched contentedly as the crowd mingled in the grassy courtyard. Jacob seemed a lot more grown up to me that night than he'd ever been before. He sat patiently next to many of our guests, using grown-up expressions and gestures as he pried them with his questions from a curious mind.

Emma and a couple of sisters she had become close with prepared a huge spread for our guests: the table was brimming with steamed corn, fried sweet potato casserole, fresh honeydew, southern-style mac and cheese, freshly baked raisin oat bread, stir-fried mushrooms, candied apples, cottage cheese quiche, dried figs, and a vintage case of NE 38 cabernet from my time on Jeju Island. The aroma was irresistible as it cascaded from the dishes; we didn't have to call the guests to the table twice.

"Thank you all so much for coming here," I said from the end of the long table in the garden courtyard after our friends had found their seats next to their loved ones.

"You've all had an enormous impact on me in the last few decades since the passing of the Old World. I learned important lessons from every single one of you, and I hope that I've been able to capture the essence of these lessons in my book.

"When I took my first few steps in the New World, I knew so little about so much. Even now as I approach one hundred years of age, I feel entirely ignorant when it comes to so many of the things you all are accomplishing now in your specialized fields. I cannot help but think of the wise man's words at Ecclesiastes 3:11. How true it is that we will *never* find out the work that Jehovah had made from the start to the finish.

"I've invited you all here to thank you for the growth you helped me to make, and for making this project possible. I'm sure many will read it and see, through your experiences, just how awesome our great God Jehovah is.

"So before we take this meal before us, let's pause for a moment to thank Him, shall we?"

And there, as the sun cast the last rays of dusky light across our evening feast and a tranquil, salty breeze glanced about our perfect bodies, I closed my eyes and said a prayer.

THE END

The following is an excerpt from EK Jonathan's second novel,
THE UNRIGHTEOUS...

WHEN JACK FINALLY OPENED HIS EYES, the world was on fire. His nostrils stung with the putrid, choking sea of smoke that blanketed the battlefield.

He could remember breakfast. They'd eaten in the canyon, having slept in a cave just like their enemies, stuffing their mouths with cold, diluted curry, knowing the next meal could be days away. There'd been twelve of them. Their camp had been engulfed in the sludgy blackness of pre-dawn. No lights allowed. No fires. They couldn't take the risk. There were eyes everywhere in these dunes and their lives were on the line. The curry was runny and tasteless and the air was dusty and stale. No one complained. Their minds were on their mission and nothing else mattered.

The intelligence from the previous three weeks had been unequivocal: small bands of insurgents were moving steadily westward, away from the front lines and towards several points believed to hide weapons caches. The experts agreed this could only mean that the enemy's supplies were running dry. Intel had also learned that an unmarked convoy would rendezvous to restock a key target at oh-six-hundred, and Jack and the boys would be there waiting for the liaison, cutting them off with a surprise assault. If all went as planned, they'd be one step closer to defeating an enemy that had until now always been one infuriating step ahead.

They'd arrived early, with plenty of time on the clock to find suitable positions to lay in wait. Two of the boys went ahead to lay detonators near the roadside, a distraction that would give them the opportunity they needed to strike.

Jack heard the fire of automatic rifles long before realizing the men at the road had been shot. He called for cover and the men scattered. Artillery shells whip-cracked through the air, tearing through the dunes. Men were screaming. Jack spotted the black metal tips of AK's peeking from somewhere above the sand ridges, lighting in orange sparks as they spat bullets into the fray. But there was nothing he could do about them, for his entire focus was consumed by a new sound, a low thud followed by a faint whistling that every soldier feared and fled from.

He winced with gritted teeth as the screams and wails of his comrades washed over him. Jack never saw who fired the grenade launcher, and he nearly missed the black, smoking canister as it bounced across his path. It was almost playful in its approach, a harmless toy to be kicked back into the shadows. Jack dove for a boulder.

The only sound Jack heard when he opened his eyes was a dim ringing in the pit of his head. The air spun crazily with dust and sand and rain. When the rain touched Jack's face he felt its slickness, its warmth. It was raining blood.

Lying on his back, Jack checked himself for wounds. He could move his arms, which was good. No serious spinal injuries. He wasn't able to get up, but that was probably safer anyhow, he thought. Jack prodded and pressed against his chest, neck, face, and ears. There were bits of metal embedded in the Kevlar fibers of his vest and his sleeves were bloodied in places, but nothing to be worried about. Jack struggled to lift his body slightly to get his bearings. And that's when he saw it.

At the base of his body were the two stumps that were, just seconds ago, his legs. Jack looked away. A violent gush of nausea and memory swept through him. Thoughts of home. Thoughts of Mom. Thoughts of cold Montana nights spent by the lake. Even thoughts of his brother.

But there were no thoughts of rescue.

Their orders had been clear, the stakes known to each soldier. They were too far out for anything to go wrong. A rescue would pose too much of a risk to command, which was already spread razor thin in the unending expanse of the bone white Syrian desert.

Despite the flames licking the air from pools of burning metal, Jack felt the coolness seep in. The creeping of death. Inevitable, unreasoning. The only warmth came from his own life force that leaked from his body and made the sand stick to his tattered uniform.

Jack snapped open the latch at his chin and let his helmet fall away. Pressing his sweaty hair into the cool sand felt good, a kind of comfort in the chaos. At least it would be quick. All twenty-eight years had been quick.

Day was approaching, and between the scraps of smoke Jack glimpsed what would be his last sight. The red streaks of dawn. There was no pain, only dawn.

For more information on this project and others like it, please visit:
www.allthingsnewnovel.blogspot.com
If you would like to provide feedback regarding the novel, email me at
allthingsnewnovel@gmail.com

Printed in Great Britain
by Amazon

55318801R10149